A REALM
OF
DEATH
AND
DARKFIRE

Emma Bradley

For Neri and Niall, who have been
in my head for 20 years now:
you've more than earned
your happily ever after.

And for Livia, who is up next.
Sending blessings because
she's going to need them.

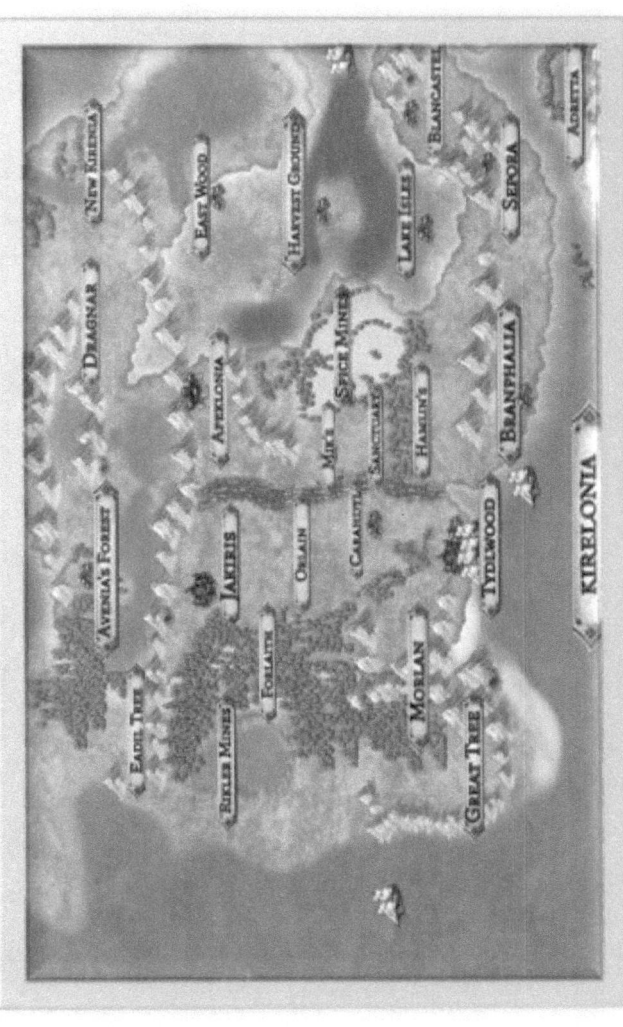

CHAPTER ONE

The candle shop was long deserted and layered with dust. Motes danced in the rays of baking sunlight radiating through the cracked shutters, and the musty scent of neglect permeated the air.

Neri eyed the mucky floor with her heart flapping like a caged bird in her chest. Her limbs ached and her head pounded, but she couldn't linger for long.

The fire shimmer had sent her to the east side of the cursed forest as planned, but she didn't get time to change into suitable clothing or to grab her cloak. She hadn't expected Niall to tackle her through the flames either. She had no idea if he had made it through the fire with her and ended up somewhere nearby, or was still safe in Jakiris.

No doubt Livia told him.

She stared at the derelict candle shop with her heart sinking. The door hung on one hinge, no doubt left to go to ruin after the Governance had stormed in and killed Hamlin. Echoes of that night when she'd escaped with Niall filled her head, but she shuddered and forced the visions of the past away.

The settlement likely wasn't safe if anyone recognised her and she had no actual friends in the area, so 'borrowing' a horse was her best bet. It would get her where she needed to go quicker than walking, although in the folk could rarely afford to lose a good working horse.

She took a grim look down at the pretty green dress and matching slippers she hadn't had time to change out of and walked to the abandoned counter. The entire shop had once been laden with colourful woven baskets full of candles but the entire space had long since been picked clean of anything useful.

I'll need to wait until nightfall and take a horse from the fringes of the settlement.

She wasn't entirely sure where to start looking for the sanctuary where her friend would be, other than 'vaguely south', but the remnants of the cursed forest would be toward the west so she would start there.

Her fire gift burned across her skin, a momentary warning, and she glanced toward the door that led to the old kitchen.

A cloaked figure stood in the doorway, tall and lithe with thin fingers curled around the handle of a short blade. Neri would have guessed a woman but she couldn't tell underneath the raised hood of the cloak.

A grey cloak, which could only mean one thing. She hadn't even considered that the Governance would post watchers in her old haunts.

I should have thought this through. No time now.

Neri slipped her hand under the counter and felt along the underside until she found what she was looking for. The blade was tiny, a safety net she'd stashed there once in the early days of sleeping behind the counter, but it would do.

With the blade tucked into the small bag hanging beneath her skirts, she darted around the counter and ducked toward the shop door.

Her gift flared as fingers snared around her shoulder, then her wrist, but she tamped the fire back down.

"No you don't," the grey-cloak, definitely female, grunted. "I can have a blade in your side before you even twitch, and I don't want to hurt you."

"Then let me go," Neri seethed

She struggled against the fierce hold the woman had on her, but short of drawing her own blade and making enough noise to draw attention, she couldn't land a successful hit.

I can't risk anyone from the settlement seeing and confirming who I am, or they'll take me straight to the Governance.

"Can't do that," the woman muttered. "Don't make things difficult and we won't harm you."

We, because of course the grey-cloaks always travelled in packs, with a cage-cart waiting outside to take captives away.

The shop door was shoved aside on its single hinge, which then broke completely. A second grey-cloak stood holding the door in two hefty hands, and he shrugged before tossing it to one side.

Neri took a steadying breath and willed her fire to calm. It tingled through her limbs but she'd trained hard to control it, to curve it to her will. Letting it flare now would only go against her, especially if she escaped and the grey-cloaks took news of her new gift to Amis, and she had no intention of killing them unless she had to.

The door-thrower, a bulky man with messy black hair and, stared at her with green wide eyes.

"Sure it's her?" he asked. "Her hair's a lot redder than I expected. It looked a darker brown on the posters. Eyes are the right shade of brown though."

Neri guessed the Governance had wanted signs of her around every settlement and main track across the east

3

after she escaped Amis the last time.

"It's her. They got the face close enough," the raven insisted.

A third grey-cloak hurried in, a younger girl with fizzy yellow hair spilling over her shoulders. She looked familiar but it took Neri a few moments to remember why. As she locked eyes with the girl and opened her mouth to say it, the girl pressed her forefinger to her lips.

If I say I know her, it could make things difficult. Neri grimaced as the woman hustled her toward the door. *No sense raging in.*

"There are signs of others approaching in the distance, so we should go," the girl said.

With the press of a blade against her ribs, Neri had to surrender her bow, quiver, blade and her pack, and let herself be shoved out into the searing daylight. The suns would grow weaker soon and winter would take hold, but for now the sunslight was still fierce on her face.

The entire settlement looked deserted as the woman forced her toward the waiting cage-cart. Even if there were folk still around, they wouldn't be coming to rescue her. She could set the whole place ablaze and find a horse to steal, but if there were no horses left then she would be stuck alone with no food and a long walk through the wilderness. Folk would take news of her fire to the Governance as well, and Amis would rip the entire realm apart to dig her out.

Escape along the way was her best option, if she could manage it. A day or two of travelling would give her an idea of the grey-cloaks' schedule, and whether she would have time enough to burn through the cage-cart itself and steal one of their horses. If not, the moment they let her out of the cart again, she could fight away from prying eyes.

"Where exactly are you taking me?" she demanded, not really expecting an answer. "What is it I'm supposed to have done?"

The woman laughed and jostled her up into the cart. There was barely enough room to stand on the dirty wooden board underfoot, but Neri stood ready as the woman slid her hood down to reveal suns-burnished skin and black hair, like a raven with fiendishly sharp grey eyes.

"You're famed in every settlement," the raven said. "The price on your head is so vast we're likely going to have to hide you from other grey-cloaks passing. We'll feed you well enough if you're quiet, and Millie there can talk your ear off if you need chatter, or even if you don't. Others mightn't be so kind though, so mind yourself."

The man had taken place on the driving seat of the cart and clucked his tongue to send the horses forward.

Neri shivered. The bumpy thudding noise from the wheels filled her head with memories, but she sank to her knees and peered out at the raven walking alongside.

"Where are we going though? The Governance stronghold?"

The raven only smiled, but the young girl's face appeared right in front of Neri's through the bars and made her jump.

"You haven't heard?" The girl grinned. "The stronghold was destroyed by some resistance forces not a few days ago. The Governance council have fled to Apeklonia, but-"

"Enough, Millie."

The raven's voice was rough with warning but Millie only rolled her eyes and clambered to sit on top of the cage instead.

Neri eyed the grubby floor for a moment then sat down

in astonishment. The resistance as she knew it was a handful of folk, and she could imagine Ma hitting someone with a pan if she absolutely had to, or Moonshine divining their future over and over until they went mad. Emelyn might talk the enemy's ear off, but blowing up an entire massive dwelling with armed guards like the stronghold? Neri guessed even the hideously irritating Finn might be able to put up a fight against folk in combat, but not enough to make an entire elite fighting force move locations.

She pulled a face at the thought of Finn. They'd not exactly parted as friends but he'd been on their side when they left him last.

Niall. Neri's heart sank. *I'm not sure if I should hope he made it through the fires with me, or that he's safe in Jakiris still.*

He would be angry beyond all fury with her either way.

The cart joined the lane that led out of the settlement and after a brief look back, Neri turned her mind to planning. They were heading west toward the cursed forest, which meant she had a better chance of finding the sanctuary or Mik's if she escaped nearer to it.

Not north though. She frowned. *If we're not heading north toward Apeklonia, then is Amis waiting for me somewhere else?*

She had no answers, and the familial band of grey-cloaks that caught her wouldn't give her any.

She pressed a hand to her chest and rubbed to ease the sudden swooping ache there.

Niall would find her. If there was one thing she could be sure of, west or east he would find a way.

CHAPTER TWO

Niall stumbled out of the blazing sunlight into the familiar calm of the sanctuary. The front door banged shut behind him and he waited in the cool, dim hallway, not able to push further into the dwelling under his own steam. He was safe for the moment, but Neri might not be.

Of all the addle-headed things to do…

He couldn't even shout at her because her inane attempt to cross through a shimmer had separated them. While it had dumped him a short distance from the sanctuary in a stretch of woodland he knew well, Neri didn't answer when he shouted for her, so he had no idea where she had ended up.

Cursing under his breath, he glanced down at smudges of old murals chalked onto the concrete floor, then at his arms. Shadow flickered over his skin, a remnant of his shade-self, but his skin was at least still visible beneath it. Unlike the first time he'd been sent beyond the cursed forest to the east, when his shade-self had turned him entirely to a being of shadow, he was still blessedly whole this time. As he moved further into the dwelling, he caught his reflection in the bucket of water Ma kept on a small table to catch unwanted energies.

An uneven pattering noise reached his ears, and he quickly swept his hands through his dishevelled chestnut hair as a flash of blonde blurred in front of him. Surprisingly strong arms wound around his middle and squeezed tight enough to hurt as a stream of excitable chatter shattered his eardrums.

So relieved to see a friendly face, he hugged Emelyn back as she grinned up at him with shining green eyes.

"I can't believe you're here! It's been ages!"

Niall winced at the loudness and shook her off, his mind swirling back to panic as he leaned one hand on the wall.

"I need you to write Neri back," he insisted. "We made it, crossed through the cursed forest. But then she jumped into another shimmer and I ended up back here chasing her. It separated us and now I need you to write her back to me. I need to find her."

A shiver of shock passed over Emelyn's face and she took a wary step back. Niall followed, stalking after her as she reversed into the den. The quickest glance told him Moonshine must have been staying there a while, because everything was in a different place. The mismatched padded chairs that Ma had restitched with various hues of purple and green thread were by the window, and the various wooden tables were all over-laden with even more plants than before.

"I can't, you can't ask me to do that." Emelyn's voice shook. "I would if I could, you know I would. But it will only twist and turn. If I do, it might cause pain or misfortune."

A dash of fury brought a snarl from his throat before he could choke it back, and the curls of his shadow gift jumped over his skin.

"I don't care. Do it."

The sane part of him tried to keep on top of the anger, but the shadow was rising even as he tried to choke it down.

"What if I did and it only brought back her body?"

Emelyn asked. "I can't."

The thought of Neri's body washing up along some stream without the most vital parts of her still inside it, shocked Niall out of his anger.

He rubbed a hand over his chin, the apology stuttering on his tongue as he noticed Ma waiting patiently to welcome him. She approached when he caught her eye, her unerring serenity and the waft of something herbal settling his fury more. He let her hug him and allowed the contact for several long moments, mindful enough to avoid her frizz of bright red hair.

"Welcome home, my love," Ma crooned, as though he were a child throwing a tantrum. "We'll find her but perhaps you need to rest first. Get your strength back."

A flowing shiver of movement brought Niall's chin off of Ma's shoulder. He stepped back. He knew better than to throw anger or petulance around as Moonshine unfolded herself from the windowsill. She straightened her usual white wrap of a dress and patted down her curling purple hair as she approached. He'd not noticed her there at all, and a tiny hint of heat leapt to his cheeks.

"Ma is right, you need to rest." Moonshine smiled at him, a greeting in itself. "The family will come together soon, but you must be patient."

Niall nodded. He couldn't do anything else. Emotion didn't seem to work on Moonshine and she could see things before they happened. If she counselled patience, then he would attempt to be patient.

Something solid landed on the toe of his boot and he looked down to find a hefty black paw. Dog had once belonged to Hamlin, but after he died Dog had aligned himself with Neri instead.

Dog's intelligent eyes bore into his and his shaggy black

tail started to wag.

"I did try to look after her," Niall muttered.

As Ma insisted they sit down to eat something, he couldn't find the energy to apologise to Emelyn. She disappeared through the door to the kitchen, but he dropped onto the nearest chair to sulk as Ma produced food in moments.

Almost as though they knew to expect me.

He glanced at Moonshine but everyone seemed to be honouring his petulant silence. Guilt settled over him when Emelyn jumped as he passed her on his way to the kitchen. The thought she was still scared of his mood was irritating, but then he heard the same sound she had.

Everyone turned and hurried toward the front door.

"All roads lead to home." Moonshine said, a cryptic half-smile on her face.

The door swung open and Niall had to take steps back as a familiar face stamped inside. His chest squeezed with relief and he got hustled forward to rebound into a strong pair of open arms.

"Here's the chaos," Mik said with a broad smile. "And yet none of you ever send word to me!"

He let Niall go in order to move further into the room and they exchanged a smile over Emelyn's shoulder as she all but strangled him in greeting.

"Did you arrange this, Em?" Mik whispered. "It all seemed rather sudden."

Emelyn shook her head and stood back, her cheeks pink.

"I have called everyone here," Moonshine announced. "The time will soon come to make a stand. Tomorrow we'll set out to join the wider group. They're on the move now, so we'll need to keep pace."

Niall tamped down on his instant anger. He needed to find Neri, but the first place to start would be calling in the odd trade or two. The wider group was the best place to do that, and to get information on any new captives the Governance might have taken.

Ma insisted she would begin a final dinner to use the last of their perishables. Moonshine continued to hold court and Emelyn sat on the floor with her arms around Dog's neck.

"We're going on an adventure," she whispered to him.

Niall rolled his eyes as Dog smiled back at her, tongue lolling out. He wanted to get going, to set off immediately, but the Governance knew many of them now. Niall, Emelyn and Moonshine all had reason to avoid being caught.

When Mik raised his eyes to Niall and asked for a word, Niall stood immediately. He led the way into the hall by the front door and his pulse picked up as Mik faced him with a serious frown.

"What happened after you left?" Mik asked, mindful to keep his voice low. "I heard rumblings that the Governance stormed the Summing ceremony."

Niall sighed. "They did, and I've got the scar to prove it, although Eva gave me that."

The memories swelled, of the woman he'd once called an acquaintance if not a friend leaning over Neri with a blade. His pulse picked up as the image flashed in his mind, and the scar Eva had given him on his shoulder twinged in answer.

"What then?" Mik asked.

"Neri and I made it west. She... I still can't quite believe it but she had that kyne with the feather in it, and the firebird came for her. It gave us a shimmer west, and we came out near the Morlan mountains."

Mik gasped softly. "That's near where you travelled before, isn't it? What happened then?"

"We made it to Jakiris, I screwed up a lot and Neri ended up with ai-tan. She almost died, but then the west was fighting the borderlands and she set a bunch of random dragons free-"

"Dragons? Really? That's amazing."

"Yeah, sure, which would have been great except she then convinced herself that she has to save Em and everyone else, so she made another shimmer out of wax and here we are."

The anger churned inside his chest but he still caught the furtive grimace Mik made as he checked they were still alone.

"I had news from a trusted source. It came whilst I was travelling from a friend who deals with the underground traders. I had folk keeping an eye out for you and Neri, just in case, and I thought it was weird when they said they saw her a day ago travelling without you."

Niall froze. "Where?"

He glanced over his shoulder. Ma and Moonshine were determined to drag everyone somewhere else, and if they knew about Neri they might even try to stop him from leaving to find her.

"She got picked up by Ciena's crew apparently, somewhere further north." Mik sighed and rubbed his chin. "You know what that means."

CHAPTER THREE

The cage-cart rattled and bounced on with only brief stops to rest the horses. Neri's shoulders ached from leaning against the wooden slats, and after two days of travelling and watching the pass of the suns, she was convinced that they were still heading west.

Any further west and they'll be passing through the cursed forest.

She entertained herself now and then with thoughts of the future, wondering what the children of folk might rename the forest if it was no longer cursed. She'd seen it herself during the battle for the borderlands, swathes of once impenetrable woodland that had turned patchy and decaying, the trees darkened to smoking columns. She assumed deep down that was because of the fire from the first time she and Niall had shimmered, when the firebird first came to claim her.

She stabbed her tiny blade idly against the floor of the cart and cocked her head to listen. While the raven had removed her longer blade, she hadn't made any attempt to remove the smaller one. Not that Neri could do much with it in confinement. She had a hatch in the base of the cage-cart for her personal business, which came in handy when moving through longer grass, and the raven insisted they weren't going to be letting her out until they reached their destination.

The food rations weren't up to much either, musty bread

and cold soup from pouches, but Millie pushed liberal amounts of fruit and some nuts through the slats at random intervals.

Neri bided her time. She could hear the subtle hum of voices over the rumble of the cart, but not what they said, and she guessed that it would come down to fighting the moment they let her out.

"Do you want a nut?"

Millie's face appeared as a shadow on the cage above her. Neri shook her head.

"No, I'm fine. Do you know what happened to the Governance?"

She hoped Millie's excitable need to babble would serve her better if she pretended.

"The rumour is that the resistance laid a trail of spark-stones beneath structural points in their stronghold. Set the whole lot off, shook half the walls down."

Millie's grin gleamed down as she paused to crunch on a nut.

"Many hurt?" Neri asked.

"Not a clue. The Governance council moved to Apeklonia to keep themselves safe, but word has it the cursed forest isn't decaying fast enough, so they're mustering strength to march through the borderlands and take the west that way."

Neri's gut twisted. After the battle for the borderlands, several of her friends could be there.

If the Governance attack, Viljo will be the one leading the forces against them, assuming he's travelled to take up the role immediately.

She had little hope that anyone would be able to talk diplomacy with the Governance, but Viljo had a steadfast notion of duty to his legacy, so he might not even try.

The cart rumbled to a halt, the absence of the wheel noise sudden and swift. Neri tensed and swung into a crouch, her hand ready on her blade. She couldn't cause much damage in the confines of the cart, but the moment they hauled her out she could strike. She contemplated using her fire to keep them at bay but until she knew exactly where she was, revealing that part of herself might not be safe.

Last resort only.

As the raven grabbed her by the arm to haul her out, Neri steadied her weight until her slippers hit tufty grass. She swung herself forwards and shunted the woman back off balance, swinging around until her hand levelled the line of her blade, even as an unyielding power snared around her shoulders.

"Nice try."

The raven got to her feet and wiped a hand over her mouth, grinning. Neri struggled but the male grey-cloak showed no signs of letting her go. Her fire simmered, but Millie stood nearby with a huge pail of water and an even bigger grin.

Almost as if they know what my ai-tan is. But how can they?

She dropped like a rock and fell out of the man's arms instead. With a mighty swing that sent one of her slippers flying, she swung sideways and flicked her leg out. He staggered against the kick and she had her blade up ready to strike.

A stab of icy water sluiced over her head and she shrieked out loud, her fire quivering inside her bones as her blade was knocked from her hand. Instinct forced her to use it to warm herself, but two sets of hands were on her shoulders and pinning her arms before she could gather herself.

"You're strong, but you're outnumbered," the raven said. "This won't take long, don't worry. He's been waiting a long while to see you again."

Neri froze as a wholly different type of icy trickled through her bones.

The grey-cloaks hadn't brought her to the Governance. They'd dragged her straight to Amis himself. It had to be him. Nobody else would have a price on her head, or be looking for her.

Thoughts of Niall filled her mind but she forced them aside as the grey-cloaks dragged her through the long grass toward a derelict dwelling with its door missing.

The man disappeared and left her in the raven's charge, but Neri was too busy fighting the pulsating fear. She had her fire, she could fall back on that, but enough to kill Amis with it? He wouldn't be letting go her free any other way. She sought for something, anything she could offer or fight with, but her blade was back in the long grass and all she had was her fire left.

The raven gave her shoulder a not-so-gentle shove and Neri tumbled through the doorway, tensed ready to run. She might not make it far but she had to try.

Amis wouldn't let her go this time, and he wouldn't risk letting her anywhere near a weapon. Running was her only chance. Or burning the entire dwelling down with him in it.

Across the empty room, filled only with a chair and signs of soot in the cracked hearth, a man stood cloaked and hooded with his back to her.

He wanted to do this where nobody would see us.

She held herself ready, one arm lifted at her side to wield fire if she needed it. When he didn't turn or speak, she charged in first.

"Been a while," she said. "Sorry to see you're still alive, but you've dragged me off course by several days so you'll excuse the lack of pleasantries."

Still he didn't turn, only uttered a dry chuckle that shook his shoulders. Neri clenched her fist, willing the flame to stay hidden until she needed it.

She stalked a few steps forward and kept the open window to her left in view. If he refused to turn around, she could keep talking and leap out of it. Grabbing one of the horses wouldn't be too tough, and she could ride fast enough. Before she could move toward the window, Amis took a step back.

"You've never been known for your manners. Probably why your old foe has been hunting so fiendishly for you."

That voice.

Familiarity flirted with confusion as the man lifted his hands to lower his hood and turned to face her.

The sandy hair was desperately in need of a wash, as was the rugged, tanned skin, but beneath the traveller appearance, the brown eyes were as wicked as ever.

Neri stared in horror as Finn smirked back at her.

"It was unfair of us to drag you the wrong way, sweet thing," he added. "But all in good fun."

Thoughts of Niall raging through the east searching for her filled her head, of Emelyn and Ma and Moonshine now so much further away than they could have been. Stunned and utterly outraged, her instinct bubbled over.

With a feral snarl, she lifted her fist and punched Finn square on the jaw.

He staggered back and lifted a hand to his cheek. Neri stood with her shoulders heaving as she clung to the barest hints of self-control.

All this time I could have been on the way to the sanctuary, to finding Niall, to-

She spun around at the sound of a rasping laugh. The raven stood with one hand on the doorframe, the other on her stomach, gasping for breath as she doubled over.

"In the name of all things sacred, Neri, that *hurt*," Finn grumbled.

Stuck between the two of them, Neri wasn't sure who to face first.

"Why bring me here?" she demanded. "Why you? Why all the secrecy and pretence? Niall's probably out there somewhere frantic."

Finn rolled his eyes and massaged his cheek.

"He'll be fine, calm yourself. After your mad dash and the summing ceremony going to ruins, the Governance have hired half the east as grey-cloaks to persecute the other half. We have to travel as grey-cloaks now to get through settlements unseen."

"If it weren't us waiting around for you, some real ones would have been only too happy to turn you in," the raven added.

"What about Niall?" Neri demanded. "How far is it to the sanctuary? Or Mik's? He might go there."

Finn sighed. "We'll be joining with a much bigger section of the resistance. It's quicker this way, and we couldn't risk anyone else catching you first. One way ticket to the enemy, that."

Neri resisted the urge to stamp her foot, or punch him again.

"What bigger section of the resistance?"

The raven huffed, an irritable noise that suggested she didn't much take to Neri's demands. Neri ignored her as Finn chuckled.

18

"You didn't think it was just the sanctuary fighting the entire might of the Governance, did you?"

She hesitated and glee spread across his face, but for once he didn't taunt her any further.

"That's not my concern," she snapped. "I need to find Niall and make sure Em and the others are okay. Then I'm heading straight to the borderlands with anyone who wants to go through."

Finn raised his eyebrows, his head tilting and some of the amusement fading.

"The borderlands? Why there?"

"Because I know who'll be ruling it after Niall almost sliced off the old lord's head."

"And who do you think will be ruling it, sweet thing?"

She hated the nickname but let it slide. This wasn't exactly her idea of a welcome party, but Finn was better than Amis. Marginally. And a whole lot safer.

"The previous Jakid-in-training of the west. He's a... friend, of ours."

Finn's grin was slow and devastating.

"If you say so. We're meeting at the edge of the forest further north, so we should get moving."

"I'm not going with you. I need to find Niall first."

Something clattered at her feet and she looked down to see her long blade, her quiver and bow, and her pack. She swiped them up to secure them over her body and eyed the raven grinning at her.

"We know his old haunts better than you would."

"And who are you exactly?" she demanded.

If this was an old fling of Niall's, she wasn't going to give the woman the satisfaction of showing any irritation.

"My name is Ciena. Niall and I are old friends." The piercing grey eyes roved over her face for a moment. "Not that kind of friends, don't worry. You're more my type than he is."

Neri shrugged. "And he's more mine than you, no offense. I need to find him either way."

"He'll have gone first to the sanctuary," Finn said. "Then he'll be following the others to the gathering further north, if he has any sense."

Niall doesn't have much sense where I'm concerned.

She didn't voice that thought, even though it gave her the urge to smile as she threw her bow over her shoulder and settled her quiver across her back. Finn hadn't betrayed them before so she would follow his lead for now. If it did lead her to Niall, all the better.

"Fine." She sheathed her blade. "When do we leave?"

CHAPTER FOUR

Niall sat on the driving seat of Mik's cart. Ahead and behind were several other wooden carts with varying styles of covering, from colourful awnings of dyed fabric to fixed wood-tile roofs. Mik didn't sleep much but Niall couldn't find a moment of rest either, so they took turns driving their cart with its wooden roof and Niall spent the rest brooding over Neri.

Eight days since leaving Jakiris and still no sign of her.

The weather had finally turned, and the heat now carried the sizzling promise of storms. The skies had gone from hazy white to rolling grey, but it matched his mood at least. He sagged against the seat as Mik hopped up beside him.

"So, it's been a while since I last saw you." He began the conversation Niall had been expecting. "How have you been really?"

Niall managed a weary smile, able to let some of his defensiveness drop around his old friend.

"I'm fine, dragged through the bushes, but fine."

He wanted to ask several questions but Mik held up a hand and gave him a serious look.

"For now, let's allow our little family some time to enjoy company before we start putting the realm to rights. Start with what's happened and work up to what must come. Ma and Moonshine will be taking over the cooking and throwing cutlery again in no time."

Niall chuckled. He remembered the fateful feastmas celebration at the sanctuary that sent Mik fleeing into his own private company.

I didn't even get a chance to see her much, let alone celebrate anything like feastmas. He scowled at the line of trees they were following. *She didn't even trust me to go with her.*

He couldn't blame her, not after he'd essentially done the same thing to her, but it still hurt. He also had the smouldering edge of the cursed forest for company, gusts of ash puffing up now and then from the decaying trees. Neri created chaos wherever she went, but it was the kind of chaos that burned away the rot so new hope could grow, and he had no idea how to handle that.

"I know you worry about her." Mik's voice tugged at his attention. "When she returns, she'll need you. She's the type who will push you away to keep you safe but you mustn't let her. Whatever you do, you need to stay."

Niall nodded. Mik was as wise as he was happy playing the fool, but he couldn't have any idea of what had happened, how it was Niall's behaviour that had pushed them apart, not hers.

She's changed a lot since I first met her, all for the better. What can I even offer her now?

"She's everything," he said.

His voice broke and he blinked hard as the emotion spilled out.

Mik chuckled. "I figured as much. We've not known each other that long, you and I, but I could see she feels the same as you do well enough. Now, distract us both. What's the west like?"

"It's alright." He shrugged. "Green, grassy, forests. We started in Morlan, but Neri was injured and ended up wandering into the *aerie* woods."

He smiled. Without that, she'd never have found the *liliam* to give him. He'd scented it at various intervals since leaping through the shimmer after her, and that alone told him she was still out there. He could only hope that she was smelling it too and knowing the same.

"Fascinating. What exactly are in *aerie* woods? We've not heard tale of any in the east for a long while."

"No *aerie* left, not that I've heard. Rumour has it they all moved north, assuming they're not a myth by now, but there's still deep magic in those trees. Flowers that lull and chime, *liliam* that scents."

Mik laughed. "*Liliam* is one I have heard of."

Niall reached into his pocket and took out the small fabric pouch he carried with him always. After Neri had given him some, he'd crushed the dried petals and put them in the pouch.

Mik took it and peered inside before giving it a delicate sniff.

"Hmm. Interesting. I imagine it has to be fresh to be potent."

"I can still smell it," Niall said. "Whenever she's thinking of me, I smell it."

Mik frowned. "I'd like to ask some questions when we find her, of both of you. There are so many aspects of *aerie* magic that we don't know about still."

Niall took the pouch back and slid it into his pocket.

"*Aerie* magic is no different to land magic. It all comes from the same source in the end."

Niall scanned the horizon irritably but it was the same mass of dying grassland and the smoking line of the cursed forest.

"You mentioned dragons as well," Mik prompted.

"Yeah. We saw six, varying sizes but all larger than a standard dwelling. Scales, various colours, some with wings and some without. The old lord had them chained with *freirer* ice."

"*Mekhan*," Mik swore.

"Exactly. Then Neri freed the dragons and I culled him down. Well, I gave my brother the kill in the end."

"My, my." Mik chuckled. "Emotional growth. Neri really is having a wonderfully charming effect on you."

Niall scuffed his boot across the footwell of the cart and scowled.

"Only when she's with me. Right now, she's not."

Mik grinned and stood to climb down to the ground.

"She's a good girl then. Keep the reins. I'm going to assist Moonshine with preparing a lunch before Ma gets wind of it."

Niall glanced over his shoulder, despite knowing full well that Ma would be somewhere right behind them as Mik made a lively hop off of the driving seat.

Ma passed by a moment after, and soon Moonshine passed with a dangerously serene smile, apparently heading in the same direction.

As the sound of Emelyn squealing pierced the air, he wondered if they'd finally come to blows with the kitchen knives.

"Niall! Come and see!" Emelyn shouted. "You won't believe it!"

Niall tied the reins to the front rail of the cart and clambered down to the ground, curiosity warring with weariness.

Then a cacophony of barking caught his ears.

Dog rarely barked.

It could only mean one thing.

Niall rounded the back of the cart and stumbled to a halt.

He recognised the dark-haired woman a short distance away. With short black hair and delicate enough features that fooled those who didn't look her in the eye, Ciena had been his friend in times past. She also had more pride than a wounded kitchen-cat. He should play nice and approach her first, but someone else appeared beside her and his insides roared.

His boots caught on the rutted grass as he stumbled forward, until he swathed enough shadow around the edges of his body to carry him to her faster. Neri gazed at him with wide brown eyes ringed with golden fire, her arms raised even as she hesitated. Her shoulders were shaking and she probably expected him to shout at her.

He was definitely going to shout. A lot. But first he folded his arms tight around her and pulled her against his chest. Her skin was too chilled for comfort and she shook against him as her tears soaked through the front of his shirt.

Anger at himself for being foolish enough to trust her not to do something mad, and at her for doing it, flared before he could tamp it down.

"What the hell did you think you were doing?!"

He pushed her away, half out of concern for her hearing as he yelled and also to keep his mind sharp. If he kept holding her he might not be able to let go again. Fury warred with the innate need to calm her shaking and take care of her. His anger peaked in continuous waves and her wide eyes staring at him didn't help.

He reached out for her again but Emelyn bounded up before he could grab hold, or possibly throw her over his shoulder and tie her down somewhere safe.

"Niall, Mik asked if you can go help him," Emelyn

sang. "You two will have plenty of time now."

Niall ignored her as the words filtered in. He and Neri would have time, and he had a strong sense that he should calm down first. Her lips parted, perhaps to plead with him to stay, but the fury won as he turned and walked away.

Ciena looked him up and down as he passed, then nodded once in greeting. Simple, curt and to the point. Her dark hair looked shorter than he remembered, but her smug expression had all the same bite to it.

"Is she permanent then?" she asked.

He choked back the instinctive growl in his throat.

"Yeah. I appreciate you bringing her here. What's been going on?"

Ciena shrugged. "We're fighting. Lavian has tasked everyone with moving the performers on to a big celebration in Apeklonia. The entire Governance council will be there."

Niall nodded. "I'd stay to talk more, but-"

"Don't waffle," she scoffed. "She's been delightful company and there's not a scratch on her. Go sulk like you always do and we can swap the gore later."

She walked away before he could say a word, heading toward where Ma, Moonshine were greeting the others as Emelyn cannoned straight into Finn's arms.

Niall hauled himself back onto the driving seat of the cart, even though the horse had continued following the one in front without any input from him. He settled back against the seat and rubbed both hands over his face.

Despite the anger, the shock and the sheer fatigue roiling around in his system, *finally* he could breathe again.

CHAPTER FIVE

Neri stared at Niall's back as he strode away from her, straight toward Ciena. After convincing herself that he must not have made it through with her, seeing him had sent her head in a spin. She'd expected his anger, but now he might take off somewhere to punish her for trying to leave him behind.

She took a step forward to follow him but a firm pressure landed on her forearm to hold her back. She glared at Emelyn and shook her arm free.

"Let him be for a while," Emelyn pleaded. "He needs to calm down, although he won't say why he's been so angry. I thought it was just worry for you but he seems furious still."

Neri sighed. Emelyn was right. Niall would need some time to let his anger cool. If he didn't want to speak to her then she had to wait for her chance to make amends. She didn't have to like it. Perhaps in time he would understand why she tried to leave him behind. She dredged up a weary smile as she noticed Emelyn vibrating with excitement.

"At least you're happy to see me," she quipped.

Emelyn all but strangled her with a tight hug.

"I want to hear everything that happened, everything you've seen, all I've missed."

Neri nodded. "I'll have stories enough to keep you going, don't worry. I just hope-"

She broke off as a ball of dark fur collapsed in a panting

heap on her feet. With a strangled cry of happiness, she gave up trying to be strong.

Dog licked her hands and her face as she dropped to her knees and threw her arms around his neck, his huge stumpy tail wagging as he made tiny whining noises.

She had to wipe her eyes after and focused on the swelling hope firing inside her chest.

There would be time for her and Niall to fight it out soon enough. Until then, she'd achieved the first stage of her plan and found everyone, and she could risk relaxing just a little as Emelyn linked their arms tight.

"Everyone will be so pleased to see you! Mik mentioned to me that you met him before, and Ma and Moonshine are here too!"

Neri allowed herself to be dragged along in the wake of Emelyn's enthusiasm with Dog padding along behind them at a much more dignified pace. Now that she knew for sure where Niall was, the tiredness and sense of vulnerability she'd been holding back swamped over her. The sight of Ma walking a few carts ahead of them, her red curls bouncing and her flowing earthy-green dress swaying in the warm breeze, made Neri feel like a kid again. She stood through the onslaught of hugs and exclaimed greetings, smiling and hugging and trying not to drop into the grass to sleep. Then Emelyn insisted on hauling her further along the procession of carts toward Mik, who gave her a swift hug.

"I'm glad you're back safe," he said with a broad grin. "Niall has been extremely annoying without you. But Emelyn, I think Neri needs to rest. We'll all need to keep our strength ready."

Neri didn't ask why that might be. Rest did sound good, and she still had to deal with Niall, to apologise and explain.

Emelyn rolled her eyes. "Fine. Come on, we have a spare bunk in our cart."

Neri let herself be guided back the way they'd come, half looking for Niall and disorientated by the carts rumbling past.

"This is us," Emelyn announced.

Neri eyed the small cart, barely more than a box with a wood-tile roof, and desperately hoped Moonshine and Ma hadn't packed a lot.

"Never mind that!" Millie appeared beside them with a huge grin. "We'll be stopping for the night soon anyway. You can sleep then. I overheard that you can make fire too, is that true?"

Chills wavered through Neri's skin. Only Niall knew about her gift so he had to have told someone. Millie cocked her head to the side and leaned closer still.

"Okay that's a lie. Ciena saw you burn something under your feet yesterday, and she said she thought you were glowing from the inside out at one point. But can you?"

Neri shrugged, trying to think of something both vague and suitable to say.

"I can when I need to."

Millie's mouth formed a perfect circle of surprise.

"I won't tell a soul, promise! Will you sit with us at dinner? No, I guess you want to see your friends. Can I come and sit with you instead?"

Neri had to say yes, but it was enough to send Millie darting off again.

The skies above had turned a tumultuous grey, the suns already receding for the evening. A vicious wind whipped around them and Neri shuddered as a splatter of rain hit her forehead. With the cloak she'd borrowed from Emelyn on she would be alright, but her slippers were already ruined and she doubted they'd manage to build fires if the rain got stronger.

Before she could ask Emelyn, someone hollered up ahead and the line of carts slowed. The moment folk halted, lightweight hide canopies were put up, fires were built underneath them, and the merry thud of cooking pans filled the air. Neri watched, mesmerised. She followed Emelyn to the nearest canopy, but Ma and Moonshine were already working fast in surprising harmony together.

When another length of hide was thrown down, Emelyn patted the ground beside her and Neri had to sit, cheered only by Millie and Ciena flopping down with them.

"Anyone got anything to trade?" Millie asked.

Emelyn frowned. "I might. Not much of substance, but I can trade you a story. What have you got?"

Neri lost any hope of paying attention to them when she noticed Niall approaching. Her insides leapt as he looked her way, but a moment later he sat on the other side of the fire next to Ciena. She grinned at him, but Neri couldn't see any hint of emotion beyond amusement on the woman's face. Niall gave her a sideways glance then returned his gaze to the fire.

"So, what's the plan?" She prodded his arm.

He shrugged. "It's undecided. From what I hear, Lavian and the others are planning to march on Apeklonia."

"We know that," she scoffed. "What's your plan?"

Neri bit her lip, her pulse kicking up. She inched closer to the warmth of the fire and let it soothe her ruffled feelings. Her mood dimmed even further when Finn sank onto the ground beside Emelyn.

"At least the company has improved now," he teased. "All I've had is her threatening to fight me," he gestured across the fire at Ciena, "and her glowering at me."

Neri rolled her eyes when he pointed at her, but it was enough to make Emelyn laugh which stopped her snapping back at him.

"That said, you are a picture when you look sour, sweet thing," he added.

Neri bristled as he winked at her, but Emelyn slapped him playfully on the shoulder. She glanced across the fire and her heart sank. Ciena sat alone and Niall was halfway across the grass already, headed for the cursed forest.

She flinched as Emelyn slapped her arm next.

"Niall won't tell me a thing but I'm not stupid," she huffed. "What's the west like? Is it beautiful? Is there a way through for all of us?"

Neri sighed. "It's beyond beautiful and it's my home now. I found a way back here though hoping I'd be able to give you all a chance to come with us, but I didn't exactly think it through."

"Is that why Niall's so mad?"

"Yeah. I tried to leave him behind. I just wanted to keep him safe, but you know what he's like."

Neri grimaced as her voice began to shake. She paused as more food made the rounds. She had eaten some of Ma's delicious cooking but couldn't stomach any more.

"Millie said about you having a gift," Emelyn prompted, ignoring Mik giving her a warning look. "What? It's not like I asked her myself!"

Neri had to laugh. "It's mainly wielding fire, warming things."

"I thought it would be! I touched your hands earlier and you were burning up. Oh, actually I brought something with me."

Emelyn launched to her feet and dashed toward their

cart and Neri shook her head, fondness keeping a tiny smile on her face. Mik gave her a weary look and that cheered her a little more. Niall might sulk for an age, but he was safe and she had to be grateful for that.

When Emelyn returned some moments later, she had a small folded blanket full of old candle stubs. Noticing the furtive looks folk nearby were giving her, Neri stood and grasped the blanket to her chest.

"I'll give you a demonstration later, okay?" she asked.

Emelyn inhaled sharply, paused, then nodded. Without a word, she held out a hand, Neri's old carving blade balanced on her palm.

"Okay. Make something pretty for me!"

Neri nodded, choked with sudden emotion. Emelyn was one of the main reasons she'd returned east, to give the others a way through the borderlands. Viljo might be fussy about things, but she was almost certain he wouldn't deny her the safety of a few of her friends.

Even after I rejected him, but we'll deal with that when it comes.

She walked away from the camp and followed the line of the trees, keeping the dancing light from the fires in sight. Once she could be sure nobody would see her, she sat down on a fallen log and took a stub of wax in her hands.

With a deep breath, she closed her eyes. Excitement at using her gift bubbled and the heat seared in one sudden rush until the wax splurged through her fingers. It splattered on the dead, dry leaves at her feet and she picked the fast-drying gloops of wax off her fingers with a sigh. On the second try, done with a calmer, more determined mind, her gift sang and sizzled to her will. The wax softened in her hands as the familiar tingle of magic warmed her skin and kindled in her bones.

A twig snapped somewhere nearby and Neri lifted her head, too weary to do more than tense.

"Not safe to be wandering alone in the darkness," Ciena called out.

Neri shrugged. "Not safe anywhere, not this side of the cursed forest."

"Is it safe beyond then?"

Neri gathered up the wax and moulded it into a ball, using the smoothing motion over and over to calm her irritable nerves.

"It is now. We fought the lord of the borderlands and won, so we can only hope it stays that way."

Ciena kicked her boot against a tree and leaned back against it, her lips lifting with amusement.

"No doubt that suits you then, what with you and Niall stepping out together and him being in line for a title someday."

Neri focused on the wax ball. "Don't know about that now. Nothing's certain, but we need to get west before anything else."

"Ah, what would you want to languish in great halls and rot slowly in finery for?" Ciena drew a blade from the confines of her sleeve and twisted it fiendishly fast between her fingers. "You've got a strong gift that could do great things if you weren't tied down. Think about it."

"What's your plan then?" Neri countered.

Ciena grinned. "Cause trouble. Fight. Other things beginning with F."

"Sounds like you're better off staying this side of the forest then for that. Well, the trouble and the fighting bit anyway."

She stood and pocketed the wax but Ciena pushed away

from the tree and blocked her path back to the camp. In the dim shadows cast by the firelight behind her, her features were almost indistinguishable.

"Winning a battle isn't going to keep your land safe, not when the forest is done dying. The curse was cast long ago but I'll bet there are folk on both sides who believe they're entitled to stuff on the opposite one. The fight's just beginning and I don't want to miss a moment of it."

Neri held her gaze, a healthy dose of her attention on the still flicking blade. Ciena could have probably killed her at any point, but that didn't make her safe to be around.

Ciena eyed the blade and grinned.

"Good call. Wise." She turned away but threw a parting shot over her shoulder. "Rumours have been spreading down through grey-cloaks by the way, about issues in the borderlands. I wouldn't count on that being a safe route back across either."

"What rumours?"

Ciena didn't answer and Neri refused to chase her.

Bet she and Niall have had a nice cosy chat about it already.

Before she could give in and follow Ciena back to the camp, the scent of frost and cake-spice hit her, so potent that she spent a moment breathing it in. There was nothing to see in the shadows, but she knew better.

"I know you're there," she called out.

Her hope fell again when nobody answered. Niall was watching over her but he clearly didn't want to talk. Downcast, she packed the candles back into the blanket and folded it into her arms.

Nobody stopped her as she walked the short distance back to the cart she would share with Emelyn and the others. As she put the candles away, she hung onto one comforting thought. Niall had come to watch over her in the dark. Even if he didn't want to speak to her, even if he was clearly furious with her, he still cared enough to keep her safe.

CHAPTER SIX

"It's smoking."

Niall glanced up at the sound of Neri's voice. Every time she spoke his head whipped up or his skin rippled with shivers.

He followed the line of her gaze to the cursed forest, or what remained of it. Some trees were nothing more than charred stumps, while others were ghostly husks against the wintery sky. Even the leaves on the ground were decomposing and sending up puffs of warm smoke, the stench of decay wafting on every available breeze.

He didn't like that Neri was walking alongside the cart in front with Emelyn, Finn and Ciena while he sat driving his, but at least he could see her.

The time would come to talk to her soon, but every time he even imagined it, the anger was still whirling sharply, prodding and piercing at his resolve to stay calm.

That's her doing. He bit his lip. *Her affinity with the firebird, her shimmer to the west, it caused the curse itself to burn.*

She loved him, he knew that, but she deserved everything he wasn't and everything he probably couldn't give her.

"It's never enough," he muttered.

"What's not?"

He flinched as Ciena clambered onto the driving seat beside him. She wouldn't let the matter go either, he knew that much.

"Her." He nodded to where Neri walked ahead. "The cursed forest is burning because of the shimmer she summoned. I could walk back into Jakiris and put a title on my head, and the locals would still bow to her."

Ciena snorted. "She doesn't seem the type to set stock by titles. Forget that nonsense. Focus on getting her to the borderlands, if you're not going with Lavian's group to Apeklonia."

"What exactly is the plan there?"

"Perform with enough might to take out their leaders. Lavian has kept the details hushed, but everyone who needs to know knows their part."

Niall managed a wry smile. "And you didn't get given one?"

"I have a blade, don't I?" She grinned wickedly. "If I'm good, I'll get several. We can't wait for the cursed forest to fall, or for your side to trudge over and start liberating everyone, assuming they even would."

Niall glanced up at Neri, his irritation settling when he saw Finn leaving her side and walking back toward the cart. Finn flirted with her purely to annoy him, but he still didn't like it.

"My sister would," he admitted. "My awful brother got the emotionless duty, I got the chaos and she got all the goodness and light in the realm."

Ciena rolled her eyes. "She sounds dull. I keep forgetting you're meant to be some high-born lord the way you sulk about."

"Nice. The forest is falling though, slowly, and we have Neri to thank for that. We're closer than we ever have been to getting enough forces to bring the Governance down."

Finn reached them, his brow lifting in amusement.

"You speak like the next alternative will be any better."

"Ever the optimist," Ciena taunted. "It can't be worse than what we've got stuck with. We even had a few folk trying to go through the cursed forest but still no luck."

Finn smile dimmed. "At least they made it back out this time."

"We won't dwell on that now," she insisted. "We're stopping for the night it looks like."

She pointed to the tiny glow of lights in the distance, the front of the group having set up camp already. Niall clicked his tongue and the horse put on a burst of speed.

The moment they stopped, Niall threw the reins to Ciena before she could fight him over it and swung down to the ground. Her indignant cursing followed him as he followed Neri, crossing the grass toward where Ma had set out an awning over the side of their cart to ward of the worst of the rain.

He hovered until Neri sat down with Emelyn on one side, then Mik winked at him and sat on Emelyn's other side, leaving the space beside Neri free. His heart lurched when she looked out of the corner of her eye at him.

They didn't have to speak, not yet. He lowered himself to the piece of wood set on the grass to ward off the worst of the water, keeping a short gap between her knee and his.

He wanted to talk to her but she turned her attention to Emelyn instead. Picking up a tiny bit of twig, she held it in her hands. A moment later, fire flared around her fingertips.

She nudged Emelyn with her elbow as her gift grew and the twig caught alight. The brittle middle burned in moments and half dropped from her fingers. It landed on the barren ground and she quickly stamped it out with her boot.

"Cool!" Emelyn managed to keep her voice to a whisper.

Next, Neri pulled a candle stub from the pocket of her cloak. She held the wick of the candle between her fingertip and thumb.

"No matter how dark things seem there will always be light somewhere."

Niall had seen her do that trick once before, shortly before he'd teased and all but taunted his way back into her life, into her affections. Somehow, because he was furious with her still, it didn't seem appropriate to tease and taunt this time.

So they sat in silence with Ma and the others chatting nearby until food did the rounds.

"Right, time for decisions has come."

Niall looked up from his rigid vigil of staring at the corner of Neri's knee at the sounds of Lavian's gruff voice.

He'd had little to do with the leader of the resistance, and knew even less about the man's past, but Moonshine was the one who dealt with him and she was someone Niall trusted entirely.

He had no idea what everyone else had planned, but he had no intention of going to Apeklonia to fight. Viljo was now lord of the borderlands and that was his fight to be had, and no doubt the Jakida would get herself involved too, both as Viljo's *ama* and as the leader of the westlands. Niall refused to see her as his *ama* as well, not after she'd abandoned him, but the westlands was Neri's home and therefore his also. He had no intention of doing anything other than wrangling her back to the safe side of the cursed forest, and possibly finding some kind of tracker to set on her tail for the rest of their lives.

"Some of us will be turning west to the borderlands,"

he announced. "Great idea you've got, but we're needed west."

Lavian nodded. "No doubt about that. Whoever wants to go west can go. I've heard rumblings about the new lord and who he's been seen with over the past days since he arrived at the borderlands, but rumours will be what they are."

"Always a grain of truth in rumours," Ciena muttered.

Niall froze as Neri nodded beside him, but she didn't speak up. No agreement to going west with him but no fight about the suggestion either.

Unless she's assuming we're not making these decisions together anymore.

Then again, as she'd once yelled at him, he was the one making all the decisions without her for the both of them before.

"Is it safe to go through the borderlands now then?" someone asked.

Neri bit her lip. "We have links there."

So distracted by his sudden urge to reach out and pull her lip free, Niall didn't claw in the disbelieving huff of laughter that broke free. She glanced at him but looked quickly away again.

"There's a man who controlled the old lord of the borderlands, all tales tell," Finn added. "He will likely try and do the same to the new one. We have to have hope that the new one has some strength of mind."

Niall didn't make another sound. If he had to admit one thing about his brother, he was steadfast in doing his duty. Whether that duty would fall as allegiance to his family or to someone able to sway his mind the other way, Niall wasn't sure.

But Neri seemed to have faith left in Viljo, something

that rankled a sour taste in his mouth.

She insists any desire between them was all on my brother's side.

He had to believe her, even as doubt crept up and tangled around his resolve.

"We'll be there in a few days either way," Ciena said, her eyes taking on an unsettlingly keen gleam. "The targets will be heavily guarded no doubt, but you've narrowed them down. I would have thought you'd want to join us though, Neri, considering you have previous with Amis."

Niall started forward as Neri's body glowed momentarily, as though a single candle flickered on inside her and guttered out.

Her reaction was nothing compared with Emelyn's.

Her feet and hands scrabbled on the wet grass but she managed to stand. As everyone stood up, Neri pushed her way past Niall to be first, almost kicking a hole in his knee.

As soon as Neri managed to drag Emelyn a few paces, Niall was on his feet to follow.

Reaching the fringe of the trees away from prying eyes, other than his, Neri halted. Emelyn's breath came in ragged gasps and her eyes were still wide.

"It's okay." Neri tried to soothe her. "We won't let him hurt you."

Emelyn began to shake. Neri removed her cloak and threw it around Emelyn's shoulders.

Niall had some ideas about what Amis had done to Emelyn during her imprisonment, but Neri had attacked him since and worry for her often pushed the thought of Emelyn's horrors from Niall's mind.

"You don't understand," Emelyn stammered. "He has a way of getting into your head. He twists things. I don't want to see him."

Neri shushed her and lifted her head, glancing past where Niall stood. He looked over his shoulder and found Ma lurking at a suspiciously convenient distance.

Emelyn didn't struggle when Ma came to cuddle her. Neri watched for a brief moment before walking slowly back to her seat by the fire. Niall joined her but she didn't look his way.

"You know something of this Amis bloke?" Ciena asked.

Niall glared at her, not wanting Neri to relive those memories.

"It's not your story to know," he grumbled.

Neri grimaced. "It's okay. Let's just say I attacked him and he doesn't like me much."

Ciena frowned, waiting.

"He hurt Em pretty badly at one stage and I tried to bash his head in," Neri added. "So he chased me around the east until we shimmered west."

Ciena and Finn leaned forward, gleams of anticipation lighting in their eyes.

"We thought you might have, but nobody was certain," Finn said quietly. "What did bring you back here though? And how?"

Niall glanced at Neri. "We made it. Neri has some kind of sketchy affinity with the firebird, but you were the one that told us that anyway. We were sitting safe enough in the west when she insisted on coming back to *save* everyone."

Neri sucked in a sharp breath and he fought the urge to start the fight then and there. They would need to have it, there was no avoiding it, but first he needed her safe. Easier to chase her across the west with access to coin and horses than worry himself sick with the Governance hounding her in the east.

"That's a bold move." Ciena looked over toward Emelyn, now seated back by the fire. "I don't doubt there are some that need saving. Rash, but I admire the attempt."

Nothing more was said for a long time and Ciena turned her vigorous attentions to carving into the side of her boot while Neri matched her with a more delicate energy, carving swirls into a stub of wax.

As the fire dwindled folk began to drift off to their own caravans. Niall half-hoped Neri was lingering with the intention of talking to him. Perhaps he needed her to start and he would be able to finish the fight, grab hold of her and never let her go. But when she stood up, she barely even glanced his way.

She drifted away from the fire and he watched her go until the unsettling sensation of being stared at, or more accurately grinned at, turned his head.

"You think she's going to run again?" Ciena asked.

Niall shook his head. "No, she's got what she came for."

"Well then." She groaned to her feet. "I'm going on personal business. I'll try not to stumble over her in the dark."

She flashed him a sinful look which he ignored, mainly because he knew if she did stumble over Neri on her wandering, Neri was safer with Ciena than she was alone.

She might be alone now though.

Niall gave it a short while before getting to his feet and striding in the same direction Neri had taken. A short distance away, he caught the tiny flicker of light and followed it to find her sitting on a fallen tree, lighting and extinguishing a candle with her gift.

Each flicker of light illuminated her face, giving him fleeting glimpses that calmed his temper. He was angry, but he'd done worse to her. She'd made peace before disappearing on him, whereas he'd technically done it first and broken her heart in the process.

It's the deception of it, he thought as he watched her. *How can I trust she won't do the same again?*

But then, how could she trust he wouldn't throw a temper and leave her behind again?

Before he could dredge up the courage to approach her, soft footsteps announced someone else's arrival.

Neri's hand was on the hilt of her blade in the darkness before she recognised Ciena approaching. She held her ground as Ciena eyed her up and down.

For a long moment nothing was said.

"Niall says you're a good fighter and that your *ai-tan* is powerful," Ciena announced.

Niall tensed as Neri stood and faced into the dry roar of the wind. He hadn't said a word to Ciena yet about Neri's abilities, but Ciena was a warrior with sharply honed instincts, so she would have noticed straight away.

Neri shrugged, but Niall saw the slight wariness in the tense shoulders and keen gaze. Both women were powerful in their own ways, but nobody he knew could best Ciena with a blade, and she better than any fighter he'd ever met in a straight body fight.

"I can handle myself," Neri said.

Ciena's stance altered. She drew no blade and held no fighting pose, but Neri brought herself up tall ready as the winds whipped at her flimsy dress.

Niall clenched his fists as he watched Ciena circle, never breaking the stare. When she feinted forward, Neri moved to hook her leg, but Ciena had already swung it out of reach.

Unperturbed, Neri steadied herself and moved her

attentions to defence.

"I'm something of a seer myself." Ciena's tone sounded like taunting. "I can't rival Moonshine but there will be a time when you need to push Niall away. You won't believe me now, but you will know when the time comes."

Niall broke out of the shadows, letting them settle and dissipate. Ciena might be able to teach Neri some fighting skills, but he wouldn't let the woman drive any more wedges between them.

"I can take care of myself," Neri tossed back. "If you're so close to him, I wouldn't want him to hurt you if I lose my head and you attack me."

He almost laughed at the sheer derision in her voice, but the taunting brought Ciena forward, another feint.

Neri managed to dance out of the way, her skin glowing as her *ai-tan* sparked against the dry leaves whisking against her and singing against her skin.

"I won't even get close." Ciena taunted her again. "Niall would separate us before it came to it. But there will come a time when you push him away and you have to do it."

Neri glanced around, her eyes darting back and forth between her opponent and the emptiness that surrounded them.

Still half-hidden behind a tree, Niall wondered if he should let them get their egos out of the way or step in. Neri didn't have the same pride Ciena did, but he wouldn't be fixing anything between them if it looked like he thought she couldn't hold her own.

His lips twitched. She'd told him off for that enough before during the battle for the borderlands.

Neri shrugged and did a mocking side-step.

"I'd never let him go. Even if I tried he'd find me, that'll never change."

His chest clenched tight, warmth blossoming and rippling over his skin, as though her words were cloaking him with her gift.

"Your devotion weakens you," Ciena insisted. "If you truly want to be invincible you have to cut the ties that bind you."

When Ciena came at her, Neri caught the intent and whirled sideways. She evaded the attack but failed to grab her own hold quick enough. Niall lurched forward but stopped himself as they returned to sparring apart.

"My devotion keeps me alive," Neri countered. "Without it, why bother fighting at all? Besides, he's not here now and you've not floored me yet."

She feinted to test the waters and dodged back as Ciena responded in kind with a roll of her eyes as her lips curled into a fearsome snarl.

"The boy can cloak himself into any shadow and you think he's not watching over you now? Watch this."

Neri barely ducked to avoid the punch, but Niall was already past her, his arm outstretched and his hand full of throat as his shadow billowed over him.

Ciena lay sprawled against a nearby tree trunk, pinned by his hand as she started laughing.

"Niall leave it, we were just sparring!"

Neri's squeak reached him even as his anger ebbed. Ciena never usually managed to rile him so easily, although she'd tried so many times, but Neri was his weakness. His grip slackened but he put more warning into his eyes, even though Ciena wouldn't pay the slightest bit of attention.

Neri's fingers slid over his arm, reaching underneath the fabric of his shirt to warm his bare skin. He closed his eyes, the torment of having her close, touching him, whisking all thought of anger and of his friends away.

"Leave it, please."

Her touch disappeared as he grunted and released Ciena, who smirked back at him. Unable to rage at her, he moved his remaining anger to Neri and gripped her shoulders tightly, pulling her face close to his.

"You may just be sparring but I won't let anyone throw punches at you."

He eyed the tiny smile creeping across her face, disarmed by the sheer sight of her so close.

"Leave us to talk, Niall. No sparring, I give you my word."

He flicked a glare over his shoulder, but if Ciena said no sparring, she would honour it. He had so many words for Neri, but they would come and he was too afraid they might be harsh ones still. With one last yearning look at her, he stepped back and walked away.

As soon as he was sure he was out of sight, he folded himself into the shadow and dodged behind a tree to listen.

"I mean it about having to push him away," Ciena said. "The time will come, and not because I have any feelings for him, don't insult me like that."

Neri raised her eyebrows. "So, definitely women."

"Stop it, you're taken. But yes."

It was enough to see Neri grin as she kicked at a pile of leaves nearby. Her vigour sent them into one of the flurries of wind and she watched them dance.

"We'll agree to disagree about the pushing away thing then," she said. "Friends?"

Ciena shrugged at Neri's words and splayed her arms out wide.

"Friends. Be nice to Niall. He's an idiot, but he's clearly in love with you."

Neri rolled her eyes. "Be better if he was actually talking to me instead of grabbing and grunting."

"Be grateful." Ciena laughed. "The fact he's letting you out here alone with someone who could kill you in one swoop is progress."

Neri glowered as the skies opened and rain began to lash down upon them. Niall risked a grin, letting his anger ebb and his panic calm. Neri couldn't argue that as Ciena would best her in a straight fight, but she clearly didn't like the suggestion that he was 'allowing' her to be out alone.

He knew her better than she probably assumed. She was quiet with Emelyn, distant with Ma and the others, and hesitant with him.

She wanted Livia. She yearned for her cottage in Jakiris so she could claim her own space. She wanted to feel like she was home, and as he followed them back to the camp at a distance, Niall vowed he would do whatever it took to make that happen for her.

CHAPTER SEVEN

The procession rumbled on throughout the day, and Neri sat on the driving seat of their cart holding the reins. Emelyn ran back and forth, carrying messages between various folk. Sometimes she would sit with Neri for a while, but then she'd run off again. Dog chose between sitting up by Neri's feet or trotting back and forth with Emelyn.

Neri barely noticed. Her gaze stayed fixed on the solid form of Niall in front of her, walking alongside the cart he shared with Mik. He never once looked back, but she knew he had to be cold. The shirt he wore provided little barrier against the biting wind and he had no cloak at all.

The moment the dreary grey sky began to darken, Neri waved to Emelyn. A large splat of rain landed on her forehead as Emelyn jumped onto the seat next to her.

"Take the reins for a moment." Neri threw the reins over and jumped to the ground.

Her legs jarred and she winced but wasted no time in peeling off her borrowed cloak. She hadn't allowed Emelyn to lend the only spare set of clothes she'd brought with her, so the dress had to stay, but at least she could borrow the cloak to keep her warm. She'd also spent an agonising few moments searching for her missing slipper after Ciena taking her to Finn, but she was glad of it now. The slaying heat had turned chilly overnight and the skies were heavy with rain as far as anyone could see.

She almost lost her nerve when Niall heard her footsteps as she approached. Almost as though he guessed it was her, his shoulders stiffened and his stride slowed. Neri clenched her fingers tight around the fabric of the cloak and forced herself to draw alongside him.

"It's really cold." She held it out in front of him.

He turned to look at her and his eyes swirled dark, some indistinguishable emotion passing through him.

"You should be wearing that then." He nodded to the cloak but didn't move to take it.

Neri's breathing skittered, her heart pounding. It seemed silly to be so nervous around him, but she couldn't help it.

"I've got blankets on the bench." She tried again. "Your shirt isn't exactly winterproof."

Niall didn't say anything. Neri waited, walking alongside him for countless moments with her arm held out. The silent stand-off continued, until Neri huffed and threw the cloak. It landed haphazardly on his driving seat next to Mik, who was driving their cart and failing to hide a broad smirk of amusement.

She stalked back to Emelyn and hauled herself up onto the driving seat.

"Look." Emelyn pointed.

The landscape dipped as the rutted track they were following snaked down a long sloping hill. A large settlement waited in the distance with lights of various fires in windows twinkling in the pre-evening gloom.

"That's not…"

Emelyn shuddered. "The outer settlement of Apeklonia. It has three, one after the other until you hit the Kahlen mountains and the great water beyond."

"We'll be fine," Neri said.

She had to be the brave one. Danger would come, and soon. It was selfish to think it, but she hoped their journey would be less perilous to the borderlands than the one the rest of the group were taking to Apeklonia.

A shadow appeared beside the cart and she flinched.

Niall frowned at her reaction, but she couldn't think of anything to say to him now. His rejection of her peace offering still hurt, especially as he wasn't wearing the cloak and hadn't bought it back to her either.

"The procession is stopping for the night," he announced. "After that, we go west. The borderlands is a day away, so we'll have to hope my brother is still as much a fan of yours as he was before."

It wasn't exactly a great peace offering, or any at all, but at least he was talking to her. Then she wondered why he'd chosen to tell her all of this. She struck around for something non-inflammatory to say, but his gaze was fixed forward even though he was walking alongside the cart with no sign of leaving her be. She half-expected Emelyn to intervene with her usual boundless enthusiasm, but Emelyn only shoved the reins into her hand and bounded off without a word.

Anticipation bubbled hot in one swift instant across her skin as Niall swung himself up onto the seat beside her. She clutched the reins tight and had to tuck them underneath her thigh before the leather began to smoke.

He noticed. Perhaps the glimmer of a smile lurked for a moment at the corner of his mouth. Neri couldn't be sure. She almost squeaked out loud as his knuckles brushed her leg, but he only pulled the reins free and took control.

"Who'll be coming with us?" she asked, her gaze fixed on the shadows of the forest alongside them.

"Ciena, Emelyn, Mik and Finn. It's not the group I'd

have chosen."

She wanted to ask why but didn't. Finn was obviously not his favourite person, but he was close with Ciena and Mik, and fond of Emelyn.

"We'll be going through forest tracks on the border of the cursed forest," he added. "We'll need to move fast and will only have one cart to share between the six of us."

Neri turned to look at him. He stared straight ahead, his profile only ever so slightly shadowed. Even in the night-time gloom, the chestnut tints of his hair caught the firelight from the carts ahead and behind, and the rough hairs growing around his mouth. His sour expression didn't do anything to dim the attractive lines of his face either.

She bit her lip as he pulled the horse to a halt. Having him alone while the others were busy setting up camp for the night would be the ideal excuse for him to escape. He swung down from the driving seat and scooted across to chase after him.

"Niall." His head lifted sharply but she forced herself to continue. "I'm sorry, about what I did. It seemed-"

"Shh."

He swung around to face her and she scowled back at him, irate in an instant.

"Don't you-"

She squeaked as his hand clamped over her mouth and he threw his free arm around her waist.

"Lights in the distance," he muttered.

She fell still, her heart pounding as the maddening scent of him wrapped around her. His lips brushed the top of her ear and her eyelids fluttered in torment as Mik hurried toward them.

"Grey-cloaks," he announced. "Loads of them. The

others are hiding but you need to as well."

He looked at Neri as he said it, but Niall was already manhandling her toward the nearest cart.

"I can walk," she mumbled through his fingers.

He didn't let go, not even after cramming them into the corner of the tiny cart beneath a huge pile of musty blankets.

His closeness frazzled her mind and her skin warmed in reply. She shut her eyes, willing it to calm, but his fingertips slipped underneath her shirt and started a subtle stroking motion across her bare stomach.

"Now is not the time for you to be glowing," he murmured.

"Then stop petting me!"

He snickered under his breath but they froze as the cart door slammed open.

"It's just the old blankets we use for the wheels when the mud gets too bad," Mik said snippily. "You want to go rifling through them? Be my guest, but I want my dinner."

That explains the smell.

Niall's hand over her face protected her from the worst of it, and that didn't smell great either, but the door slammed shut again and silence fell.

Neither of them moved, Neri with her eyes shut against the maddening emotions, until a knock came at the cart door.

"They're gone," Mik called out. "Close call but Ciena started a fight and off they ran. They'll be back soon enough with more grey-cloaks though, so if we're leaving the group it has to be soon."

Neri sagged as Niall let her go and used the cart wall to haul himself to his feet. She looked up at him, but he didn't make any effort to help her up or even wait for her. He stalked out of the cart, and she found him pacing the soaked grass outside.

"What's wrong?" she asked. "They're gone, it's okay."

"It's not okay. None of this is okay. How am I supposed to keep you safe when I can't even get you to trust me?"

"I do trust you-"

"You don't. You left without me. Even now, I'm telling you to be quiet because there's danger nearby and you're still trying to argue with me."

She bit her lip. "Because I had no idea what was happening, and with the shimmer, I thought it was a good idea at the time. I wanted to keep you safe, that's all. I know it was a stupid idea, I know that now. But I stand by it. I heard Zel and the Jakida talking about the cursed forest coming down, and I had to try. I wanted to give folk like Em a chance to be free."

He scoffed loudly. "I can see the logic in it. You dance into danger yet again, assuming you'll be lucky enough to find them, let alone save them. Then you hope to find a way home, if one actually exists. Just explain to me, in all of that masterful planning, what if you hadn't ever found a way back?"

He tortured her with the thoughts she'd been avoiding for days, and she clenched her hands to fists.

"I know, I didn't think-"

"You didn't *think*?" He grimaced and lowered his voice again. "It didn't cross your mind that in going without me we might never see each other again? Did it really all mean that little?"

Neri began to shake. She tried to hide it but guessed he could tell anyway given her limbs were trembling. She fought the urge to fight back, to argue her point, and failed.

"If I had told you, you'd have stopped me."

"Of course I would have stopped you!"

She eyed the darkness behind them and briefly considered running. She could run into the woods and hide, although it wouldn't solve anything. Even in his irate mood Niall would come after her.

The sound of him taking a slow, deep breath to calm himself didn't help. She didn't want to argue with him. Arguing with him wore her out worse than fight training with Livia, worse than hours kneeling on stone to make candles.

The pent-up emotion spilled out and her clenched hands sparked flames into the cold air. She wiggled her fingers and shuddered as the flames retreated and the familiar chill crawled into her bones. Niall stood with his shadow flicking over his body, his dark eyes whirling and his face twisted in frustration. Tears burned her eyes and she turned away, determined not to make the situation any worse.

Before she could take a single step, soft warmth tucked underneath her chin and guided her head upward. Niall's face was shadowed, but she could see the weariness in the slope of his shoulders and she stared at him, unwilling to look away for even a moment, hardly daring to breathe.

"You can't," he murmured. "You mustn't do things like that. You can't just disappear."

Even as she yearned to close the distance between them, her *ai-tan* rippled indignantly. He had left her before. The circumstances had been different, that he had left her in safety and journeyed into a relatively un-hostile land where he could return to her any time he chose. But the resentment still echoed deep.

"We can't go on ignoring each other." His hands settled on her shoulders. "Things will be dangerous in the coming days and I don't want to spend it arguing. If we come out of this alive and if we get back home… Well, there are a lot of if's now."

Neri sighed. He offered her exactly what she wanted and yet she couldn't bring herself to agree. Her guilt at being so headstrong coupled with the knowledge that he hadn't truly forgiven her stuck like a blade in her mind, needling away.

She bit her lip and kept her gaze fixed on his chest.

"Neri? You understand what I'm saying don't you? Us not talking is almost as bad as me not knowing where you were. I can't tell what you're thinking and it scares me."

That feeling she knew all too well. Her gift ebbed along with her anger, not a release but a quiet concession that they'd deal with the issues later.

We don't tend to 'deal' with issues as much as fight them out.

"I'm not used to you when you're not yelling at me," she muttered.

He sighed and shuffled the tiniest step closer. Short of resting her nose on his chest, she had to look up.

"I can yell at you if you like, but it's not really something I enjoy." His eyes flashed darker. "I prefer, well…"

When he gave her the tiniest hint of a smile, she settled her cheek ever so tentatively against his shoulder. Only when he wrapped his arms around her waist did she let herself relax enough to breathe deeply, soaking in the scent of clothes that desperately needed washing and the subtle hint of him beneath it.

"It's just a shame we have to share the cart now," she murmured.

His soft chuckle vibrated under her cheek and she took it for the simple blessing it was. He might well end up rubbing what she had done in her face further down the line, but she would take that chance.

"I'm sure we can work something out," he said. "Let's join the rabble anyway. We're missing all the chores."

She smiled. "With Ma, Moonshine and Emelyn rushing around, I imagine we'd just get in the way."

He wrapped his arm tight around her shoulders and held her close to him as they joined the others around the fire. His arm remained stayed around her as they ate, and she relished the feel of his leg warm against her own. She even managed to return the conspiratorial grins Emelyn sent her from across the fire.

Not that Emelyn was paying too much attention, too busy sitting with Mik on one side and Finn on the other, both completely entranced by whatever she was saying. Neri stifled a giggle.

"What?" Niall asked.

Glad she had an excuse to lean closer, she nodded to the others.

"I think Emelyn has attracted a few suitors," she whispered.

Niall chuckled. "It makes a change. Usually I have to beat men away from you. I'm glad to be amongst friends again. At least I don't have to worry about them."

And there's the first sting.

She straightened up away from him and slid her cold hands into the gap between her knees. He didn't notice as Ciena collapsed on his other side, the hilt of a blade spinning back and forth between her fingers.

I'm tired and overwhelmed. Neri dredged up a tight smile. *I need to sleep before we discuss anything.*

"Neri? I found this for you!"

Emelyn all but sat on her lap in her excitement. Neri

pushed her irritation with Niall aside and eyed the small blade with a carved wooden handle that Emelyn held out to her, well-worn but suitable for carving.

She took the blade as Emelyn held out her other hand with a candle, barely burnt down at all.

"These are gifts." Emelyn sat down with a smile. "Would you carve me something like you did before?"

Glad of a distraction, Neri nodded. She thought for a moment, then her head dropped and she began.

The concentration drew away all thoughts of Niall and of where they were. She forgot about missing home, about Emelyn watching her carve and about Niall's mixed messages.

She lifted her head briefly once or twice as some of the other groups set up a small circle between the carts to practice their talents. The subtle flicker of fire caught her attention and she watched someone dancing through it as though it was water, questions whirling in her mind. Others danced, and one woman made a sparkling show of colours and shapes using strategically placed spark-stones.

Neri carved on even as the jollity wound down and folk began to go to their own carts for the night. She didn't hear Emelyn hiss at Niall that she felt frozen to the touch, or that he should get her cloak for her. She didn't notice Niall get up to fetch it.

Something draped around her and she jumped. The blade almost sliced over her knee and she looked up to find Niall wrapping the cloak around her. Then her head dropped again and she was lost once more. Only when the last swipe of blade on wax had been made did she sit up with her back muscles screaming.

She struggled to stand up, less than impressed that Niall chose to watch instead of helping her.

At least he stayed.

She ignored him and turned to Emelyn, who was half asleep with her chin resting on her hand. She handed over the candle and drew Emelyn's ear close.

"It's a secret message. You can put some paint or colour on it and roll it over paper to get the message."

Emelyn's mouth dropped open. She stared at the candle and darted off with a grin, then she stumbled to a halt, reversed a few paces and span around again.

Neri laughed as Emelyn rushed back to hug her with a gleeful shout of thanks. She guessed if Millie and Emelyn talked at all, she'd have to make another one fairly soon.

Except Millie isn't coming with us. We might never see them again.

She bit her lip and glanced around. Everyone else had retired to their carts long ago, leaving her and Niall by the dying embers of the fire alone. After his comment about not having to worry about his friends, she couldn't bring herself to smile like nothing was wrong but tiredness warned her not to bring it up.

"You're mad at me."

His voice echoed softly through the silence. Exhausted after having worked so long on carving, she couldn't find the energy to lie.

"I'm not mad, but you said before that you don't have to worry about your friends. I don't mean to worry you but it makes me sad that I know you won't ever properly forgive me for it."

She refused to look directly at him as she burbled on, unable to stop.

"When you left me, I know it was different. You could come back any time you wanted to, but you didn't."

"I left you safe!" he thundered.

She winced. "And I thought you were going to be safe in Jakiris! Furious but safe. I didn't even consider the idea of not being able to get back to you. The plan was to find everyone and get them to the borderlands."

She sucked in a heaving breath as Niall tilted his head back and huffed loudly.

"What would have happened if the grey-cloaks really caught you?" he asked with a steadier tone. "What if Ciena hadn't found you first?"

She folded her arms and angled her gaze away.

"If she hadn't been there, nobody would have found me. The settlement was deserted and I know how to take care of myself."

Niall sighed. "I know the idea came from a good place, but it was so risky. We can't be doing that, not when it puts an impenetrable cursed forest between us."

"I know. I couldn't risk it though, you said as much yourself that you'd refuse to let me come."

He lifted a hand and smoothed it over her cheek. His fingertips curved along her jaw and his smile turned wicked.

"I would, absolutely. But we're here now, and what's done is done."

She frowned. "No more digs?"

"Digs?"

"Yeah, like you casually slipping in that you don't have to worry about your friends."

"I meant that I don't have to worry about them being interested in you, like Mik and Finn." He dropped his hand from her face. "Although Finn's not a friend but still. You seemed almost oblivious to my dearest brother showing an interest back home."

She held her breath as his expression turned sour and

the air around them froze the very marrow in her bones.

"I could deal with that," he continued. "You chose me and that was everything. Then Livia comes to tell me that you're off to conjure shimmers alone. I had no idea what was going on and I almost didn't catch up with you. Then I woke up here and you were nowhere!"

His shadow flicked around his body and his eyes turned to simmering wells of anguish.

"Don't you see, you dance into danger and I blame myself for not looking after you?" he demanded. "If I hadn't left you back then in Jakiris, maybe you would have trusted me enough to discuss it with me. I could have kept you safe. At least part of this is my fault, and I feel awful about it."

Neri's insides clenched tight and her *ai-tan* grumbled awake at the overwhelming wave of guilt. The leaves and debris underfoot began to smoke and she shuffled a step sideways to wave her foot, then the other. The smoke followed her, a sad trail of emotion that she didn't have enough energy left to turn to fire.

"I'm a grown woman," she mumbled. "I'm not your responsibility to keep safe."

Niall groaned and slammed both hands to his head as he turned away, then swung back to face her.

"It's not about responsibility! I love you and every time I think about you being hurt it kills me. I'm not saying to wrap yourself up in cotton wool or hide away. I just want to share the dangers with you."

His voice cracked over the last few words and she stopped trying to get rid of the smoke. He flinched as she took his hands in hers so that smoke and shadow entwined, binding them together in darkness.

"I'm sorry," she said softly. "I was tired and still hurt

and I didn't think enough."

Niall's fingers snarled into her hair and got stuck. She couldn't remember the last time she'd washed or teased out the tangles, but he quickly gave up trying to free his hand and held her close instead.

"Please don't leave me again," he mumbled. "I understand now how you felt when I came back, and why you were so angry with me. I'm sorry I left you then. It won't happen again."

The apology that she'd never fully received soothed the lingering poison inside and she pulled back so she could see the truth of it on his face.

He smiled, and brought his thumb up to wisp across her cheek.

"I can't follow you in." He nodded to the cart nearby. "Not with Ma and Emelyn inside, but tomorrow we'll separate from the circus and you can ride with me."

Neri glanced toward the horizon and the natural hue beginning to form amid the dark shadows of the cursed forest.

"It is tomorrow. I doubt there's any point in going to sleep."

A cart door banged open nearby and Niall groaned quietly.

"You spent most of the night carving and shivering," he muttered.

"And you spent most of it watching me and sulking." She smiled to take any sting away. "I can drive the cart for a bit. You need to sleep properly."

He scoffed and grabbed her hand instead. His touch sent warmth tingling up her arm, enough to give her a jolt of energy she needed as Mik appeared, his sandy hair a mess and his eyes dredged with sleep.

Mik gave them a wave and grabbed a harness from the side of the cart for the horse, but Niall held Neri back when she took a step forward.

"I'll be driving the cart," Niall announced, giving her a dominant stare. "You go inside and sleep."

Neri said nothing as he led her toward the cart, but the moment he let go of her hand to open the door, she clambered up onto the driving seat. He gave her a look, and she gave him an equally arctic one back, until he groaned and hauled himself up beside her.

"I need my head healing," he grumbled.

It became an entirely different sound when she rubbed a hand over the chestnut strands next to his temple. She put the last dregs of her *ai-tan* behind it and he preened like a kitchen cat in the suns.

"She's actually got him trained, look."

Ciena's glib holler from nearby had several folk laughing. Neri blushed but Niall only shrugged with a smug grin curving across his tired face.

"She can train me to do whatever she wants," he retorted.

Neri closed her eyes and soaked in the relief thundering through her.

Finally.

"I mean it," Niall murmured, his voice right by her ear. "Whatever you want. I have some ideas that have been brewing and bubbling over for the moment I get you home."

Moonshine and Ma arrived alongside the cart before Neri could do much more than blush, but she managed to get a subtle dig of heat into Niall's forehead first that made him yelp.

"This won't be the last time we meet," Ma insisted. "I

need to go with Lavian's group, keep Moonshine out of trouble."

Moonshine smiled. "I heard that. Best fortune in the west. We'll take good care of Dog too, don't worry, and no doubt we'll see you there one day soon."

Neri nodded, hoping that was one of Moonshine's fabled instinctive knowings and not merely vague hope. She held back tears as Dog jumped up to the driving seat and she gave him a firm hug, but when Ma clicked her tongue he jumped back down again and sat wagging his fluffy stump of tail.

"Ciena, I'll be expecting you to keep them all safe," Ma added. "No fighting unless you have to, mind."

Ciena snorted. "Okay. No promises."

As Niall moved the reins to set their horse walking, Neri leaned over the side of the driving seat to wave goodbye.

"We've got everyone?" she asked.

Niall nodded. "Emelyn's inside muttering, which means everyone else has to walk alongside for a bit."

Neri looked back again to find Ciena, Finn and Mik walking beside the cart as they left the rest of the camp behind. Only once they were out of sight did she face forwards again.

"Wrap up and sleep, at least for a bit." Niall threw a blanket over her. "We can take turns once the day is properly here."

Neri opened her mouth to argue but a yawn escaped instead. Niall wouldn't give in, stubborn to the end, so she settled the blanket over both their legs and rested her head onto his shoulder.

"I'm not sleeping," she muttered with her eyes closed. "As soon as your pride is soothed enough, I'll take over."

Her consciousness ebbed to the soft sound of him

chuckling and the gentle vibration of his shoulder under her cheek.

"That'll be never then." He pressed a kiss to her forehead. "But for you, I might consider compromising."

CHAPTER EIGHT

The morning waned with no sign of the forest around them changing, but Neri couldn't calm a sense of growing urgency. Niall didn't take a turn at sleeping but he seemed to know where they were going, content to sit beside her with Mik and Emelyn walking ahead murmuring to each other. Neri grinned, wondering if Emelyn had any idea yet how devoted Mik's furtive glances in her direction were.

Mik's shoulders stiffened at something Emelyn said, but Neri's senses were distracted the moment Niall leaned close, his lips brushing her ear.

"Mik's in a mood, look," he murmured.

She nodded, barely able to stop from closing her eyes to soak in his closeness. She craved it with startling intensity but Mik joined them before she could succumb.

"Emelyn needs proof that I can handle myself in a fight," he announced.

Niall laughed and his weary face lit up.

"Good idea." He reached an arm behind him and banged on the wall of the cart. "Fight break!"

Ciena cascaded out of the cart with a wicked gleam in her eyes, but before Neri could jump down Niall's hand ghosted over her shoulder.

"Not you," he added. "Not that I think you can't fight, I know you can, but I want you to rest. You're the one who'll have to convince my awful brother to play nice."

She pulled a face at him, but it was worth sacrificing her

pride and a release for her irritable energy to see him smiling at her like that again.

Ciena threw Mik and Niall a blade each and stood to wait her turn, while Emelyn joined Neri up on the driving seat to watch.

"Can Mik fight?" Neri asked.

Emelyn shrugged. "I don't think so, but I've clearly wounded his pride by saying it. I think they're just trying to pass time and cheer us all up."

Mik threw off the old cloak he'd been wearing and Niall rolled up the sleeves of his shirt. Neri had seen him fight enough times before to not worry for his safety, but she hoped he was going to be generous if Mik couldn't match him. It didn't look like it as Niall lifted his blade with a flourish and Mik copied him.

The blades clashed and Neri bolted forward to lean over the cart's front rail. Emelyn squeaked in alarm as the blades whirled and swished through the air at alarming speed, and Neri clung to the rail with rigid hands.

Niall's blade scraped down the length of Mik's, and Mik stepped back with his chest heaving. They edged away from each other, blades pointed down and Emelyn breathed a sigh of relief.

"You're both slacking," Ciena called out. "Tension out the shoulders and absorb the weight in the knees."

Mik pulled his shirt over his head as Niall untied his.

"You're making the cart smoke," Emelyn muttered

Neri flexed her glowing fingers as the wooden rail charred underneath them, but she had to let go as the blades began to slash once more, both men fighting faster. Niall swung his blade one moment, and the next Mik lay on the floor, his blade a short distance from his grasp.

As Emelyn scrambled down from the driving seat and

shot across the grass, Neri eyed Niall, marking out his bare skin for nicks or cuts and finding none. He laughed as Emelyn dropped to her knees beside Mik and pressed her hands to his chest.

Mik heaved a breath. "Em, get off me please."

Emelyn sat back on her heels and glared up at Niall, but he only dimmed the remnants of victory dancing across his face, failing to look in any way apologetic.

"Yeah, that's all really showy, but if we carry on we can be fighting real folk," Ciena grumbled.

Neri slid down from the driving seat and rounded the front of the cart to stand at their horse's head. Her *ai-tan* jittered restlessly in her limbs and she wanted a chance to fight next.

"This will be our final rest point," Niall said. "We go any further and we're in the open. There's no stopping after that."

Finn nodded. "Hate to agree with him, ever, but he's right. We should probably scope out the boundary and see how many guards we might be facing first."

"Fine." Ciena grabbed her blade and started stabbing it through the air. "Finn, Niall, Mik, you know the area best, go scout. I'll keep the others out of trouble."

Neri scoffed before she could claw the sound back in, but Niall distracted her by sliding his arms around her. She closed her eyes as he pressed a rough kiss to her forehead.

"We'll be back in no time," he promised. "Keep a sharp eye out."

"Likewise. Be careful."

He hesitated, his gaze roving over her face, and she threw any shred of reservation aside. She got the blurriest glimpse of his surprised smile as she snagged the front of his shirt and pulled him close to claim his mouth with hers.

Now I'm home.

She smothered a laugh as she drew back and he tried to follow, grumbling under his breath before letting her go.

"We'll be back even sooner," he said.

Her gaze drifted over his shoulder and she clung onto him.

"Just, stay there a moment, or you'll ruin it," she whispered.

"Ruin what?"

She stared over his shoulder as Mik fitted a small blade to his belt and faced Emelyn. Ciena and Finn were further ahead, discussing things that Neri didn't even want to imagine, but she could hear Emelyn and Mik's conversation clear enough.

"What exactly are you lot going to do?" Emelyn asked.

Mik's hand landed on her shoulder. "Don't worry about me. I'll be back before you know it."

Emelyn's squeak echoed through the trees as he pressed a sudden fleeting kiss onto the top of her head, dashing any pretence Neri had of them not eavesdropping.

"What, what happened?" Niall hissed.

"He kissed her."

"Finally."

Neri watched Mik walk off, an unmistakeable swagger to his step, while Emelyn stood watching him leave.

She grinned. "Go, if only to bring him back safe."

Niall stole one last kiss and jogged after Mik, leaving Emelyn a statue and Ciena walking around the perimeter of the cart on guard. Neri joined Emelyn's side just in time to hear her groan quietly.

"Okay, spill," she demanded.

So Emelyn spilled. She kept going and going and going until Neri was almost dizzy.

"I'm not even sure if I like him," she babbled on. "What if somehow I had a dream of him, wrote it into existence, then didn't remember it? That's happened before. I've dreamed about stuff moving and I wake up to Ma moaning because it moved."

Neri frowned. "Well, I can see how that might be worrying, but ignore how he feels about you. How do you feel about him?"

"I have no idea. He's a friend, always has been. I mean, I had a teeny crush on Finn for a while, a long while maybe, but I never thought of Mik in that way."

"And now?"

"Now... I don't know. I get all hot and bothered when he smiles at me. But what if that's just because I wrote it into existence without realising somehow?"

Neri glanced past her as neither of them had been keeping watch, but Ciena was still stalking the boundary.

"Maybe take a look at him for himself and figure out how you feel first," she suggested. "No pressure, just who is he and do you like him."

Emelyn shrugged. "I don't know. He probably doesn't even like me like that and I'm being ridiculous."

Neri couldn't hold back a loud snort and Emelyn glared at her.

"Sorry, I'm sorry." She tried to remove the grin from her face. "But him not liking you isn't going to be an issue."

Emelyn's eyes widened, her mouth dropping open.

"What do you mean?"

Neri hesitated, but she had an inkling that Emelyn's worries were a veil for more deeply lodged emotions that she didn't want to face yet.

"Apparently, and I say this with reservation because it's

not like I've ever asked him, Mik has been half in love with you for ages."

Emelyn gasped. "How could you possibly know that?"

"It's pretty obvious by the way he looks at you. Just figure out what *you* feel first and go from there."

Emelyn nodded, pensiveness falling across her face as Ciena strode up to them with a loud huff and two blades in hand.

"I'm bored," she announced.

Neri nodded. "Yeah. How long do you think they'll be gone?"

"Who cares?" Ciena shrugged, holding one of the blades out to her.

Neri grinned. Niall might not want her fighting Ciena, or anyone, but Niall wasn't around. She grabbed the blade and stood ready as Emelyn moved back.

"I won't go easy on you this time," Ciena taunted.

"Good, neither will I."

She ignored the first feint and attacked while Ciena was still moving back. Her enthusiasm spiked the harder Ciena fought her, the whirl and dance of the blades settling a restlessness that had been raging inside her ever since reaching the east.

A flicker of shadow caught her attention, just enough to distract her for a moment.

Ciena's blade whirled.

Neri twisted to avoid it.

Emelyn gasped loudly as an arc of blood spattered through the air. It landed on the ground and Neri stepped back. Even Ciena was staring with some apprehension. As Neri looked down at the bloody gash bubbling on her upper arm.

Emelyn hurried forward but stumbled to a halt as Neri's

eyes burned in her direction, irritation flaring at being caught so easily.

"I'm fine," she snapped and raised her blade. "Again."

As her chest began to hammer and her breath began to catch, she realised she wasn't fine after all.

CHAPTER NINE

Niall saw the slash of Ciena's blade and a shout tore from his throat as blood spattered from Neri's arm. Ciena knew better than to approach or apologise as he strode past her, wisely stepping out of his way instead.

"I barely leave you alone for a moment and now you're bleeding?" he snarled.

Neri blinked up at him, that guileless expression mingled with determination driving him to distraction.

"It's just one graze," she lied valiantly. "Stop overreacting."

He gripped her shoulders with both hands and held her firm as he inspected the cut. Shallow enough because Ciena hadn't been intending to wound.

But if she had been…

"Niall?"

Even her voice sounded pained which jolted him out of the anger straight into protective mode. He settled a gentle arm around her waist and gave her a stern look instead.

Seeing she had his attention, she pressed a firm hand against his chest and nodded to something behind him.

"I'm not falling for distraction," he muttered.

She widened her eyes to insist wordlessly that he look behind him, and he turned far too obediently for his own liking. He couldn't see anything that she might be using to distract him, but then Emelyn barrelled past and ran straight into Mik's arms. He barely had the presence of mind to open them in time and staggered back when she cannoned into him.

"Steady on, Em." He laughed.

Emelyn blushed and wriggled free, her gaze dropping immediately to her toes. Niall turned back to Neri as she took a clean cloth from Ciena and held it to her bleeding arm.

"What did you find out?" she asked.

"Don't think you can distract me from this." He hesitated, then relented. "Hardly any guards on the border at all. We could probably stroll right in before anyone stopped us."

"And that's bad?"

He held her gaze as Ciena snuck up with some dark green gunk on another cloth, Ma's famous ointment if he had to guess by the stink.

"Before the borderlands were all but impenetrable. Guards on every spare bit of wall, every culvert."

"Maybe Viljo's relaxed precautions?" Neri frowned. "Which would be foolish."

She squeaked and looked down in horror as Ciena merrily swabbed her arm.

"Stings a bit?" he asked, and she nodded. "Good. Don't get hurt next time."

She winced in reply, then her gaze hardened with determination.

"How many of them are there though?" she asked. "How many is hardly any?"

Niall glared at her as he took the bandage Finn held out to him and wrapped it around her wound.

"Around ten milling in and out," he said. "But don't even think-"

Neri freed her arm the moment he finished binding it.

"That won't bother us much, but we're not going in to fight." She ignored Ciena's indignant huff. "We're not the enemy now. Come on, let's get this done. The sooner we go in and play nice, the sooner we can be out the other side."

"Desperate to get out of here, are you?" Ciena asked.

Neri shrugged. "I might even have friends staying there as we speak and the Governance wants my head, so yeah."

"We should probably have some kind of plan in case things do go wrong though," Mik said.

Ciena lifted a blade with a feral grin. "Got a back-up plan right here."

"Hardly what I meant and you know it."

Neri opened her mouth, probably to intervene, but Niall used the distraction to grab her by the waist and lift her clean off her feet.

"What are you doing?" she squeaked.

He ignored her protests, her squirming and the laughter from the others. Only once they were past the first line of trees and out of earshot did he set her gently on her feet again. Now was the time for them to talk, before his brother tried to steal her again, but she was glowering at him so charmingly that he had the infuriating urge to kiss her instead.

"Before you say anything, I was irritated and bored and it's not Ciena's fault," she muttered. "I pretty much danced into her blade so if you're going to sulk at someone, it's my fault."

He took her hands in his, and surprise flickered across her face when he said nothing.

"I'm sorry." Her voice wavered. "Em was sulking about Mik and it was torture doing nothing. Please, yell at me, push me about, do something. Just stop looking at me like that."

"Like what?"

"I prefer it when you're angry at me," she mumbled. "When you're sad it feels like dying."

He folded his arms around her with a frustrated sigh and nestled her tight against his chest.

"You need to understand that I'm going to freak out if you cut yourself chopping vegetables. If an animal bites you, my first instinct will be to twist its neck. When we have children, if we decide to have children, I'm going to want to kill it coming out of you because you'll be screaming your head off. At least, I'm told it's not pretty and there's a lot of screaming. You are my only priority, Neri. You're mine and seeing you hurt kills me."

Neri said nothing, her body tense against his. He wondered idly if it was the mention of children that had stunned her to uncharacteristic silence, but he had no qualms about children with her. When they'd seen the whole of the land and the wars were long over, he'd be happy with none, one or a whole bunch. Whatever she wanted.

"You think about that kind of stuff, having children?" she asked, her voice muffled by his shirt.

He tucked a finger under her chin and brought her uncertain gaze up to meet his.

"I'll do whatever it takes to make you happy. I doubt I'll survive more than one of you running around causing chaos, but I can't deny the thought of us having a family is a nice one."

Neri took a deep breath but no words came out.

"That said, if I get you all to myself forever, that has its benefits too," he added.

"We need to deal with getting home first."

He nodded. "We'll discuss it all later then, *when* we get home. I'm a fool dreaming if I think I can keep you from getting into trouble, but I will keep you safe with everything I've got."

He entwined her fingers with his own and led her back to the others.

She can't be in any doubt now about how I really feel.

The thought settled his lingering panic, but he'd be keeping her right beside him until they were back in Jakiris all the same.

He kept a tight grasp on her hand as they approached the group and crossed the grass to Emelyn.

"Em, I'm sorry," Neri said. "I snapped earlier at you. I shouldn't have and I really didn't mean to."

Emelyn's wicked smile was instant. "You think that's bad. Niall once almost threw me across the room."

"I so did not."

"You'd gone missing when you all came to rescue me shortly after we first met you," she explained. "Niall came back to tell me to write you safe again. I said it didn't work like that and he grabbed my arm. Thought he was going to pitch me ten paces."

Neri bit her lip. "Did you? Did you write me safe?"

"No. I can write small wishes that don't always come true. I can write that someone finds their cloak or that they escape something, but not forever. I forge links, I don't create realities. If I write that your arm will heal super quickly, it won't. If I'm lucky, you'll feel less pain, but there are consequences."

Emelyn sighed and raked her fingers through her hair.

"If I write that your arm heals in a day, it won't but you might feel no pain. Then thinking you're fine, you do too much too quick and make it worse. The bad stuff is necessary to teach us about life, our limitations. I am cursed as I am blessed. I don't meddle unless I have to."

"The responsibility must suck," Neri said.

"It does. Everyone expects me to forge lands, to manipulate time and to save everything. I hate that I can't, but nobody should have this much power. That's why it came to me, because I'm too scared to use it."

Niall knew that feeling well enough and guessed Neri did too. By most accounts, gifts had been diluted across the east through a combination of the land-wasting from the Governance's greed and sheer lack of knowledge. What most saw as *ai-tan* on the west side of the cursed forest, was seen as skill on the other. He had no clue what the north and south would be like, but in the flightiest moments of his dreaming he imagined exploring them all with Neri.

"It's not a matter of being scared," he insisted. "Power isn't something you wield. You're a rarity because you have the ability to use absolute power but you don't let it corrupt you. You're stronger, whether because of fear, or reticence, or wisdom, than anyone I know."

Emelyn blinked, the touch of tears in her eyes.

"That's the nicest thing you've ever said to me."

He shrugged, choosing to wrap his arms around Neri's waist instead of facing the emotional waves pouring off both girls.

"I'd love to say I'll find you a suitable man when we get back to Jakiris," Neri suggested. "But I don't think anyone could deserve you."

She winked at Emelyn then glanced innocently in Mik's direction. Emelyn flushed bright red.

"Um… shouldn't we be leaving soon?" she asked.

Ciena nodded. "Might as well. it's now or never. Fine,

we can take the cart, but it's nowhere near as atmospheric as sauntering in on foot."

Niall rolled his eyes, too focused on getting home to argue with her.

"You saunter in on foot then," he grumbled. "We'll take the comfortable route. I know the way so Neri and I can drive the cart. If you're lucky, we may even wait for you."

She stuck her tongue out then pointed at Neri.

"She's on every wanted sign from here to the Kahlen mountains. Sure she should be up front for all to see?"

Niall hesitated, but Neri shot him a fierce look.

"Niall and the new lord of the borderlands don't get on," she said sniffily. "He seems to like me, so-"

"Like, if that's what you're calling it," Niall muttered.

"-*So,* if anyone sees me approaching, it'll get the news to him all the quicker, won't it?"

Niall sighed. "I won't argue, no matter how much I want to. But if he makes one wrong move in your direction, or even looks at you funny, I'll end him."

"Fine. Let's go."

Ciena, Finn, Mik and Emelyn got into the cart, with Ciena grumbling something about at least having the element of surprise if nobody could see her, and Niall hauled himself up onto the driving seat. The moment Neri was beside him, he sent the horse forward and dropped the reins into one hand so he could curl the other around Neri's fingers. She squeezed and smiled back at him.

"It'll be okay," she insisted. "Imagine the scandal Livia would cause otherwise."

Niall chuckled. "You miss her."

"I do. Much like I missed everyone here. All I wanted was for folk to have the choice, but now they've made it I want to go home."

They cleared the fringe of the forest, vast swathes of it still charred and smoking, and she shuddered. Niall eyed the subtle glow playing beneath her skin as the wind danced her hair about and guessed it wasn't cold that was affecting her.

"I know it's like that because of what we did, or so everyone keeps saying, but it's still creepy to see an entire forest like that," she said.

Niall grinned. "What *we* did? I don't remember having any affinity for fire to burn a whole forest down, smiting an age-old curse in the process."

"You practically forced me into the woods, thank you very much."

She settled her head on his shoulder and nudged it affectionately with her nose. He kissed the top of her head as the horse picked up speed across the open stretch of grassland. They were closer than he wanted to admit, and nobody mentioned stopping for food or to rest the horse as the day wore on. Up ahead against the horizon were the hazy brown-grey tips of the Kahlen mountains, but between that and them was the line of the cursed forest, with the stone walls of the borderlands getting closer fast.

It took him a moment to notice the streak of movement in the distance, but Neri sat up and that drew his attention.

"Oh, here comes the welcoming committee," he muttered.

She nodded. "A lot of guards, but I can't see who they are from here."

"I can, and sadly my brother is leading the pack."

He slowed the horse to a steady walk and focused on the firm warmth of Neri's hand in his as she blinked remnants of sleep from her eyes. He could see his brother clearly now, dressed as finely as ever in a flowing bright blue cloak and riding a showy white horse. Niall stifled a snort as the group drew close enough for him to see Viljo's dark green hair swept back from his forehead to support a delicate silver crown.

She's mine. She knows it, Viljo knows it, and she won't let anything come between us again. Not even his sparkly little tiara.

The thoughts didn't soothe the doubt clenching in his gut, the dizzying swirl of panic in his chest surging on as Viljo, Lord of the Borderlands, brought his company to a stop in front of them.

Niall had to let Neri's hand go as she slid down to the ground, but he did the same and strode around to reclaim her instantly.

Viljo didn't dismount and neither did his guards. He only glanced at Neri with a guarded smile, then his expression turned icy as he faced Niall.

"Brother, I didn't expect to see you on this side of my lands. It seems there are many secrets being kept after all. Many indeed."

CHAPTER TEN

Neri caught the not-so-veiled hostility Viljo sent Niall's way. Niall tensed, but she rubbed her thumb over his knuckles and took a step forward.

"We've no idea what you've been told or not," she said. "Or what's happened in recent days. Is Livia okay?"

Viljo blinked, as if the sound of her voice had roused him from some distant state. He glanced at her, then back to Niall before dismounting and handing his reins to the nearest guard.

"I think the usual greeting between friends is still a hug," he announced. "We are friends, aren't we?"

He opened his arms wide and she noticed a sparkling circlet of silver nestled in his green hair. He was a lord now, the Jakid of his own realm in a way, and he was indicating she should greet him with a hug.

Niall wouldn't like it but she couldn't refuse without making the situation worse. She grasped her arms around his chest momentarily before stepping back and getting ensnared in his embrace.

Neri struggled for a moment but he had no intention of letting her go without a prolonged physical greeting. She had a funny feeling that his eyes would be boring into Niall's, but she heard no sounds of dissent behind her.

Finally, Viljo let her go. She stepped back with her cheeks flaming and her *ai-tan* ready to riot.

"Hopefully we're not inconveniencing you too much," she said, fighting to keep her tone civil. "I assure you, we'll only ask your indulgence until we can cross the border. I'm sure the Jakida will give us the same courtesies you can offer."

Darkness spanned his face as she mentioned his *ama*, but she stepped back until her shoulder bumped against Niall's chest. Niall wound his arms around her waist from behind and, despite the further darkening of Viljo's expression at the possessive gesture, she let her hands settle firmly over his in answer.

"So formal." Viljo smiled, but there was no real warmth in it. "We can definitely offer you suitable courtesy, Neri, don't worry. I hope you will repay us with your presence for a while. There are a good many things happening which I'm sure you will have an opinion on."

His tone didn't intimate whether her opinion would be a positive or negative influence, but it suggested it was required regardless. Neri nodded despite the sudden tensing of Niall's arm around her.

"Perhaps you'd like to ride along with me?" Viljo added. "That seat doesn't look at all comfortable."

Neri squeezed Niall's fingers tight before he could utter a word.

"It's much cosier than it looks, don't worry. We're grateful of your hospitality. My friends and I are keen to find out how things are going."

Viljo's expression darkened, his brow furrowing as the likeness between him and Niall became more and more similar.

"Friends?"

Neri nodded. "We have a few friends with us."

She reached back and tapped the side of the cart, having

to twist because Niall stubbornly clung on while his gaze remained locked on his brother.

One by one, Ciena, Finn, Mik and Emelyn stepped out, but Viljo only gave them a cursory glance before nodding.

"Come along then," he said. "You must dine with me tonight, I insist."

He remounted his horse and rode to the head of his guards, setting a smart pace as the others scrambled to get back in the cart.

"Well, that could have gone worse," she muttered.

Niall held her closer to delay them from following.

"Be careful what you say to him. He's touched by something and I don't know what yet, but there's a mark on him and it's not good."

Tempted to put his attitude down to his previous issues with his brother, Neri only nodded as they got back on the driving seat and set off after Viljo's group. Niall and Viljo openly hated each other, but Viljo clearly had more lordly intentions to sway her to his side than he'd shown before.

Maybe disappearing through to the west immediately isn't going to be as simple as I hoped.

She soothed herself with the knowledge that the borderlands were at least a safe mid-point compared to the east, but the sense of foreboding curling like a swelling stone in her gut didn't agree.

The towering wooden gates of the borderlands came into view and she glanced down at her dirty dress and ruined slippers. She'd been wearing exactly the same thing when Viljo tried to convince her to join him instead of Niall, and clearly she wasn't giving a great impression not having changed since.

As the gates rumbled open, she got the first glimpse of double-level dwellings made from stone pillar corners and finished with wooden planking for walls. Many had straw-thatch on the roofs, but there were so many signs of neglect and disrepair that her heart sank to her toes.

Up ahead through a maze of lanes, an imposing round tower of dark grey stone loomed over the entire settlement. Several circular balconies jutted out from the central column, but if she squinted she could tell most of the rooms inside were in darkness.

"What's betting you can see all the way to Apeklonia from the top of that tower," she muttered.

Niall clasped her hand tighter and leaned close.

"Or as far as Jakiris with keen eyes. Whatever they suggest, don't let them separate us. Something isn't right here."

She wanted to tell him he was being paranoid, but her *ai-tan* was roiling in anticipation and she knew he was right. Even when they arrived at the bottom of the tower steps, surrounded by a vast settlement square full of folk going about their day, she allowed her *ai-tan* to guide her instincts. Viljo dismounted his horse and handed the reins to the nearest guard with his usual stiff posture, but there was something was different about him, a less yielding aura than before.

"We have rooms for you," he offered. "You will be comfortable here. I can offer you the chambers besides my own, Neri, and perhaps we can discuss how to proceed."

Neri caught the flicker of determination in his eyes and lifted her gaze instead to avoid it. She scanned the square then looked up to the doors of the tower. A woman she didn't recognise appeared in an extremely fine dark blue dress that covered her entire body to the neck.

"That would be great." Neri tried to keep her tone civil. "We need to rest first, then maybe we can catch up after."

She made a point of clasping Niall's hand to her chest and staring Viljo right in the face, determined to make her meaning clear. His mouth twisted, but the well-dressed woman descended the steps and arrived at his side before he could answer.

"You've returned," she announced. "Who are your guests?"

Her voice was laced with suspicion, guarded against what the answer might be.

"This is Neri, Harelda. She and her guests are staying with us." He hesitated, eying Niall for a long moment. "That's my brother too."

Niall filled in their companions' names, probably just to waste Viljo's time, and Harelda offered them servants to accompany them to their rooms.

"It's getting late in the day," she said. "Come inside. You'll want to rest a while no doubt."

Neri eyed the suns already sinking low as they followed her and Viljo through the tower doors into tunnel-like halls of stone.

"I'll put you in the west hall," Harelda suggested. "You can see almost to Jakiris on a clear day from there."

Viljo stopped dead, which brought them all to a staggering halt.

"It's unusual custom in the borderlands to share quarters without union or kinship," he announced. "Unless you've united in the days we've been apart, you might wish to observe our traditions. Perhaps the rooms in the west wing will do for everyone else, but Neri can take the vacant one in the central chamber."

His gaze was fixed on her again, the dedicated intensity giving absolutely no doubt of why he wanted to get her alone. She suppressed a shudder and smiled sweetly instead, even as she fought the urge to melt the silver crown to his mind-addled head.

"We're as good as," she countered. "If it's too much trouble, we can stay in the cart. Small squeeze but then-"

"It's okay," Niall interrupted.

"Er... what?"

He kissed her forehead and moved a strand of hair away from her temple.

"We can observe the customs, and I'm sure his lordship will be more than happy to observe ours. Ciena and Emelyn can share a room with you."

Neri bit her lips between her teeth to quell a smile as Ciena nudged her arm roughly.

"Yeah, I don't snore, much. I fight in my sleep though."

Niall smiled. "She does, I've seen it. Full parries and everything."

Viljo's lordly mask slipped as disgust curled across his face, but he set off along the hall again without a word. Harelda paused long enough to give them a 'what can I do' kind of look, then swept after him. They opened a couple of doors at the far end of the hall, but while Viljo threw his open without ceremony, Harelda peered inside each as if to check they were fit for guests first.

"You may as well take this suite of rooms," Viljo said. "Take a moment to refresh yourselves, then you can join me in the main hall for drinks. There's someone who will be very keen to see you again."

He strode away before Neri could query it, but a thrill of excitement leapt in her chest at the thought of seeing Livia again. Even the Jakida's domineering presence would be a welcome lift to the hideous atmosphere.

She walked into the nearest room and Niall followed her in. As he shut the door behind them, leaving the others outside in the hall, shadows leapt around him like a billowing cloak.

"This isn't ideal," she muttered.

He threw up his hands, then paced across the flagstone floor and slammed them against the wooden bedpost.

"I have to sit in the kingdom of someone who evidently still wants to jump you and pretend to play nice like I don't want to plant my fist right in his smug face."

His low growl almost made her smile, but she knew how to quell his anger.

"Almost like me planting mine into Finn's."

He looked her way. "What?"

"Yeah. When Ciena picked me up at the candle shop, he had her drag me to some random inn. She had a great time pretending to be a grey-cloak for a few days, so I thought it was going to be Amis I was facing. Then he turns around and it's Finn. I was so furious that they'd dragged me out of my way to finding you that I punched him straight in the jaw."

Niall stalked toward her but she held her ground even as her pulse leapt.

"I don't know whether to be furious at him or really turned on."

"By him?" she teased.

He wrapped a hand through strands of her hair, tilting her head back to his liking before dropping a lingering kiss on her lips.

"That is a disgusting thought," he murmured. "How about we skip dinner? Leave my brother stewing. We're in the borderlands now. Nothing stopping us waking at dawn and walking straight out the other side. Or going now."

"That wouldn't be very diplomatic."

"Don't care. I want you home. I want you safe.

Something's not right here, I can sense it, and my brother's got something to do with it. He may be a lord now, but I don't care about him or his new land."

"That, and this could have been your land if you wanted it."

The thought popped into her mind and out of her mouth before she could stop it.

Niall's eyes darkened even further as his lip curled in disgust. He let go of her and stepped back.

"Oh yes, I'm bothered about my little brother usurping my kingdom. He's already managed that so maybe you'll run off with him as well before long."

Neri lifted a hand to his arm but he shook her away. Frustration boiled over and she folded her arms, already eying the door over his shoulder.

"I don't care about that, or him," she snapped. "But we're here. It's not exactly easy to leave the others behind either. I know it was their choice but I'm going to worry all the same. We don't even know what their plan is."

Niall was still for several moments and she mirrored him, letting him work through whatever he was working up to telling her.

Or working out to hide from me.

"Lavian is preparing the circus performance to basically wage a war on the governance from the inside," he announced. "The performance is said to be in the Apeklonian square."

"But that's perfect."

"Lavian is known for his strategy, so I've been told," he muttered.

"Not that." She frowned as the plan unfurled in her mind. "If we can get Jakirian fighters through the borderlands here, then we can hit the Governance in

Apeklonia from both sides."

Niall folded his arms across his chest as his expression turned icy.

"I suppose you'll have to cosy up to his lordship after all then, if you want to get permission to march a fighting force through his lands. You'd need a mass of fighters to see off the grey cloaks as well."

Do I let this slide and do it anyway? He wanted me to tell him everything before, but I'm so tired of fighting.

Neri sighed and turned toward the door.

"Well, you do what you want. I'm at least going to try and find some positive action in this rather than sit around sulking. I have to do something until I can grab a horse and head home."

Niall growled in response but it was a half-hearted sound.

He's not slept in days, barely eaten.

When he glanced at her, his mouth crooked with regret, the irritation ebbed away. She crossed the room to force her arms around his waist and held on until his anger settled and his arms wrapped around her once more.

"I reckon I've terrorised you enough for a while." He kissed the top of her head. "I don't know what's the matter with me, but I'm done. How about we test the comfort of our 'generous' host's bed and sleep?"

Neri smiled, the weariness and relief tugging at her eyelids even as she shook her head.

"Nice try but if Livia's here, or the Jakida, they're our fastest route home. I do want to get back too."

Even as she said the words, nobody had come to show them where dinner was being held yet, so she dropped like a dead weight onto the bed.

Niall settled beside her and pulled her close. She laid

her head on his shoulder and allowed herself the small luxury.

"The borderlands may not be Jakiris, but it's close enough. We're almost fully home now."

He murmured his agreement and Neri closed her eyes as he started to whisper about places he wanted to show her once the upheaval was over. She let her mind drift as Niall continued to mumble words to her, but a loud bang had her eyes open before she could properly fall asleep.

She sat up in alarm and almost tumbled off the edge of the bed, grumbling with sleepy indignation at Niall who tried and failed not to laugh.

"I apologise, she ran straight past me!"

A wide-eyed maid hurried after Emelyn as she burst into the room. The maid cast a quivering look of nerves at Niall, and Neri allowed the disconcerting notion that they were all being watched to swill through her.

"No harm done," she said. "Emelyn you've terrified the poor woman. We're used to you dropping in but she's obviously not. Is everything okay?"

Emelyn nodded. "We've been summoned to drinks."

Neri forced herself to her feet as Niall groaned beside her. She didn't have any fine clothing to wear but Viljo would need to take her as she was.

Eww.

"Also, there's someone here who says she knows you," Emelyn added.

Neri beamed at the thought of seeing Livia again, and even Niall managed a weary smile as he hauled himself up and rounded the end of the bed to grab her hand.

"I'll not get a moment alone with you now if you've got Livia and Emelyn buzzing around you," he grumbled.

She smiled at the hint of shadow around his eyes and

pulled him along with her out of the room.

"Or they'll get to know each other so well they'll forget all about me and you'll have me all to yourself."

He grinned as they started down the hall.

"Now that I can get behind."

Neri tried not to feel too intimidated as they walked through the dark, gloomy stone halls. She would be gracious as a guest and remain until the next day. Then they could set out for Jakiris, on foot if necessary. The thought fluttered from her mind the moment she stepped into the wide entrance hall and recognised the woman grinning at her and Niall.

Hardly unable to believe her luck, she hurried forward, but Cori grinned and held up her hands between them.

"Don't hug me, or from what I hear Niall will have my head," she joked.

Neri rolled her eyes and her cheeks tinged with embarrassment. Then Cori reached up to hug them both, her head settling between theirs.

"Careful what you say around here, and to whom you say it. I'd caution you to get out of the borderlands as soon as possible. I'll send word to Lady Livia as soon as I'm able to that you're here, but things are only marginally less strained than before all the battles. I'm here as a spy."

She let them go and slapped Niall on the shoulder as though they'd all been sharing a friendly joke.

"It's a good place to learn healing," she added. "I'll be sad when my time ends."

Neri smiled too and pushed the whispered information to a safe part of her mind. Then she noticing Emelyn standing a few steps above them and hastened to make introductions. Cori opened her mouth to say something, but her lively expression dimmed instantly and Neri turned up to find Viljo waiting for them at the top of the steps.

"Already taking in the sights without a guide," he noted. "Follow me and we'll have drinks in the main hall. I really do what you to meet my guests."

Neri frowned as she pulled Niall along by the hand to make a point, linking arms with Emelyn as well.

If Livia isn't here and Cori was talking about sneaking messages to her, then who are Viljo's guests?

Neri pressed her head close to Emelyn as Viljo stopped to talk in low tones to a passing guard.

"Where are the others?" she asked.

Emelyn leaned closer. "They insisted they didn't want to intrude."

Neri heard the unspoken addition that they would likely be doing some kind of spying among folk of the settlement. She wished she could escape the same way, but Viljo continued on and she had to follow. Niall's hand tightened around her fingers as they walked into what had to be the main hall and she squeezed back.

Fine tapestries hung along the stone walls, with the floorboards and long dining table polished to a high shine. Wooden bowls and tankards that resembled wine goblets sat at each place setting, but as they headed to the far end of the hall, Neri noticed dust lingering in several of the bowls.

Viljo took his place at the head of the table and gestured to the seat beside him. Emelyn grinned and slid onto it before he could say a word, so Neri settled onto the chair next to her and tugged Niall into the one on the other side.

Whilst servants served drinks in wooden cups, Viljo fixed Neri with an appraising stare.

"I suppose you've seen quite a few things since you've been back home?" he asked.

Neri forced a smile. "I haven't been back home to Jakiris yet, but the east did throw up a number of interests. I doubt we'll trespass on your time much longer. We're keen to get home."

Viljo's mouth twisted and once again Neri could see tiny glimmers of his sibling link to Niall in the movement as she waited for the next curveball.

"I would caution you about going back to Jakiris." He seemed to struggle with his polite tone. "Things are not as they were when you left them. Livia was quite distraught to find you'd disappeared without a word. I don't know what kind of welcome you'll receive."

He at least had some shred of decency to look at his plate as he uttered the lie, but the audacity of it brought Neri's *ai-tan* roaring to the surface.

Niall had to loosen her grip on his hand and she took a steadying breath, with didn't help. If she wanted free reign of his settlement, at least enough for them to leave it by choice, she had to be polite. But she didn't want Viljo to think that he could dictate her movements either.

"That is a shame." She frowned. "She was so supportive when we crossed through. Maybe it'd be sensible to send word first. Perhaps you could show me to a messenger after we've had the drink who can do that for me?"

She was sure that Cori would give Livia the message, and that Viljo would be sure not to. He inclined his head in agreement to her request and it seemed they were at a stalemate.

"Had time to do any improvements yet?" Niall asked gruffly.

Viljo's mouth thinned. "No."

"Seen off the scourge ruling the east yet then?"

"No." Viljo looked up as the doors opened. "Oh, on that

matter, let me make some introductions, or should that be re-introductions?"

Neri looked up at the man walking into the room and scrambled out of her chair. Even as Emelyn did the same, Neri shoved Emelyn bodily behind her.

The man noted her reaction with a slow, predatory smile.

"Hello, my dear."

Amis nodded to her as she fought the urge to burn him where he stood. He'd plaited his long white beard and she could see the hint of his Governance tattoo peeking out over the collar of his shirt. Her skin burned but she willed her gift to stay hidden as Niall joined her side with one hand ready on the blade at his hip.

"We've come full circle rather, haven't we?" Amis added. "And is that Emelyn? Well, this is a cheery reunion."

Neri willed her fire to calm, anger and fear blending until she wasn't sure which one was burning rampant through her limbs and searing her insides.

"Amis mentioned that you knew each other from prior days," Viljo said.

Neri forced her fire down and straightened her shoulders, aware of Niall blocking her as fiercely as she was blocking Emelyn.

"You could say that. We definitely didn't part on pleasant terms. How's Eva?"

Amis raised his brow. "Not a friend of yours, last I looked. Her story was a tragic one. That is in the past now though, and we honour the sanctity of the borderlands as was set out during the creation of the cursed forest itself."

Neri had no clue what the sanctity of the borderlands was, but Niall huffed something under his breath before glowering at Viljo instead.

"You're honouring that?" he asked.

Viljo nodded. "While the remnants of the curse remain, I must."

"Then we're done here."

He pulled Neri forward by the hand and she clung onto Emelyn as Niall towed them both past Amis' smug face.

"Not a word," he muttered

Neri focused on Emelyn's quaking fingers gripping hers like a lifeline as Niall hauled them through the halls.

If Amis is here, as Viljo's guest of all things, then we need to leave quickly.

The moment they left the tower and saw the square winding down, Neri allowed herself the tiniest sigh of relief. They weren't in any kind of safe situation if Amis was lurking around, and the oppressive dark halls of the tower were unnerving her anyway. After spending time in Jakiris and the palace there, she didn't know how Viljo could stand such a place.

Niall slowed his pace slightly as they walked along winding lanes toward a bustling square, but there wasn't much happiness in sight from those they passed. Even the lanes leading off the square were narrow and oppressive. As she turned into one it occurred to her that Viljo's *ai-tan* was of the earth, and yet most of the plants on windowsills and the trees around the square seemed to be wilted or withering.

She had no idea if the proximity to the cursed forest had caused the decay, or just bad management, but either way she wanted out.

"Niall! Neri!"

Neri lifted her head and caught sight of Cori pushing through the crowd. Niall changed course toward her, but

Emelyn pointed out Mik and the others coming from the other side of the square.

Cori smiled as they met in the middle, but her eyes were serious as she nodded to them. It took Neri a few moments to realise that the nod meant Cori had managed to get a message to Livia, and a few more to realise that she wasn't alone. Worse yet, Neri recognised her companion.

She managed a weak grimace of recognition as Hareili gave her a dismissive glance, then turned a bright smile in Niall's direction. Her eyes grazed over him and Neri could understand in that moment why Niall hated his brother so much. Memory of Hareili's prowess as a fighter leapt to mind, and she wondered who would win in a fight if Hareili was pitted against Ciena.

Niall greeted her like an old friend with a broad smile, but he pushed both arms around Neri's waist from behind and settled his head next to hers as he did it.

"How have things been since we've been away?" he asked.

Neri let the others do the talking, already weary and irritable.

We're standing here while the enemy is dining inside with the lord of the borderlands. We've all but lost an ally there.

Hareili detailed that the revelry had continued for days after they'd disappeared, and how their sudden absence was discussed at length, but Cori gave her sister a sour look.

"It wasn't that drastic," she insisted. "I was in the group that arrived here with the royal entourage, and we set off three days after the celebration in the square. The Jakida wanted to stay on here, but his lordship insisted she not embarrass him. His advisor prefers the power that comes from the old ways of ruling, and from what I can see, he's listening."

Neri took a deep breath to calm her temper at the mere thought of Amis worming his way into Viljo's mind so easily.

"We'll leave you be anyway," Cori said. "It's good to see you again."

They turned to leave, but Niall's hold tensed as Hareili turned back to them with a suspiciously sweet smile.

"I must congratulate you both, I almost forgot. From what I hear, Niall, you're back in line to rule Jakiris now."

Neri stiffened as Niall pulled away from her. It wasn't a conversation they'd managed to have yet, but he'd been adamant that the title wouldn't land at his feet.

"Wouldn't it be Livia's now?" she asked.

Niall shrugged and set off across the square with his hands in his pockets.

"Not unless I die. I can refuse it but then it may go to Viljo instead and he'd rule all. The Jakida only took the role because her three older siblings didn't survive infancy. It's always the oldest available that rules."

"Did you know this all along? Is that why you always wanted to go back to the west?"

She kept any accusation out of her voice, mainly because it wasn't her right to demand the knowledge and she truly was curious. She didn't care either way but living in her cottage might not be what he had in mind for their future after all.

He turned to face her, his jaw taut and his shadows flitting over his skin.

"Well I hoped it would be a positive thing, especially if we're talking about children someday."

She halted at the bitterness in his tone.

"Hold on, you were the one who mentioned children."

"Ah." He smiled bitterly. "And you weren't. Is Jakiris not to your liking then? Perhaps, having seen a settlement as fine as this one, you've decided you'd rather take your chances with my darling brother."

Neri turned to block his path and stood nose to nose with him, the glow of her skin from her gift reflecting in his eyes.

"Well I must be really bad at loving you then," she hissed. "If you seriously think that I'm here for some random kingdom, or any land at all, or that I'm even thinking about having children with someone who doubts my morals like that, you are absolutely addle-headed."

Mindful of the square full of locals, she turned away. She'd done what she intended to. She'd brought her friends through to safety. Viljo had no reason to be malicious to her friends, and Niall could do whatever he pleased.

Livia at least will be happy to see me. I'll borrow the first horse I can find in the barns and ride home.

"Neri, I didn't mean..." He trailed off.

Both of them knew he didn't mean it, not really, but he'd said it all the same.

The hot splash of tears fell on her cheeks, her *ai-tan* determined to explode something soon. The only thing keeping her from controlling her temper and thinking rationally was that Niall didn't trust her love for him.

I left without him and he'll never forgive me for it.

Like last time when he'd left her behind in Jakiris, he was trying to push her away. All her hopes for coming home and finally having some proper time with him tumbled into ruin.

She stormed back to the tower with Ciena and Emelyn tailing behind her. Neither of them said a word, not even

Emelyn. They sat in pensive silence in the bedroom while she paced up and down, accompanied by the rhythmic stab of Ciena's blade-tip as it carved the edge of the wooden bedframe.

A knock on the door made her heart lift, until she conceded that Niall probably wouldn't have bothered knocking. Ciena opened the door and stood back to let a servant hurry in.

"His lordship has summoned you to dinner," he announced.

Neri rolled her eyes. "I bet he has. What are those?"

She nodded to the pile of cloth in the man's arms and he hesitated.

"His lordship demanded that suitable clothing be provided for you for dinner."

"For all three of us?"

"Um… no, just you, Lady."

She winced at the honorific and pointed to the nearby dresser.

"Set them down there then. Is his guest still here? The awful one with the long beard?"

The servant nodded, then glanced over his shoulder at the open doorway.

"He has been here since before his lordship took control. The old lord was very… fond of him. Lady Harelda not so much."

"They don't get on?" she prompted.

"Lady Harelda is the last of a noble bloodline of ladies and lords of the borderlands. Her mother had to concede control to the old lord for the sake of our folk, but Lady Harelda still stands."

Neri recognised the echo of pride in his voice, and the meaning it stood for.

"Thank you. I understand."

He left and closed the door behind him, and Neri eyed the clothing Viljo had sent for her.

So the old lord took the borderlands by conquest, and now Viljo has done the same, all under Amis' control.

"I should have known it wouldn't be this simple with him," she muttered.

Ciena shrugged and spun her small blade between her fingers.

"You mean Niall?" she asked.

Neri grimaced. "No, he's happily throwing a tantrum somewhere else. I mean that lump of absolute filth has wormed his way into the borderlands and I never even considered it could be a possibility. Now he's got Viljo under control as well, so it's not safe here for any of us."

She wiped both hands over her face with a groan. If she didn't go to dinner, Viljo would likely find some way to bring the fight to her.

Because that's what this is. It's a fight Amis is waging on us, and he's using Viljo as his next puppet to do it with.

She stalked toward the door, leaving Viljo's offer of clothing untouched on the dresser.

"Neither of you have to come to dinner," she said. "It's probably best you don't. Instead, take a walk through the settlement. Find the exit to the west. First thing tomorrow morning, we leave. Let Finn and Mik know. The less I know the better."

Ciena nodded. "Consider it done. Do you need a smaller blade to hide on you?"

"No." Neri managed a weak smile. "I at least have enough of those."

"Can't ever have enough hidden blades, but fair enough."

Neri left the room and closed the door behind her, her pulse picking up as she wound through the sombre corridors to the main hall. Usually she would have thought to stop some passing maids and ask some questions about the settlement, but she couldn't find the energy as they scurried by like frightened birds.

Once we're home, we can sort this.

She wasn't sure, but she had to cling to it all the same as she stepped into the main hall alone.

Everyone already seated stood, but Neri's blood burned as she eyed Amis across the table from Niall. Viljo patted the seat between him and Niall and she had to make the long walk to it with Amis staring her out, his amused smile never faltering.

Her bravado lasted until she reached the chair and looked at Niall, but he didn't even lift his head to check on her. With her eyes close to tearing and her heart about to break, she forced herself to face her enemies with a smile on her face.

"You didn't like the dress?" Viljo asked.

Food was served onto their plates, a far cry from the serve yourself attitude that was common in the main hall of the Jakirian palace. She thought of Livia, of home, and the fact that she'd survived Niall's moods before and would do so long after he'd finished whatever he was playing at.

Then she smiled wide and entered the game.

"I'm comfortable enough in my own clothing, and Livia's already given me enough dresses to last lifetimes. I can't wait to get back to be honest. Oh, no offence."

Viljo's mouth crunched as though he'd bitten into a wasp.

"I see, and I believe you've already met Amis as the

head of the council that governs the east. He was advising the old lord here before I took over and has been a big help since I arrived."

Neri controlled her involuntary shudder, the fake smile stuck to her lips like candle wax to wood.

"It'll be interesting to see how your leadership of the borderlands unfolds," she replied. "You mentioned a sanctity tied to the forest, is that impartiality?"

Viljo nodded. "Of a sort. No harm shall be committed, and no blood will be spilled between our walls by either side."

She jumped as Harelda appeared from the shadows, as if she'd been born from them. Neri glanced at Niall next, but he didn't even bother to look up from the food he was pushing back and forth across his plate.

"This was once a meeting place of peace for both sides," Harelda said quietly. "Then communications broke."

Neri remembered what the servant had said and went desperately for a potential ally in the pool of enemies.

"You're local?" she asked.

"My family ruled the borderlands long ago, since even before the border was made." Harelda's gaze lifted, granite in her steely blue eyes. "Now we exist as fodder for marital politics."

Amis smiled but Viljo's taut expression grew ever tighter.

"Perhaps we are done with dining," he announced.

Neri still had most of her plate left but she didn't utter a word as servants arrived to whisk the plates away.

"Drinks," Viljo insisted. "Let us stand a while."

Neri risked a long glance at him the moment he was looking elsewhere. His face, countenance and figure looked the same. Handsome enough in a broad-jawed, statuesque sort of way, but Niall was right, there was something off about him.

Not that Niall's all-pervading sourness is much better.

"We must look to a new future now," Amis said.

Neri took a silver cup of wine a servant offered her, determined not to drink more than a convincing sip or two.

"One guess who you think should control that new future," she countered archly.

Amis smiled. "Well, someone has to. Without any rule at all, there would be chaos. The rest is purely negotiation."

Thoughts of dark alleys and dead family filled her head and the glass began to burn in her hand. So used to wooden ones in Jakiris, she set the metal down before it could melt.

"Slaughtering folk purely for not agreeing with you isn't the way I would choose to run a land though."

Amis continued smiling as though he found the whole thing utterly delightful.

"The forest will fall soon enough," Harelda said. "When it does, alliances will shift. Nobody truly enjoys a cage, even a gilded one."

Neri nodded. "Well said. When the forest no longer works, it isn't the scant handful of lords who decide which side the lands stand on. If the battle of the borderlands taught us anything, it's that the folk decide in the end."

She moved across the room toward Harelda but kept the others visible in the corner of her eye. Picking the oldest thing she could see, which happened to be a heavy set of thick brown drapes, she pointed to them.

"These are nice. Are they heirlooms?"

It was as good an excuse as any to escape the conversation and avoid burning their bones to kindling. She didn't dare look at Niall, couldn't bear to. He hadn't uttered a single word all evening, hadn't looked her way once.

She buried the hurt down deep as Harelda's expression softened the slightest amount.

"Thank you, they are, yes. Do you have many such things in Jakiris?"

"Many, although our library is my favourite, second only to our kitchen's cooking."

Harelda turned to point out a tapestry and the moment their backs were to the men, her voice dropped low.

"You must leave, you and your friends, at first light."

Neri hesitated. "Honestly, I would love to, but Viljo seems intent on keeping us here."

Harelda pulled a face.

"I know, a tournament!" Viljo exclaimed. "Tomorrow, in the square. You must stay for that."

And now we can't openly plan to leave without being rude.

She managed a weak smile before turning her attention back to Harelda.

"You'll take part, brother?"

Neri froze as Viljo challenged Niall next. She had no idea what kind of tournament he had planned, but if he was involving Niall she could make a confident guess.

"If you insist," Niall replied. "I've bested you before in more ways than one. I can easily do it again."

Neri closed her eyes in torment. Niall could beat Viljo with a blade, she'd seen it done, but Viljo wouldn't fight fair with his folk looking on, and clearly his pride was winning over any sense of morality he once had.

"The west gate will be open at first light," Harelda murmured. "If you're to leave, it must be then. No, I've barely left the borderlands but I would enjoy visiting Jakiris, if your offer stands."

Neri had no idea if that meant Harelda was leaving with them come morning or just covering her deception, but she nodded.

"Of course, we'd be happy to receive you." With a slight grimace at the thought of her current state of relationship with Niall, she ploughed on. "I think I'm exhausted from travelling. Would you excuse me?"

Harelda nodded, a hint of amusement beneath her haughty expression.

"Of course. I'll have someone escort you back to your room."

Neri knew it was coming before she heard it, and it took all her effort not to cringe noticeably.

"Allow me." Viljo swept to her side. "Niall will be fine on his own I'm sure."

Neri eyed Niall, wordlessly begging him to save her. The look he threw her way, completely devoid of any emotion, almost brought her to her knees.

"I'm always better on my own," he muttered.

Neri refused to let her expression crack or the tears to fall. She held her head high and walked past them without a second glance, even though her heart felt like it was breaking fresh cracks deep to the bone. Amis's willingness to let her leave frightened her, but she focused on remembering the corridors she'd taken before to her room, not trusting Viljo not to lure her off course.

"You will grace me with your company at the tournament tomorrow?" he insisted. "We can talk more. I know the others might seem somewhat heavy-handed in their ideals, but together we can guide them into a better way of thinking."

She flinched as his hand landed on her arm. He truly believed what he was saying, she realised. He arrogantly assumed he could sway such warped, power-hungry minds away from complete dominion of all they could capture.

We leave tomorrow.

Once she was in the west, Viljo wasn't her problem any more. She would ask Ciena to ask Mik to tell Niall the plan for the morning.

She would be going home, with or without him.

"Of course." She faked another smile. "I have a lot to say."

He chuckled. "You always do. Goodnight, Neri."

"Goodnight."

She slipped into the room and shut the door firmly in his face. Ciena and Emelyn were absent but she expected that. Tiredness zapped her energy but worry kept her awake.

Pacing the room, Neri waited for someone to return. She sat down on the bed occasionally but soon stood up again and paced, constantly extinguishing and reigniting the candles dotted around the room to calm her *ai-tan* as it fed off her panic.

Untold atrocities entered her mind, of Niall being unfaithful, or caught up with in a dark corner by Viljo's men and disposed of, or worse, just walking out of the castle and once again deserting her.

By the time dawn was tinging the sky through the window, she was getting close to setting the curtains alight and dragging the entire tower down until she found Niall and made him fight it out.

The door opened before she could act on it, and Emelyn slipped inside.

"I need to tell you something Neri, and I hate it but I wanted to be the one to tell you."

She came in and sat down on the bed, making Neri sit

down also. Neri jumped in first, the realisation of the truth hitting her so hard she could barely choke the words out.

"Niall's gone already."

"I don't know about that. I mean, nobody's been able to find him since you both left dinner, but we haven't looked that hard."

Emelyn rubbed her face with her hands in dismay.

"No, what I wanted to tell you is that I overheard that horrible man speaking to Niall. He told him that he's an empath and that he can tell you want children. He said that you've been enamoured by the borderlands and the idea that Viljo might go on to rule Apeklonia too, and he worries that Niall might want to protect his heart."

"But that's ridiculous! Niall's an idiot if he thinks otherwise."

Emelyn shushed her, a worried look crossing her face.

"He says he has read it in your mind. We know it's utter dung, but he mentioned that Viljo has a land and Livia might even inherit Jakiris, which leaves Niall with nothing to offer you."

Neri groaned. "Where did you hear this?"

"After you left the dining hall. I'm surprisingly good at going unnoticed, and Ciena wanted someone listening outside the window. I think that woman almost saw me when you were wittering on about drapes, but she didn't say anything."

"Then I'm guessing Niall left?"

"The hall he did, but there's nothing to say he's left the settlement." Emelyn didn't look convinced. "Perhaps he just needs a bit of time to get his mind right."

Neri shook her head and sat up. It was still early enough for her to leave. Amis was after her, not Niall, and had an interest in Emelyn also, which meant the borderlands wasn't safe for either of them, Niall or no Niall. She stood up, grabbed her blade and left the room with Emelyn hot on her heels.

The halls were deserted and the firelight burning low, so she led them straight out of the front doors and down the steps to cross the square. She would let everyone know where she intended to go and tell them that they could come with her. If Niall wanted to talk, he knew where she would end up.

"Out for an early morning stroll I see."

The voice kindled her *ai-tan* into anger and she clenched her fists. Viljo strode toward her, his face a picture of dark discontent. Only now with juxtaposition of light from a lantern in his hand, could Neri see what Niall referred to when they'd first come across Viljo again. A sort of darkness surrounded him that hadn't been present in Jakiris, all the more visible now compared to the bright smile emanating from the woman beside him.

Neri choked back a cry and tumbled forward on unsteady feet, all thoughts of Niall blissfully absent for a few beautiful moments. She took in the shining golden hair and the radiance of the elegant woman before her. Then she jumped into Livia's open-armed embrace.

After a long moment of blubbing, Livia drew back but she clung onto Neri's arms tightly.

"I'm so glad you made it back! I've missed you so much! We left your cottage waiting for you. Where's Niall?"

Neri's happiness ground to a halt. Her mind wavered between breaking down and telling Livia of her fresh pain or keeping the pretence up in front of Viljo. He would no doubt pounce on a chance to use the information to his advantage.

"Niall has been difficult to locate since last night," Viljo said, finally amused about something. "He didn't seem too happy either. I do hope he's not strayed too far, but then that is his usual routine."

Neri closed her eyes for a moment of torment, but Livia scoffed loudly.

"Well thank you, brother. Now leave Neri and I to catch up. I'm sure given the circumstances, you can wait to start your little tournament thing."

She didn't make any shooing motion with her hands but the sentiment radiated from her voice. When he didn't move away, she took Neri's hands and towed her toward a nearby lane. Emelyn fell into step behind them as Livia led them to the inn, but Neri still had no idea where Ciena or the others were, and dawn was breaking fast. Viljo wouldn't let them leave, and he insisted on Niall fighting in his ridiculous tournament, which would delay their leaving another day.

The thoughts cascaded around in her mind but she didn't say a word as the three of them walked up the stairs and toward a door. Livia opened it with a key and ushered them in.

"We can talk freely here," she said. "I have friends in a few places and I often stay here when I visit. *Ama* stayed behind in Jakiris, as I'm sure you've gathered. Now, what are we going to do?"

Neri caught sight of Emelyn standing by the door, hesitation scrawled across her face. Livia didn't seem at all regal to Neri, and Emelyn had shown no reluctance to be herself in the tower, but now she hovered and stared.

"I need to speak to everyone I've brought with me," Neri said. "I should give them the opportunity to make the journey west but I'm meant leave at first light, and Harelda said I should. Then Viljo's planning this mad tournament and he wants Niall to fight in it, so we can't leave without being rude, but the head of the Governance is here so Em and I need to leave. I hoped Niall would come back and we could talk, but he's pulled the same old trick of running off yet again."

The words seared in her throat, but there would be time to sulk later.

Livia sighed. "The time is soon to come when the fragile links will break, but I am glad you're back. I'll be honest with you too, although you may not like it. Niall may disappear, but he loves you above all else. He will return just like he did last time."

Neri's tears threatened to fall once more but she bit her lip and focused on action. If Niall had left then she had nothing left to keep her in the borderlands. On her request, Emelyn left the room to fetch Ciena and they returned almost immediately, so quickly that Neri wondered if Ciena had been given the task of watching her.

It's something Niall would do. Send a friend to stalk me so he can stomp off and brood somewhere else.

"Finn and Mik are doing their own thing," Ciena announced. "They'll be safe enough, but you're not."

Neri did brief introductions, then Livia stood with a determined gleam in her eyes.

"Nobody can know we're leaving, so we need to go now."

Neri nodded and forced herself to stand as Ciena huffed and braced her shoulder against the doorframe.

"We could rally a fighting force," she suggested. "If this lord is as dodgy as he seems then we need to bring order. Oh, no offense." She glanced at Livia. "That's what we've been trying to do all along."

Livia frowned. "*Ama* has been keeping the peace for now. Since our last wars folk are fewer than before and they don't deserve to be dragged into another battle. I trust her counsel."

Neri nodded her agreement when Ciena glanced her way. No war would fix things, at least not yet.

"Are we ready?" Livia asked. "I doubt we can wait for long."

Neri sighed. "I told Niall my plans but he clearly doesn't want anything to do with them. Or me, apparently."

"Don't be silly. He loves you." Livia hesitated. "He's just a bit..."

"Spoilt?" Ciena offered.

Emelyn nodded. "Pig-headed, definitely."

Neri wiped both hands over her face. The borderlands weren't safe for any of them with Amis around, and the thought of leaving Niall behind made her queasy.

"We need to get moving either way," Ciena said. "The early morning will give us some cover, but I've scoped out the watch-points on the west walls and they'll be able to see us before long."

"Fine." Neri took a couple of steps then halted again. "Cori's still here, right?"

Livia nodded. "And I can get word to her easily enough if it's important."

"Ask her to find him then. If he's still in the borderlands, ask her to get him home or at least through to the westlands, even if she has to kick him through the gates."

"Why do other folk always get the fun bits," Ciena grumbled.

The moment Livia promised, Neri forced herself to walk through the doorway and out of the inn. Niall was a grown man, and he could make his own choices. She had to make hers.

I can only hope his choices do bring him back to me.

They followed Livia down the deserted lane, but she paused and shuffled them all into the shadows of the nearest dwelling.

"Voices," she whispered.

With a whirl of her gift, a soft wind picked up and carried the murmur of folk toward them through the otherwise still air.

Neri's blood chilled, her *ai-tan* momentarily swept away by fear as she recognised Amis' voice. He appeared to be bargaining with someone. Neri dwelt on the possibility that Viljo could have turned darker than she'd thought.

"The young lord is amenable but slow to convince. It will take time but it will be done. He will see that your ways and ours are the same. None can prosper when equality drags down those that are truly gifted and those that play with elemental folklore and insist on communing with nature. There are subjects and rulers, we both know that, but power is what makes one unique. When you crossed over you came into my realm, and I very much look forward to your continued part in it."

Neri shivered and backed away. She had no idea who he was talking to if he was talking about Viljo as the 'young lord', but she guessed there would be many a noble lord from other parts of the land willing to help him desecrate and gain dominion over all.

"Hopefully together we can make this realm glorious in power once again," Amis continued. "The West will not be able to withstand us."

Neri caught Livia's eye, then glanced at the tinge of light hitting the sky behind her.

"We have to go," she whispered.

Livia nodded, turning toward the west gate beyond the tower.

"If we follow the mountain line it will lead us to a settlement. From there I will be able to get us more suitable transport once in the west."

Neri nodded and they set off. Just once she turned back and the old shards of pain, buried from the last time Niall had deserted her, rose up to claim her. Her *ai-tan* brought necessary warmth to keep her putting one foot in front of the other.

She had no idea whether she walked away from him or toward him, but she had to hope he was heading home same as she was.

CHAPTER ELEVEN

Niall opened his eyes and sat up. His immediate alertness came less automatically than it used to in the days before Neri slept at his side, but she wasn't at his side now. He didn't even recognise the gloomy small room he was in, but Cori sat at a small table in the corner, watching him with a sad smile.

That triggered the hazy echo of memory, of the *mekhan* sliding thoughts into his head. He groaned as he remembered the carousel of bitter thoughts about the Jakida discarding him as a baby, Caden berating him over and over as a child, and even everyone at the sanctuary seeing him as Hamlin's chosen protégé because of a heritage he didn't even truly belong to save for the blood in his veins.

He even soured the memories of her. He shuddered. *How could I have doubted her so easily?*

He stood and folded his arms, cloaking a little of his shadow around him. Finn and Mik stood waiting expectantly by the door, but neither of them said anything as he got snared by the memories again, flashes of Neri looking utterly heartbroken at dinner, and his body doing absolutely nothing to go to her.

"Where is she?" he asked. "How bad is it?"

Cori grimaced. "We still don't know the full effects, but let's just say your mind hasn't been your own for a bit."

"We found you wandering down a lane, mumbling to

yourself," Mik said, his tone the gentle hum he might use on Emelyn when she was skittish over something. "The things you were saying… well, they didn't sound like you. We brought you here."

"What happened to me? Where's Neri?"

Anger fired as they exchanged wary looks, but Cori stood up and placed a brave hand on his forehead.

"The man you met last night, Amis, is entrenched deep in some dark sorcery. He can manipulate minds, and he had great fun with yours last night at dinner."

Niall frowned. Another fragment of hazy memory filled his head, of Neri staring at him with desolate eyes, and of her walking past him.

Why wasn't his body moving? Why didn't he reach out as she passed?

He shook his head as Cori stepped back.

"You feel dizzy?" Cori asked. "Sick?"

"Hungry, and seriously furious."

He cloaked the shadows around him to dodge past Mik and Finn, but their arms formed a barrier across the door before he could open it.

"Let me out," he growled.

Finn had the sense not to smirk at him, while Mik only sighed.

"You're not going to kill your brother, no doubt that's what you're planning."

"Him, his council, I'm not fussy."

Finn rolled his eyes. "He has guards and you only have us. Think sensibly for once. Neri has."

Niall stilled. "Where is she? Is she okay?"

"Livia arrived just before first light and escorted them through to the west," Cori said. "Viljo isn't going to be happy when he finds out, but Amis is the one pulling the strings here still, as he did with the old lord and rather successfully with you."

"They were planning to leave?" Niall whipped around to face her. "Why? Why didn't Neri tell me?" He slammed his hands against the wall. "I pushed her away. They all told me not to do it but stupid pride I did it again. I don't deserve her, I knew it."

The pain in his chest grew and he put his hand to the charm around his neck. Memories of when he'd been more shade than man swam around him, when the charm had become a part of him. Now that he stood alone, with Neri possibly halfway to Jakiris already, the scent of *liliam* wafted to him. Somehow she had tied them together with it long ago, when he was forced into permanent shadow and he'd forced them to part. The scent of it, bitter and sweet in equal measure, brought the damning realisation that he'd screwed up yet again.

Finn stepped forward and placed two strong hands on his shoulders and held him firm. Niall looked into the swirling irises of Finn's eyes as they changed shade to deep night-time purple.

"Neri is hurting, anyone can see that. I can read thoughts in her that run beyond simple anger. But something else is in there, and I don't think she's aware of it yet. She's safe in the west now but we need to find our own way out. Then you can go raging about flinging threats like a noble."

Niall frowned, but Finn had a point. Neri was in the west so they were wasting time hanging around in the borderlands.

"What do you mean, something inside her?"

Finn let go of him and stepped back to block the door again.

"It's like a soft murmur she has speaking inside her. It could well be her gift, I'm not sure, but it's there. Whenever she started to look at you or get upset, it fluttered, that's the only word I can use."

Niall had no blade, no clue where he'd lost it or when, and nothing other than the clothing he stood in, but it didn't matter. Either they would barter for horses or he would walk back to Jakiris. The first western settlement would likely loan him some if they recognised him.

I shouldn't have let the mind play bother me. I should have trusted her, should have been stronger.

"What are we waiting for then?" he asked.

"Viljo won't let you go," Cori said. "Once he hears that Neri went this morning, he'll want to keep you separate. It's her they all fear, and easy enough to see you're at least part of the reason she fights them for everyone's freedom. Stay here until dark. Then I can give you another route out of the settlement. The west gate won't open again for a long while now."

Niall growled in frustration but nodded in irritable agreement and sat on the bed in the corner to brood as Cori stepped into the hall.

"I'll fetch food but I should be seen about. I'll probably get interrogated about them disappearing, but there's not much they can take from me. There's food enough on the table."

She left the room and Niall stood to pace and contemplate his options. Neither Mik nor Finn seemed in the mood for talking either, which he appreciated. Mik produced a book, Finn slumped on the end of the bed to sleep, and Niall moved back and forth across the tiny strip of floor with his mind racing.

He trusted Cori but had no notion of how viable the

escape route would be.

I'll fight my way out if I have to. She's forgiven me before, and I've let her down over and over. Not this time.

She had Emelyn with her now. When the forest finally burned away, the east and the west would meet in battle. There was no avoiding it unless the Governance were quelled for good, but with folk like Amis pulling mental strings, Niall had little hope for Viljo siding with family over his new puppet master.

The door swung open and Niall reached for a blade he didn't have. Finn was on his feet in an instant and Mik almost launched his book.

"We have to go now."

Cori hurried in and grabbed a cloth bag, swinging it over her shoulder. Niall eyed the cut on her cheek and Cori pulled a face.

"They assume I helped the others escape, but I think Viljo is more worried about where you've disappeared to. He's rallying every guard in the settlement to tear homes apart to find you, so the time to go is now."

Niall followed Cori out of the room and down a narrow corridor to a mound of hay and the scent of horses. Cori kicked the hay aside with a grin.

A small wooden hatch lay in the ground, and Niall bent to haul it open.

"Down you go. Whenever you reach a fork, keep right. It should bring you out in an old barn on the other side of the border wall, but keep moving fast. The boundaries of the borderlands still aren't entirely controlled by the west."

Niall nodded and gave Cori's shoulder a thankful squeeze before dropping into the hole. Cori passed the bag to Mik and hovered over them once they were all in the tunnel.

"You're not coming with us?" Niall asked.

"Nope. We need someone here, and I need to keep an eye on my sister."

He'd forgotten Cori and Hareili were related, so intent on pushing the girl out of his head in case Neri somehow read his thoughts and assumed the wrong thing. She was tetchy where Hareili was concerned for some reason.

"West will always be your home," Niall offered.

Cori grinned. "I know. Go. Keep moving fast. There should be a settlement half a day's walk if you keep to the edge of the forest. The others might even still be there."

That alone was enough to set Niall walking. He strode along, resisting the urge to run because he would need his strength to keep going through the night. He wouldn't stop until he knew exactly where Neri was. All he had to do now was find her, apologise and hope she understood. He knew one day she wouldn't forgive him again, but he wanted one more chance to prove to her that he could manage it.

"Light up ahead," Finn called a while later.

Niall hurried toward the soft glow, only to find an open hole in some rotting floorboards. The first broke in his hand when he tried to haul himself up with it, and Mik had to give him a boost from below. He hauled Mik out after him next, then left Mik to struggle with Finn as he inhaled the sweet air and looked back to the boundary wall of the borderlands behind them.

"We keep just inside the line of the trees," he said. "We don't stop until we reach the settlement."

"Who made him leader," Finn grumbled.

Mik sighed. "Heritage, sadly."

Niall grinned as his mood lifted instantly. They were finally home, albeit a long way from a familiar bed. Neri might even be at the settlement still, or knowing her she would have insisted on horses and a swift gallop back to Jakiris. Either way, he would keep their pace going until he found her.

At least this time it technically wasn't my doing.

It was a small comfort, because she was either going to shout at him a lot or worse, push him away.

I'm stubborn enough to bear it though.

He was certain the Jakida wouldn't exile him if Neri asked her to. Almost certain. Even as the woman who birthed him with a mind that was duty incarnate, the Jakida had a soft spot for the woman he loved.

The occasional scent of *liliam* kept him moving forward. Whatever Neri thought of him, it meant she was still thinking of him, and he hoped she would get the scent as strongly as he did to know his thoughts were still only of her.

He delved his hand into the pocket of his trousers and ran his fingers over the small pouch that never left him. He had no idea whether getting rid of the *liliam* fragments inside would destroy its effects or not, but he didn't want to run the risk by trying.

"So, do you want to tell him, or shall I?" Finn drawled.

He'd been ignoring their furtive looks, but now he slowed enough to keep pace with them.

"Tell me what?"

"We've been hearing rumours," Mik said. "We all know that some folk can wield the element of fire. Neri is one of them."

"So?"

"Amis, that man with the mind tricks, can apparently wield darkfire," Finn said.

Niall stopped walking. "Darkfire is a myth."

"So's the firebird. So are dragons to some. Even Neri would be considered mythical to the right minds. Darkfire can't be doused with water, can't even be rocked by most gifts. It incinerates all it touches. If he truly wields it, then there are next to none in this realm that can stop him."

Niall sagged and started walking again.

"I heard voices in the walls," Finn added. "I can tell truths when folk speak, but I can hear them without words better than most too. Their minds are almost too afraid to think. Those that do are frightened. They fear the old ways, and that their families will be targeted. They are frightened of raising questions and none of them have any confidence in their new lord. Sadly, it appears Amis and therefore the Governance are running the borderlands now."

Finn had always insisted he remained entirely chivalrous and never dipped into the thoughts of others unless totally necessary, but Niall had never quite worked out whether to believe him or not. Either way, Amis and his darkfire would have to wait. He pointed out a settlement in the distance.

"We need to barter for some horses. A wise woman I know, Zel, will have some idea about darkfire, better than any of us can."

He didn't admit that Neri was his only real reason for rushing, but he knew they both guessed it anyway.

They ate as they walked and the suns waned around them, but nobody mentioned stopping to rest or for the night. Niall focused on the settlement ahead with unerring dedication, knowing that Neri had almost a full day's distance on him. If she'd set out for Jakiris already then he might not see her for a few days more, but he would see her at least.

He almost missed the sound of hooves up ahead, too

stuck in his own mind until Finn and Mik dragged him into the dark gloom between the trees.

They waited for the riders to pass, but the hoofbeats slowed, then stopped.

Niall didn't have a blade, but he would let the others engage first if needed, then fight by hand if he had to.

A subtle glow lit the trees ahead and for a long moment, he thought it was a lantern. But lanterns didn't glow as pale as the light approaching. They didn't have flowing hair and a soft glow about their wholly female body either.

Niall stared into wise dark eyes and let a proper sigh of relief tumble out. With a chuckle, he stepped forward.

"You're a long way from home."

CHAPTER TWELVE

Neri sat on the hard ground as the night fell above and watched the stars dance dazzling dots of brightly coloured light across the inky sky. Livia attempted to talk to Emelyn, but once again Emelyn was being strangely reserved, almost sulky in return. Neri had expected the two women to get on well, they were so similar, but she didn't have the energy to mediate. She reserved her attentions for Dog alone and sat with her arms around his neck. Even Ciena had long since given up trying to suggest they mass a fighting force to storm the borderlands and sat digging her blade into the hard earth instead.

Neri let it all pass her by, but the occasional waft of *liliam* haunted her. She had no idea if Niall was back in the borderlands still or whether he'd left her once again for reasons unknown. Either way, beneath the guilt of leaving him that warred with the determination to get home, she hoped that he was safe.

"It's a shame we can't find dragons and ask them to incinerate him," she muttered.

"Who, Niall?" Ciena asked.

"No, Amis. Just have one swoop by and snap him up. Niall said the rest of our group in the east are marching on Apeklonia and hitting it from the inside, so if we got rid of Amis then it might all be over."

And Niall could stop screwing about being sulky.

Livia sighed. "Nice idea in theory, but you'd need an

animal-talker to even get close to a dragon, and the only one I've heard of is in Carahdyl."

Neri stilled. Carahdyl was a fair ride south, but perhaps that was what she needed. As much as she yearned to go home, there would be no plan for the future. The Jakida would protect the west and wall them in if she had the chance, leaving Amis to destroy everything.

And when the forest does come down, what then?

She thought of Ma and Moonshine marching to Apeklonia with the rest of the camp, and the slaughter that fight might bring.

Carahdyl and an animal talker, that was where she had to start.

Even if the dragons don't fight, the ones that breathe fire might understand the dangers of darkfire. They could tell us how to fight it. I have to try.

"We will reach the border by tomorrow." Livia raised her voice to capture attention. "I can arrange a quicker way home for us then. Are you looking forward to seeing your cottage again?"

Neri faked a smile and nodded in answer. She did want to see her cottage, but now she had another mad plan burning in her mind instead. She would wave the others off to the safety of Jakiris and set out alone, hopefully with a horse. If she succeeded, then she would not only learn more of use about dragons, but also find something to stop the Governance from ravaging the land before they turned their attentions west.

She didn't sleep, her mind drifting but never succumbing. When the others woke to the dawning light and passed around a meagre breakfast from the supplies Livia had 'borrowed' from the tower kitchens, Neri took her share and stashed half of it.

She wanted nothing more than to swaddle herself in the comfort of luxury and let them spirit her away to her cottage. There she could shut out her pain with the rest of the world. If Niall cared, then he could find her there.

Each time she considered it, her *ai-tan* grumbled. Amis would always be hunting her. He needed to be stopped and she would need to sacrifice things to achieve it, like going home straight away. She could follow the suns easily enough to get her to Carahdyl, but it was worth journeying on with the others for a while longer until she could find enough goodwill in the west to get a horse.

The settlement they stopped at next was smaller than the ones they'd already passed. A long circular lane of stone and wooden dwellings ran the length of the settlement walls right down to the square in the centre. Some of the dwellings even had their own gardens, the odd riot of colour coming from various crops and herbs, but Neri focused on the long, single-floor dwelling at the far end of the square. The thought of an inn, with warm water and fresh food that she could save for the journey, plus ample access to horses, gave her strength.

Livia walked straight to the inn and proceeded to speak with the barman, who seemed to know her well. He insisted he had rooms for them all and Neri allowed a brief moment of gratitude for a comfortable bed.

They ate and talked in low voices, Neri and Livia indulging Ciena and Emelyn in reminisces of their previous experiences. When discussion dried up and Livia began to explain the recent history instead, Neri let it all flow over her, grateful that they let her sit there and stew in her own mind.

She retired to her room as soon as the second drink was finished. With a modest yet comfortable mattress and downy, soft blankets similar to those she remembered from long ago at Mary's in Carahdyl, Neri allowed herself to relax enough to drift into fitful sleep.

The *liliam* woke her several times, dragging her from dreams of Niall calling for her through endless shadows, but it was the sound of her door banging open that had her sitting up in a sweat. She winced and blinked against the bright sunslight streaming through the window of her tiny room as Emelyn knelt on the end of the bed and crushed her toes.

"There's a huge procession outside." Her voice all but bounced off the walls. "I think half of Jakiris must be here!"

Neri pushed her aching body out of the comfort of the soft covers with a groan. She didn't bother to freshen up, still cursed with the ragged dress and nothing to change into, but Emelyn had new clothing on as she led the way out down the hall.

As they emerged into the square, Neri stared.

Maybe I should have at least scraped my hair back a bit.

A parade of folk on horseback filled the lane, servants mostly, but Neri saw the Jakida at the head of the riders. The Jakida dismounted with the innate grace of royalty and Neri stood for the excruciatingly unimpressed once-over the Jakida gave her. No matter what Niall said, this was his *ama,* and Neri still had the notion she should make a somewhat good impression if she could.

"We will talk later." The Jakida's tone invited no discussion. "For now we will stay one night here, if you have room?"

Neri turned to see the innkeeper with red cheeks and shaking hands at the idea of having royalty as guests.

He bobbed his head several times, alternating it with bowing, and Neri realised Livia probably hadn't ever bothered to tell anyone who she really was. Then he remembered his manners and waved at the door to invite them inside. Livia caught Neri's gaze and rolled her eyes. Neri had to smile. She knew Livia's despair at being high-born but it did have its uses.

Everyone followed the Jakida inside. Ciena, Ma and Emelyn were introduced and greeted with friendly attention. The innkeeper hurried back and forth, bringing out what seemed to be his entire kitchen and the complete content of his bar.

Folk made excuses throughout the day to go in and out but the Jakida held court by the window. She chatted quite easily with local folk, including their quivering land owner who considered himself in charge. Neri found an ideal quiet moment to take a seat opposite.

"I have something I need to do." She hesitated. "I don't want to impose but I need to borrow a horse. I don't want the others to know either. I'm sure you know better than anyone that Livia would insist on coming along, and Emelyn is much the same. I will be coming back to Jakiris but by a slightly longer route."

She had the Jakida's attention but knew she had to pick her words carefully.

"There's a very evil man currently in Vi- the lord's confidence. Viljo seems to be agreeing with his opinions, and I have a bad feeling they'll try to bring about the old ways again. I might be able to bring that to a halt, but I need information first and that requires travel."

Neri cast her gaze to the Jakida's unreadable expression as the sounds of folk echoed around them. As Livia flopped into the chair between them, the Jakida nodded.

"Viljo's adviser used to advise the old lord." The Jakida gave no sign of emotion as she mentioned her son. "We have been aware of this but not who the man was in relation to the east. This was an oversight on our part, and Zel and I have had words over it, but the last time I spoke of my opinions to Viljo, he asked me to leave his lands and that our link was at an end. I have not attempted contact since. If anyone has a way to bring the scourge down, and any others that happen to have corralled to their banner, I would like to know it."

She fixed Neri with a no-nonsense stare, then looked away. Knowing that the Jakida was giving her permission to take a horse at first light the next morning, Neri faced Livia with every intention of distracting them both until she could leave. Livia would start to ask questions soon enough, and perhaps they could firm a better friendship between her and Emelyn as well.

First, I need to do something rash.

She left the inn and hunted around until she found Ciena throwing blades at a wooden wall. Ciena turned her head as Neri approached.

"How are you holding up?" she asked.

Neri shrugged. "I'll live. I need to ask you to do something for me."

"Something boring, no doubt."

"Not exactly. I think there'll be a time to raise a fighting force, and soon, but you have to do it quietly. Never do it under the Jakida's nose, but a few well-chosen words whispered in opinionate ears might get others to do the work for you. The Jakida will fight if her folk want to, but they need persuasion."

Ciena regarded her for a moment and then threw another blade with a wicked smile.

"I take it you don't want the others to know you're going until you're gone?" she guessed.

"No, Livia and Emelyn are scarily alike. They'll both be on the first and second horse behind me."

Ciena chuckled. "Fair. They don't get on so the ride to Jakiris for the rest of us should be interesting at least."

"I don't understand why."

"Oh please."

"What?"

Ciena rescued her blades and sheathed them in various holders and hidden places about her person.

"Em get attached to folk, you being one of them. She sees your friend as someone who's going to take you away from her."

Neri frowned. "That's mad."

"Maybe, but that's Em for you. Is it mad when Niall does it?"

"Well, no, but he's…"

"Addle-headed over you? The poor boy will be right behind us, so do you want me to tell him where you've gone?"

Neri hesitated. Niall would be straight after her the moment Ciena told him. He'd probably insist on dragging her back to Jakiris and forbidding her from having anything to do with dragons.

"No, not immediately. I'll send word when I've done what I need to. Tell him… tell him I'm safe, but this is something I have to do for myself, and I can't risk him stopping me. He should understand."

He wouldn't take it well and they both knew it, but Ciena's grin only widened.

"Long time since I've had to fight him. He's a bit shabby with his blocks but it will at least give me a bit of practice to toy with a while."

Neri snorted. "Just don't cut any necessary bits off, that's all I ask."

"I promise nothing."

Neri went back inside with the uneasy awareness that Ciena meant it too, but Niall could handle himself.

Her thoughts turned to the journey she needed to take, and as she joked with the others that evening, she wondered if she should ask Ciena to give Niall a letter instead. She hadn't spent much time perfecting her scribing as a child, but it would be legible.

Livia threw her the odd suspicious look that made her temper her mood, but she didn't say a word, and Neri stayed with them all well into the night to avoid any questions.

By the time she made her excuses and retired to her room, there was little point waiting for morning. She checked the halls were empty and tiptoed out of the inn to the barn, mindful to check every spare corner and spot of shadows for Livia.

She selected one of the Jakirian horses, a solid, steady-looking black mare, and sent the horse at a smart pace out of the settlement.

Indecision swirled around her mind, but she kept the pace steady and headed south as the suns rose over the horizon, tinging the land in ethereal, dusky hues. They veered east until they found the fringe of the cursed forest, then Neri kept the suns above her. They took the longer route occasionally to avoid settlements in the distance, but by the time the suns waned again and the stars danced their gentle glow, the horse snorted and slowed their pace.

The lip of the hill up ahead would provide a better resting place, more secure in case of any nighttime wanderers, but the horse plunged sideways as Neri urged her forward.

"Easy," she muttered. "Just a bit further."

The horse avidly refused to go forward, and veered right or left instead, so eventually Neri had to dismount and tie the rein to a nearby shrub branch.

"You're being silly. We've gone up and down loads of these hills today."

The horse snorted again in answer and Neri frowned as her *ai-tan* fluttered over her skin, echoed by the faint trilling noise it seemed to make lately. She hadn't even had time to barely notice it, but she didn't hear it with her ears, not like the crackle that came with the flames when they danced over kindling. It was more like the warmth she felt when it caressed her skin, the comfort of a lullaby in her mind that she knew rather than heard.

She shook her head and wiped a hand over her face. The hill ahead was more of a steep incline than previous ones, so perhaps the horse was simply tired.

"I'm going to check there's nothing on the other side while we rest a bit," she told the horse. "But it's just going to be another rolling drop, so hopefully you'll cheer up after a break and we can get going again."

Aware she was talking to an animal that couldn't understand her, she headed toward the slope and peered over the lip of the summit.

A large quarry of bare earth lay below, and there was no way the horse would be able to stumble down the cliff face on the other side.

Neri sighed. *I owe her an apology.*

The pit ran in deep, rutted lines illuminated by firelight, and she could make out wooden carts of powder in differing colours being run back and forth.

Lumps glimmered in the powder that took her a moment to place. The only time she'd seen anything like it before, pearlescent and pale, was on the battlefield. The *freirer* ice had chained the heads of the enemy's dragons to coerce them into obedience.

Neri shuddered and focused on the folk running the carts back and forth, their strides uniform right down to the footfalls. So many shadow-folk, shades like Niall, except these had no sign they'd ever known skin or the emotions that dwelled within. They ran back and forth with no faltering, each movement identical to the next.

One slowed and fell, but the rest only dodged to avoid him. A man emerged with a small hand cart and gathered the fallen shade onto it. Without ceremony, he wheeled the cart to the side and dumped the shade onto a pile of others, as though they were nothing more than items to be used and discarded.

Neri moved away before her *ai-tan* could flare bright and give her away. She walked back to the horse and settled her nerves before remounting.

She couldn't shake the thought of shades like Niall being worked into the ground, and in the west too.

If the Jakida is mining freirer ice in the west, what is she planning to do with it? Assuming she even knows.

She set the horse trotting back the way they'd come to take the long way around, but the thought plagued her as she rode on. It would be something she'd have to question when she eventually returned to Jakiris, but the thought of horrors behind her and Carahdyl ahead kept her going. She stopped so the horse could rest and eat, but she didn't dare sleep herself whilst travelling alone, so they pushed on through the cold remainder of the night.

No doubt Livia and Emelyn would be furious at being

left behind, but she consoled herself with the knowledge that they'd be well on their way to Jakiris by now. She hoped Emelyn would warm to Livia and the two would become friends. If she didn't return they would be good for each other.

Either that or Ciena will have them fighting each other before dawn.

It wasn't a particularly helpful thought, but she was struggling to keep her mind clear of Niall. It would be so easy to turn the horse around and ride back to Jakiris. He'd find her there, she was sure of it, and whether they were still fighting or ready to forgive each other, everything in her screamed to go back and find out.

Only the thought that he'd try to hold her back, to stop her fighting the war she had on her hands, kept her going forward.

The sight of the Morlan mountains, just tiny little tips on the horizon, brought her a small dose of hope. She had to be close to Carahdyl, and they stopped as often as they could to get water from streams and pools. She dodged any possibility of coming across other folk but by the time the suns fell again, a tiny familiar dot appeared up ahead. It took an age to grow into a settlement but finally she rode into Carahdyl almost delirious with hunger and exhaustion. She slumped over the horse's neck but she continued to walk with wooden, ingrained practice into the barn and straight into a stall.

Someone helped her down from the horse's back and she heard a familiar voice, the fluid, rolling accent enough to open her weary eyes.

"Hello love, what happened to you?"

Neri had no idea when she fainted, but she woke with a throbbing head in a comfortable bed with soft bedding.

Testing her limbs in case she'd had a fall and been found by some unknown stranger, she stumbled to the window and looked out on a familiar scene.

At last her spirits lifted.

Still in the same dress and slippers that had seen her cross past the cursed forest twice, Neri made her way slowly down to the bar of the inn. She glanced around the familiar room, the chaos of tables and chairs all polished to a bright gleam, and smiled at Mary.

"You were in a state," Mary announced and patted the bar in front of her. "What brings you this far south, and in such fetchingly disgusting clothes?"

Neri perched on one of the stools.

"It's been a long journey. If you have spare clothes, I'll trade for them."

Mary laughed. "We'll go over the difficulties and awkward bits in a moment. First, have something to eat and to drink, warm your insides a little."

Neri couldn't say no. Mary might ask for coin, which she didn't have, or trades which she'd give willingly if she could, but even without the price agreed, she ate two helpings of bread and whipped egg with berries. Then she happily accepted the spiced wine that swirled the scent of cake-spice and Niall through her mind.

"So, still heartbroken and this time travelling alone huh?" Mary asked.

Neri shrugged with a sigh. She explained briefly about Niall and venturing east. Before long, the whole thing came spilling out about Niall, their troubles, his moods, the east, the west, all of it.

Mary listened as she wiped glasses and unpacked bottles, all while making sympathetic noises in the right places.

"Niall's a good boy." She smiled. "He came by here shortly after you did the last time, half a day to be exact, frantic about finding you. His heart will be in the right place no matter what his mistakes."

"I didn't know you knew him," she muttered.

"Ah, he stayed here a while. Had a girl travelling with him all doe-eyed, but he wasn't the kindest to her when they parted."

Neri tried so hard not to feel a surge of elation at the thought that might have been Hareili in previous times. She failed and covered the smirk behind her cup. As much as she wanted to ask all about his time there, she had other more pressing questions.

"I came here because I wanted to ask you a few things. I'm guessing you hear a lot in here and have no reason to lie to me. I could help out in here if you needed it, if you could spare a room but I can always sleep in the bar. I just need somewhere safe."

Mary regarded her for a moment, shrewd blue eyes assessing her. Then she moved to refill Neri's glass and smiled.

"Help me a bit setting out in the mornings. I'll do the evening food, but you could help by pouring the drinks. The room upstairs is yours as long as you need it. I don't know what use I'd be to you though."

Neri leaned across the bar and cast a glance round the early morning silence, just in case.

"I need to find out the myths and rumours first. Then I need an animal-talker to find dragons."

CHAPTER THIRTEEN

Niall stared at the woman in front of him, the soft glow emanating from her illuminating the greenery around them. She stood surrounded by four horses with shaggy brown coats, but she held none of the reins.

"I've come to bring you home," Zel said with an amused smile. "We've had a few rumours that you were not with Neri when she left the borderlands. Your *ama* was concerned."

Niall snorted. "Sure she was. So you know where Neri is now?"

"She's safe." Zel lifted a hand to indicate the horses. "You'll reach Jakiris quicker on horseback."

Niall grinned. If Neri was still on foot, he might even catch up to her before they got home. He clambered onto one of the brown horses and waited impatiently for the others to do the same. The moment everyone was ready, he urged his horse forward.

He would find Neri wherever she was and make amends. Like last time, he'd prove he still loved her.

Assuming she believes me. He sighed. *She does these things for noble reasons, I do them for weak ones.*

He tensed as Zel rode her horse up alongside him. She didn't have a hand on the reins but he guessed part of her *ai-tan,* powerful and unchallenged as it was, transcended the need to ride like the rest of them.

"Such sadness on returning home," she said. "But you

are home and so is she. That's got to be a start."

She already knows, or more likely guessed that I'm the reason Neri isn't with us now.

"I doubted her. I'm jealous because I don't deserve her. I'm not enough."

He heard the general grumbling of Mik and even Finn behind him. To his irritation, Zel chuckled.

"What counts as enough?"

He shrugged. "I don't have a great living to offer her. The most my skill can lend itself to is fighting, and I have no plans to leave her following the westland warriors from place to place. I'm no fancy lord."

She'd said she didn't care about that, and he believed her, but she was stubborn in her own way about things. One day, she might decide otherwise.

"Do you think titles dictate love?" Zel asked.

Niall looked her way and for a moment he could see the whole universe reflected in her eyes. She shook her head at his lack of response and continued.

"It's our actions that make us good or bad folk, our choices. Yet we all make mistakes, some with good intentions. It's up to us to fix those mistakes. Your impatience, your frustration, comes from fear. You fear that she will one day tell you enough is enough. Neri loves you and she is stubborn."

He let the soothing calm of her words settle over him. He sensed some kind of sorcery among them, but he couldn't bring himself to struggle against it.

"The Jakida is riding to collect them," she added. "She will no doubt have them in her company already. We will need to ride a slightly different route. Things must happen as they must happen."

Niall wanted to argue, but something about Zel had

always awed him into a weird sort of obedience.

"What different route?" he asked.

Zel pointed to a dense crop of trees swathing the land at the base of the Kahlen mountains. It was the only thing that the cursed forest hadn't been able to cut off, but Niall had roamed enough to know nobody went into the mountains unless they wanted to face the Kiren-folk, lawless savages that hunted in huge hordes.

Even the *aerie*-caves where he'd seen Caden were part of the Kahlen mountains, but set forward enough from the main line of peaks that the settlement below was safe from the Kiren.

"There are relics in those woods I'd have you see," Zel said.

She gave him no more information than that, and even sent her horse on ahead before he could ask. His mood soured ever further when Finn appeared alongside him, Mik on the other to hem him in.

Niall glanced back toward the track that would take them on to Jakiris. His friends no doubt wanted to explore, and he would have considered it if he had Neri at his side. As if he sensed this, Finn smiled and looked ahead.

"You're lucky to have someone to race back for. I doubt she'll be going anywhere soon after returning home. Whoever that woman is, I reckon she's safe enough to follow."

Niall smiled. The thought of anyone not trusting Zel's word was strange to him, but then Finn and Mik had no idea who she was.

"She's safe enough," he agreed. "I can promise that. Even I know better than to go against what she says, but we're going to be quick about it."

No doubt Neri would be alright without him for a few

more days.

She might even need a few more days to calm down.

He smiled. She would forgive him in time. They might dance around each other and spar with words, but he'd won his way back into her life before. He could do it one more time.

The moment they entered the trees, the silence seemed to shout around them. Not a flutter of wings or a snuffle of ground animals, as if they were the only ones there.

"There are whispers in these woods," Finn murmured. "Nothing awful, but it feels sad. Old."

"These are echoes of souls that have been severed," Zel said.

"Severed?"

She nodded. "There are laws of the land even the ancients and the *aerie* wouldn't dare challenge. Some say souls are mined back into the land they came from. Others, well they think the idea of souls is fanciful nonsense."

"And is it?" Niall asked.

"Nothing is nonsense if believed in, and in a way, everything is nonsense to some. See that clearing ahead? That used to be a shade mine."

Niall froze, and his already tense horse skittered in alarm.

"Like that graveyard further west the Jakida sent me to?" he growled.

Zel frowned. "That was ill-advised of her. Shades weren't always what they are now. A long time gone by, shades were known as shadow-folk. They loved and laughed and lost and lingered as much as any other."

Niall hadn't known that. In all of his time recently, Zel hadn't mentioned it. He pushed his reins into one hand and clenched the other tight against his thigh. In all the winterspans growing up, Caden had never once thought to mention it either.

"Why?" he demanded. "Why now? Why here?"

"There are many intricacies of shimmers, we all know this." She glanced at Finn and Mik. "But while Neri has the affinity for fire which power hers, there are more than fire-kynes that can cast them. Allow me at least the indulgence of getting to where we need to be before I explain further."

Niall flicked an irritated hand in her direction, and urged his horse to follow hers.

They stumbled over roots and more than once he had to rein away from a low-lying branch. The trees provided a soft canopy that allowed dapples of light through, but the irritation was getting harder to ignore as his shadow flicked over his skin.

Moments later, they rode into a clearing in the trees, and even he had to stop and admire the overwhelming essence of unsullied natural beauty. Wide purple trunks towered above them, and long grasses swayed in an almost non-existent breeze as tiny little flowers grew wild in the thick of it all.

He frowned. "I've... been here. Except I haven't."

"Ah. Memories imprint in strange ways with shadow-folk," Zel said. "You have been here once before, but you were a baby then, barely born. Your *ama* brought you here in the hopes the shadow-folk would take you, or be able to remove the shadow from you."

"But they didn't."

Zel shook her head. "They refused. Took it as an insult. A few winterspans after, we had word that the shadow-folk had left the forest. We don't know where they went, but so many shades were appearing by then."

"I heard once that a shade is devoid of emotion," Mik offered quietly.

Zel nodded. "Shades, yes. Some are born that way, but most are shadow-folk who lost or traded their emotions. Who knows what the land takes or why. Perhaps it was a choice, or perhaps it was penance of some kind."

"So, the Jakida sent me and Viljo to that graveyard out west because she thought some of them would be shadow-folk instead?"

Zel looked around at the clearing a long while before answering. It gave Niall time to notice a rotting wooden post beside a wooden platform overtaken with branches. He rode toward two thick lines wood hammered deep into the earth, another hazy memory flickering.

"Caden mentioned tracks once. He told me, find the tracks and follow them. I went searching and ended up in Carahdyl instead, then Morlan."

"Ah yes, all roads lead to Carahdyl at some point," Zel said sagely.

She still hadn't answered him, but the puzzle was beginning to piece itself together in his head.

"Caden wanted me to find the shadow-folk on my own. The Jakida, she... I don't know what she's playing at, but if I'm one of them instead of a shade, then why did I start losing my emotions?"

"How old were you?" Zel prompted.

"Fourteen winters. I was worried, snapping at folk then feeling nothing for days. I was harsh to folk who didn't deserve it and emotionless to those who did."

Niall looked around. He wished Neri could have seen the tracks with him, because she would have understood. She wouldn't have rushed him or given him half-truths of veiled hints.

Mik joined him at the dismal remnants of the tracks and clapped a gentle hand onto his shoulder.

"There's time to work all this out, but it won't be here. Whether you choose to find your own folk, or to let it be, we're here for you. Until then, Neri's waiting at home for you."

It was exactly what he needed. He hadn't even considered having a 'folk-kind' of his own, but then he'd seen himself as a shade all his life. He wiped a hand over his face and nodded.

"Good point. Are we done here?"

Zel nodded. "I thought you should see it and know, that's all."

"You thought? Or she thought?"

Zel smiled, but there was an echo of sadness in it.

"I'm not in the habit of referring to more than myself if not accurate. Come, let's get you home to Jakiris, and to Neri. Perhaps there everything will make sense."

Niall took the lead back through the trees, the echo of truth haunting him from behind.

If Neri decides she does want children, will they be shadow-folk too? Are there risks, or would it be possible?

He also had to consider that the Governance wouldn't stop hunting them, or destroying everything in their path. If children did happen, whether their own or welcomed from elsewhere, the Governance would be their problem too. If not theirs, their children and descendants might one day suffer from the growing power of the enemy.

Understanding began to dawn on him about Neri's urgency to save everyone. She wanted a family and a home. She wanted love and safety for her family and fought in the hopes it might one day become real. He almost thought he smelt jasmine around him. For the first

143

time since returning to the westlands he realised that he was in a position to help.

"If we destroy the darkfire, and anyone associated with it, then I want to see if the tracks can rebuilt and the folk invited back to live there."

The idea of ever getting free of their enemies seemed impossible. It remained a mere dream to dance along to, with no hope of ever bringing it to reality. Despite that, Niall knew he had to keep fighting just in case.

"What if the tracks could be rebuilt? Would you see that as your home, your folk?" Finn asked.

He couldn't even consider it unless Neri wanted him to, and he felt pretty sure she called Jakiris home. He smiled at the thought of her getting home, airing out her cottage, being dragged up to the palace by Livia and forced into training immediately.

"No, Jakiris is our home. But I doubt we're ever going to see it again if we can't get out of these woods. Are we going to rest here tonight or blunder about in the trees?"

Zel broke through the trees to ride alongside him, her usual serene smile firmly back in place.

"We ride straight and will reach the plains before long. If we move through the night then we will be in Jakiris soon enough."

Knowing that he was finally on the home stretch, Niall's mood finally lifted. Neri might be upset with him still, but at least he would finally be able to see her.

The moment they left the forest and rejoined the track leading to home, he sent his horse forward fast. He barely gave anyone time to stop at pools for water, but nobody complained on the brief stints he allowed for them to rest the horses.

Neri would take some convincing, but she had what she

wanted now. She had Emelyn safe, and even if she did still have some mad plan to attack the Governance again, he would find ways to support her without her being in danger.

He turned his head to look at Mik and Finn riding behind. Ever since Neri had pointed out Mik and Emelyn to him, he had forgotten it completely. Now he wondered if perhaps his hunch about Mik's permanent single status had been right. He'd seen Mik watching Emelyn for years. The quiet devotion had completely passed her by as she got over her crush on Finn. He had half a mind to speak to Mik and tell him to go for it, but he didn't want to interfere.

He grinned to himself.

Not unless Neri tells me to.

By the time Jakiris came into view, he couldn't bear the suspense any longer. They hadn't seen Neri or the others on the journey home, so no doubt their stop to look at the tracks had kept them behind. She would be there already, and his horse plunged forward at the insistent dig of his heels. The wind swept past his face and his eyes watered from the onslaught, but still he didn't slow down.

He ignored the startled guard at the front gates of Jakiris and forced his horse to clatter up the main track toward the palace. The others weren't behind him but he guessed they'd taken a slower pace, so he jumped off the horse and threw the reins to the stable-master's waiting hands.

Jakiris was home. It was still strange to feel it so deeply in his bones, but there it was.

He turned toward the palace steps and grinned to see Livia with her mouth open at the sight of him. She seemed to fumble slightly as he strode up the steps, and she didn't even hug him in greeting.

Maybe she's mad at me too.

Then he noticed her expression and veered back, almost falling as he went down a step. He opened his mouth to ask but Livia beat him to it.

"She's not here."

She glanced around at the sight of others pouring onto the steps, Emelyn and Ciena both clamouring to say hello in their own way. Emelyn hugged him tight, but Ciena looked him up and down as if she was ready to cuff him on the ear.

"We reached a settlement near the border," Livia said. "She seemed alright, but then *Ama* arrived to escort us home. She and Neri talked, and the next thing you know Neri's taken a horse and disappeared. We have scouts looking out but not a word has come yet."

Niall inhaled a sharp breath and walked toward the nearest tree. He didn't care that several folk nearby gasped as he slammed his hands into it, and when he yelled, the area cleared like magic.

Find her.

It was the only thought revolving in his mind as he turned Ciena, Livia and Emelyn waiting behind him with various looks of irritation. Mik and Finn arrived, and Emelyn hugged them both, but the only thing Niall could focus on was that he was in Jakiris and Neri, once again, was nowhere to be found.

"We will find her," Livia promised. "It'll just take time. We've got birds in the skies and everything."

Niall barely heard her as Ciena appeared in front of him, arms folded.

"When you're done throwing a fit," she said, waiting until he glowered up at her with as much ferocity as she was glaring down at him. "I thought you might want to know that Neri gave me a task to do."

"A task. Neri gave you something to do, then flitted off without a word?"

The idea of Neri issuing orders would have amused him in any other situation, but now his anguish was turning to worry-fuelled fury.

Ciena nodded. "She told me to be discreet, but to whisper into the right ears of the locals that the enemy is on the prowl. We should be getting ready to stand and fight. I think she *finally* wants me to gather a fighting force."

Niall let that sink in. Some time ago, he would have feared that deathly calm, and assumed his shade self was taking over. Now he clung to it.

He had no idea where Neri was. He had no idea who with, or how safe she was. He had no clue what her plan was, but it would be mad and dangerous. He also knew she would be just as furious with him as he felt with her now, but the old desire to bait and fight her on something that he couldn't blame on himself felt good.

He let every essence of that anger flow into the shadow cloaking his skin as he uttered the next question between clenched teeth.

"She wants you to gather a *what*?"

CHAPTER FOURTEEN

Neri wiped glasses and watched the first few of Mary's locals enter. Their work-worn chatter filled her grateful soul with the sound of normality. It was her fifth day working for Mary and she had come no closer to finding anything about dragons or darkfire that might help her fight Amis.

Pushing cups to the newcomers, she smiled and continued cleaning bowls. Mary ran by just as one woman made a joke about her getting ideas above her station and hiring help.

"She's a shining star." Mary winked in Neri's direction. "She sings when she sweeps the floor, thinks nobody's listening but it fills the place with light."

Mary continued on her way and Neri flushed at the praise. The only trouble with Mary noticing her humming was that it didn't originate from her. The notes she hummed were the same echoes of her *ai-tan* that fluttered in her chest and warmed her skin. Almost like having a tune stuck in her head, she could hear rhythms she didn't know as though they'd existed forever. Even more unnerving, the trilling notes almost sounded like birdsong when she hummed them.

Zel would be the ideal person to explain such mysteries to her, but even though she'd not succeeded in finding anything, it had only been a handspan of days since arriving, and she had some serious reservations about going back. Either she'd find out Niall was still missing and be tempted to go back into danger looking for him, or she'd find him in Jakiris and their age-old argument would begin all over again.

So instead she served drinks and swept floors and had even managed to sleep without dreams for a short while each night.

Mary reappeared and bent her head close to Neri's. Neri tensed as Mary nodded toward a man standing at the far end of the bar.

"If you want to know the rumours about dragons, Sav over there is your man."

Mary straightened up and started pouring a cup of ale.

"Oi Sav, time for you to go to work now. My girl likes dragon stories."

Sav turned his scarred face their way with a broad smile and nodded in weary agreement as Mary slid the cup across the bar to him.

"Dragon stories? How about the story on how I got this scar right here."

He pointed to his cheek with a chuckle. Neri moved her washing bowl and tray of dirty bowls to the other end of the counter. Playing innocent excitement didn't come easily, but Sav regaled her with several tall tales, and she waited until the bar had filled with the chaos of local chatter before she risked a few questions.

"Do you know where they dwell?" she asked.

Sav grinned and downed the remainder of his tankard.

"The dragons and unicorns aren't commonplace now. Most folk believe they've travelled to a better realm along with the firebird. Nobody's seen that for an age either, although a few have stories on it, all more fantastic than the last. The Lord of the Borderlands had some dragons but thankfully he lost them in the battle."

Sav spat into his cup and promptly apologised. Neri grinned and filled it up again without washing it. She pushed it back to him and winked as she noticed Mary wasn't around. Sav nodded in gratitude before continuing in a low tone.

"Some say they dwell over the border mountains, hidden there from folk who try to enslave them. In truth, I don't know where they are, but I would ask the birds to find them. Folk think I just got into a lot of bar fights when I was younger and use dragons as a cool way of explaining it."

Neri shrugged. She could never admit that the firebird had graced her with fleeting visits on a couple of occasions, twice to help her through the cursed forest when she needed it most.

"One little known thing about dragons and this'll be my next drink I'm paying for," Sav added.

Neri grinned again and nodded her agreement. She didn't gain anything useful really. She could possibly ask Zel in time to advise her on finding dragons, and if she did then she might be able to use her fire to convince them to help her side through persuasion rather than force, but that seemed a long and unlikely option now.

"That piece of scum that controlled the Lords of the Borderlands, the 'high adviser'." He looked close to spitting again as his face twisted in disgust. "They say he has somehow managed to gain mastery of darkfire, the fire of dragons. Whether he stole it from them, kindled it, or made it, I don't know, but darkfire could easily raise the whole realm to dust."

"Darkfire's no more than a myth, like dragons," someone called out. "You've been drinking too much of

Mary's special brew. Makes you see all sorts of wonders."

"Oh, no doubting this land has wonders," Sav insisted. "Time was we'd have dragons in the skies and on land, in the water too. Small thin ones darting up streams like rushes of gold and silver, and enormous ones that flew with trails of fire or stampede the very tunnels far beneath the grass."

"Ever seen a dragon, have you?" Mary chortled.

Neri hesitated. "I have."

All eyes turned to her, doubtful and curious in one sweeping glance.

"The battle for Jakiris recently," she added. "The Lord of the Borderlands had six chained with ice. They're free now, as they should be."

Her mind twisted back to the mine of shades she'd seen, something she had to ask the Jakida about when she inevitably had to return.

Low mutterings spring up around tables and she ducked her head to wipe more cups as Sav cleared his throat.

"Dragons have been seen. No, what I'd love to meet is a unicorn."

Neri frowned. "The magic horses? Now those must be a myth."

"*Elemental* horses, actually." He grinned. "And not to be sniffed at. One time there were unicorns of all elements roaming, with horns and thundering hooves, or wings, and those born of seaform, and fire horses that dwell near the whitefire lakes."

"That would be a sight to see," Mary admitted.

"What about shades then?" Neri pressed him. "I heard rumour there were still shades on this side of the cursed forest?"

She didn't dare look Mary's way, because she vaguely

remembered mention of Niall and Mary knowing each other, but Sav's sigh made her look at him instead.

"Shades are a tricky one. Seen odd few pass through but they never stay long. Rumour had it there were a bunch killed much further west than here, but only hearsay. Either way I hope not. Poor souls still deserve humanity, even if they can't feel the sting or kiss of it."

"I heard there were a few working in mines somewhere, that's all," she said with her heart sinking.

Mary sighed. "There might well be. Shades haven't always been treated rightly but the nearest mine to here is past Acerinth, and that's long been abandoned."

"Near the cursed forest?"

"On the border of, yes. Folk don't venture near the forest now for fear of getting sucked inside and other such nonsense."

Neri asked no more and even Sav made his excuses to follow the last wave of drinkers out the door.

If they think the mine is deserted, it would be so easy to spread superstition about the forest and use shades to mine there. Question being, is the Jakida aware of it?

She pressed a hand to calm the sudden warm fluttering in her chest, like tiny wings beating to get free. The soft echo trilled in her head and she wiped her weary eyes on her forearm.

"To bed with you," Mary insisted. "The woes and whys will still be here in the morning."

Neri opened her mouth to argue, or to ask more, but Mary smiled knowingly.

"I wouldn't go around asking too much about darkfire," she warned. "It's a fable and nasty stuff at that. The dragons, I hear, have tiny quantities of it in their make-up and they alone have control of it. It's a fire that water can't touch, can't extinguish, kind of like a fire made from oil. Do you want a drink yourself for bedtime? You've earned it."

Neri nodded and spirited the drink up the stairs to her room. Tomorrow she would plan. If the dragons had darkfire, or elements of it, she would need them if Sav's suggestion about Amis was in any way true. Mulling this over as she drank her wine in bed, Neri wondered what she would do next and how long she'd wait.

Getting a message to Cori at Apeklonia would be difficult. The only way she could get the message safely without detection would be to send a bird. Unfortunately, she had nobody to tell the bird the message. Sighing, she vowed to enquire tomorrow if Mary knew of any animal talkers.

She slipped into sleep and realised the next morning that her slumbering hours were getting slightly longer. She woke feeling more rested than she could remember being for a long while.

Humming what she thought of now as the firebird's tune as it rolled in her mind, she waved to Mary and started sweeping.

When Mary interrupted her and suggested they take a trip to the market, Neri stared at the open door. She'd not left the inn since her dramatic arrival. Catching sight of her face, Mary forced the broom out of her hands and her out of the door.

Blinking in the daylight, Neri looked around the little market, alive with activity. Gratitude to Mary overflowed once again as she got swept up in the hustle of it all.

She followed Mary around the stalls, chatting to folk she knew already. Mary instructed her on what items to put in the basket and Neri almost forgot that for most of her life she'd had to pay or barter for things. Mary made the wine and gave the folk drink. They in turn gave her the ingredients to cook her food and anything else she needed.

One man suggested Neri might like some clothing for a new outfit, but she smilingly declined, insisting she only worked at the bar and had nothing to repay his kindness with.

She often warmed water with her gift and Mary gave her the leftover candles to play with, but she didn't want anyone knowing about her fire. It might cause wagging tongues to carry rumours to the other settlements and tell everyone where she was.

She imagined the Jakida wouldn't care much about her being found. Emelyn and Ciena would just be glad she was safe, but she didn't doubt for a moment that Livia would be on the first stolen horse out of Jakiris, probably with Emelyn in tow.

Or Niall would, assuming he left the borderlands safely. She winced and clenched her hands tight around the basket. *I shouldn't have left him.*

She knew she had to, and he was a grown man with the ability to fight and fend for himself, but even then the guilt made her queasy enough that she struggled to draw breath.

The man at the stall was still looking at her with doleful eyes. When she smiled at him and took a step to move on, he held up the cloth again.

"It's very good cloth, strong quality," he insisted.

"I'd love it, I'm sure, but I can't repay you with anything."

She could sneak him drinks but it wasn't her wine to offer. To her surprise, he smiled.

"What about gifts or skills? You must have something beyond sweeping and singing in you?"

Neri hesitated and dropped her gaze to the basket. She couldn't tell him about the fire, couldn't risk it, but she noticed he had his feet in a bucket of water. When he caught her looking he grimaced.

"I have bad circulation. The healer tells me to keep them warm but also to keep them in water when I can so it's a stuck situation. I hate the feel of soggy footcloth."

Neri balanced the basket with one arm as she knelt down and stuck her finger in the water. She let her *ai-tan* warm the water and left a tiny kernel of it there. It would simmer for a while, longer than it should, and it would help him a bit at least.

She looked up at his amazed face and he smiled with sheer relief.

"For that, I have this nice green top here, softest cloth, all yours. Please."

He held the cloth out. Mary had given her a shirt and some trousers, but Neri couldn't remember the last time she had clothing of her own that wasn't borrowed or a gift from Livia. Knowing not to reject a gift, even though she'd done very little in return, she took it and held it out for closer inspection.

As she stood there holding the top, she looked up. A large blue bird swooped above, its plumage catching the sunlight as it flitted over the square and dived away across the grasslands. It reminded her that she had yet to ask Mary if she knew any animal-talkers.

"What material is this?" she asked.

The man smiled and twisted in his chair. He pointed toward a lane running between two buildings. It led to the fields beyond and Neri could just see black lumps against the grass. She squinted enough to make out large animals oblong animals with squat legs and curling horns.

"It's spun from the finest Mathoen fur. Sav, I believe you know him, he raises them and gives us the fur."

Neri smiled. She hadn't found anything quite so fine for fabric in Kirelonia and wondered why on earth the palace at Jakiris weren't stocking it. She said as much and the man laughed.

"I don't doubt they would want it. Sav is very particular who he trades to. The royal envoy came many winters ago to inspect our crop but perhaps they preferred to support their local tradesfolk."

Neri heard the diplomatic response and decided it was best not to comment further, so she thanked him for the top and hurried to where Mary was waiting for her. They finished Mary's errands and Neri returned to sweeping the inn floor with a lighter heart. The goodness of folk around her made her think of those in Jakiris. She missed her cottage and her friends.

Jakiris will always be home.

The echo in her head flowed at the thought, trilling a sadder song of lament and Neri hummed it out loud as she worked.

The firebird had chosen to appear to her even when she had no *ai-tan*, and from what everyone else said, had honoured her with the gift of it since. It had to mean something, and she had to hope that something allowed her to find a way to fight Amis and his darkfire.

Lunch and the afternoon were supposed to be her own time for dragon hunting or whatever she chose. Rather than venture out, she found an old story book of Mary's and settled up in her room to read it.

The tale of Kalen the Adventurer had all the qualities of fantasy. The writer appeared to have dreamt a realm all of his own full of floating islands in sparkling waters. Neri thought back to Emelyn's book and its tales of ancient Kirelonia, and she wondered whether Kalen's stories were anything more than myth.

As the suns fell lower, she got up and went to tend bar. Sav came in and gave her a wink as she passed him his drink with a small smile. She almost dropped the cup in her hand as a shadow passed the door, but it was just a large bird that perched on the windowsill. She huffed at her flightiness and focused on warming the cup of wine for the clothes trader, who accepted it with a big smile.

Some of the younger folk set up in a corner to play drums and wooden flutes, and Neri nodded her head to the music as she worked, pleased that her mind had decided to give her a night off from its own songs.

Someone came in and said something to Sav, and Neri noticed him leave, but she continued serving and cleaning with her mind settling.

I can't avoid going home anymore.

Even Sav and Mary were adamant finding the dragons was a lost cause. She would have to go back to Jakiris and speak with Zel instead. The cursed forest would give them some time but soon enough the Governance would start bursting through and waging another war.

I can't avoid the inevitable fight with Niall either.

She missed him, achingly so. The distance and time since they spoke paled their argument into pathetic insignificance. When she saw him again, she would keep her temper and insist they speak calmly. Whether her emotions could manage that she didn't know.

If I see him again.

Someone slammed through the inn door and she breathed through the panicked surge of heat readily springing to her fingers.

"It's Sav, he's injured himself," the boy panted. "He got gored by one of the bulls or whatever the hell they call them here."

Neri dropped the cloth and dashed out from behind the bar to get to the door, along with several others.

"Where?" Mary demanded.

The boy led the way across the square, up one of the side lanes and out onto one of the fields. Several carried fire-brands but Neri hadn't thought to take one, so she stumbled near the front of them with the grass illuminating from behind. Sav was being tended to by a healer but his eyes were closed and blood seeped from a large gash in his chest.

Neri caught Mary's arm.

"Get rid of the crowds. Get them back."

She kneeled by the healer who she didn't know by name.

"What's happened?" she asked.

The healer grimaced. "Caught a hoof to the chest. Nothing too bad normally, but he landed on a sharp bit of blade. He's too cold and the wound won't weave fast enough."

"I can help." Neri winced as her voice shook. "If you need me to warm him or anything else, I can help."

The healer nodded and fumbled for something in his bag.

"Warm him then."

Neri focused on taking the tingle of her *ai-tan* along with every good thought she could dredge up and passing the kindling warmth into Sav. Her gift crooned inside her, the lyrical notes encouraging her on. In that moment, she could almost feel the flow of life through the heat.

When the healer sat back a while later, Neri opened her

eyes but maintained her flow.

"You can stop now." The healer smiled. "That helped a lot, have you thought about joining our ranks?"

Neri shook her head and turned her attention back to Sav. Maybe one day, if she ever had kids, she'd be that kind of *ama*.

She watched Sav open his eyes and he sluggishly felt around with his good arm until he found her hand with his.

"I knew you were good luck girl," he mumbled. "I figure I owe you now."

Neri hesitated, then lowered her face to his ear.

"If you know any animal talkers, I need to get a message to any dragons. If not, then perhaps you can name one of your animals after me."

Sav laughed then groaned at the pain in his chest.

"Am I good to get up?" he asked the healer, who rolled his eyes before nodding. "Good. Help an old man get back to his home with dignity."

Neri and the healer hefted him to his feet, but he leaned his weight on Neri as she supported his good side.

"I'm alright!" he croaked to the crowd. "Now I think this pretty girl is going to help me to my door."

The crowd cheered and relieved shouts of laughter echoed through the evening. Neri guided Sav toward the dwelling he pointed to at the far end of the field and the woman hovering there.

"I told you to clear that field," she grumbled even as she smiled with sheer relief.

Neri sagged as the woman took Sav's weight from her, but before she could escape she was herded inside with him. The door shut behind her and she hovered as the woman dropped Sav unceremoniously into a chair.

"I can't thank you enough, you and old Dernie. I've

been telling him to clear that field for handspans now."

"Yes and you've been telling everyone you've been telling me that for even longer," Sav replied cheerfully. "Now I'm fine don't fuss. If you want to fuss, go open the shutters."

The woman huffed but went to open the window shutters before going to their separate kitchen just visible through a small archway.

Sav made a chirping noise and Neri tensed as her mind issued its own lyrical note in response. Cocking his head to the side, he stared at her with curiosity narrowing his brow, almost as though he'd heard it. Neri had no idea what to say, but then Sav turned his attention to the window and a bird flew in.

Sav made a soft twittering noise, then asked Neri for her message.

"Message? To the dragons?"

He nodded. "I can commune with the birds. Dragons not so much, although I tried long ago. Only birds. But they have their own skills among many types of bird, so if there are dragons that can be spoken to, you can consider the message sent."

Neri bit her lip. She had no idea whether she should give Sav the whole message and hope, or ask the dragons to meet her somewhere.

Where would I even go to meet an enormous beast without being seen?

"If you can just tell them that we need to find out how to get rid of darkfire, to fight or snuff it out. If they know how, can they find a way to tell us. Or show us. But not if it hurts anyone. Or we don't want them eating dwellings or something. Maybe don't tell them that bit though."

Sav rubbed a hand over his mouth.

"That's bold, but I owe you."

He twittered to the bird, which cocked it's teardrop head and issued a responding chirp. Neri watched it sail out of the window and sighed.

"I won't ask," he added. "Far beyond my desire to delve into. Do you want to stay for dinner?"

Neri opened her mouth to refuse, although how she could without being rude she wasn't entirely sure, but a flash of fire caught her eye outside. She stood, fully believing that either Sav's farm was on fire, or her firebird had somehow escaped her mind and fluttered free. Wild thoughts thundered on until she saw the fire come into view again.

The blaze wasn't from fire but from the coat of a horse cantering around the smaller field fenced off from the larger one beside the house. The horse's coat shone in the firelight from the dwelling like the shiver of a flame in a breeze, its long mane and tail flowing freely.

"That's a beautiful horse," she said.

Sav grinned. "Ah, she's useless. Fine for a riding pony but I've no kids to ride her. She won't mix with the bulls and hates pulling the cart. I've half a mind to take her to market and trade her for a bucket of Mary's wine."

Neri caught the amused gleam in his eye and bit her tongue. She couldn't buy or trade the horse from him, not without contacting someone in Jakiris to bring her things to trade or her small collection of coins.

"She's worth more than a bucket of wine," she said wistfully. "Even Mary's. I can't stay for dinner, but you rest up and I imagine Mary might stand you a drink for your recovery."

The horse trotted up to say hello at the fence as she left the dwelling. Neri paused to stroke her nose and wondered if perhaps he might consider keeping the horse until she was able to go home and come back for another visit. Maybe then she could make a deal with him.

She waited until the horse had tired of her attentions and walked across the field to the inn alone. As she served the stragglers still in the bar, a little tipsy from the wine that Mary pressed on her, she glowed in the wealth of good wishes folk gave her for helping Sav.

Neri had already chastised herself into setting off for Jakiris in the next day or so, but hadn't found the nerve to mention it to Mary. She couldn't resist taking the chance to ask a few questions as the bar emptied out.

"If one did find dragons, would they be able to claim the darkfire themselves do you think?"

Mary sighed. "They may not even understand. They have no need to fear darkfire like we do. Whatever you're planning in that pretty head of yours, I'd probably try and find another way to a solution."

She had to smile as Mary dropped another drink in front of her.

"There was an old tale about fire," Mary continued. "Ancient, all told, about lakes of whitefire underground, then folkfire gifted by the firebird, and finally, darkfire grown in the dank pits of air within deep, fetid waters."

Neri grabbed a drying cloth automatically as Mary began to wash cups beside her.

"Whitefire is unwieldable," she explained. "Darkfire is near impenetrable, but folkfire in its purest form can mute them. So, unless you have a firebird about your person, darkfire isn't to be messed with. Oh for the love of..."

She hustled out from behind the bar, her attention fixed on something outside the inn, but Neri stayed in place.

Firebird beats darkfire. I wouldn't need the dragons.

Maybe I wouldn't need anyone, and they'll all be safe.

She could go back to the borderlands alone and face Amis. It wouldn't be easy, but no doubt he and Viljo would delight in taking her captive.

Niall might still be there.

She lifted her head as shadows filled the inn doorway and a soft gasp puffed from her lips. Standing in the bar were several folk she knew, but none of them were folk she'd served over the past days.

Livia, Finn and Mik stood smiling at her.

"What are you doing here?" she asked, astonished.

Ciena must have told them where I was.

Livia snorted. "I've had birds hunting the skies for you since you disappeared."

Of course she has.

Neri rounded the bar and let Livia bundle her into a tight hug, the sensation of nearing home and missing it even more swelling painfully.

"Oh." She sniffed against the burn of tears. "Why are you here though? Not that it isn't good to see you."

"We need you. There's talk of the west marching on Apeklonia to attack."

"What?" Neri wiped a hand over her face.

She managed a frazzled smile at Mik and Finn.

"It's why we've come to get you. It's all anyone is talking about, you demanding a fighting force then disappearing without a trace."

"What's the need for said fighting force?" Mik asked gently. "Perhaps we should start there, because Ciena said you asked her to find one, and she's taken it far too seriously."

Neri grimaced at the image that summoned.

"I didn't, I just said she should ask around and see if

anyone's willing to join should the need arise."

"Ah yeah, you asked the wrong person then," Finn said with a laugh.

"But why?" Mik asked.

"Viljo is in-thrall to Amis, and rumour is that Amis can wield darkfire now," Neri reminded them. "Seems silly now but given what *ai-tan* I have, I wanted to see if I could find the dragons. They're said to be the only thing that can quell darkfire."

"If that's correct, then we are at a distinct disadvantage," Livia said. "Are you coming home now? We really could do with your help."

Neri sighed and rubbed her hand over her eyes.

"I guess I have no excuse not to. Is..." She bit her lip, unable to ask.

"We'll have a walk around the square," Mik said, giving Finn a pointed look. "We should leave as soon as you're ready, Neri. Tonight if possible. We can rest on the road easily enough."

He hustled Finn back out of the bar and Neri braced herself for Livia, who smiled wickedly.

"Is...?" Livia prompted.

"Don't make me ask it."

"Fine. He's in Jakiris. I think you've had a weird effect on him because he asked to see *Ama* the moment he found out where you were."

"He didn't want to come get me himself?" Her heart sank.

I deserve that. I should have stayed, should have fought it out with him.

Livia shrugged. "He wanted to, but he and *Ama* are in counsel and wouldn't let me join them. So I insisted on coming to get you instead. Much more fun anyway."

Neri decided not to answer that and glanced around at the bar. In Carahdyl with Mary around, she felt strong alone. If she went to Jakiris the sense of home would anchor her and leave her vulnerable. If Niall discarded her for leaving him this time, she might actually break.

But Jakiris was home. If she did intend to fight, to wage a war on Amis, then she wanted to be home before she did.

"I'll need to say goodbye to Mary," she said. "I probably still owe her for the food and board."

"No debt owed."

Mary appeared from the storeroom behind the bar with a grin and dumped a couple of drawstring sacking pouches onto the bar.

"These will see you home," she added. "Come and see us again soon, stay a while. Now, I believe a friend outside has a gift for you, and don't give me any of the nonsense about not accepting it because I had to run like the wind to let him know you were leaving."

Neri forced herself to smile. War notwithstanding, she could return to Carahdyl any time she chose. She accepted the pack from Mary and rushed up to fetch her own pack. It fit inside the new one without her having to move the contents so she shouldered the extra weight and followed the others outside.

Neri glanced around, wondering what friend could be waiting with some mysterious gift. The square was empty but a flicker of brightness caught her attention. At the far end nearest the lane leading to the plains beyond the settlement, Sav stood waiting with a broad grin on his face. In one hand he held a set of reins and attached to those reins was the same horse she'd admired in his field.

"She's for you." Sav held the reins out as they approached. "Nothing doing with her in the fields, but she'll be a good traveller, steady enough if you keep a light hand."

Neri took the reins. She couldn't reject a gift, Mary had warned her as much, but she had nothing for him in return.

"Thank you. It seems you're getting the poor end of a trade," she said quietly.

"Ah, be off with you." He laughed and waved her away. "Come visit us again soon, and we'll look after Mary until then for you."

She nodded, her thanks stuck in her throat as emotion swelled up. She held her hand out to the horse instead, *her* horse, and admired the shining golden coat.

She mounted with Livia's help and waved goodbye once more as Mik took the lead, with her and Livia in the middle and Finn at the back. They left the settlement and started across the open plains with the stars dancing above them, and Neri settled into her horse's stride.

"What's the Kirelonian word for 'fire'?" she asked.

"In the old tongue, the word for fire is *Fiorja*," Livia said. "Although mostly people drop the second 'i' sound, so Fiora. Is that what you're calling her?"

Neri nodded. Fiora suited the horse that seemed to have been born from the same element she now wielded. Then her thoughts turned toward home, and what was inevitably waiting for her there.

Even a horse of fire isn't going to save me when I have to face Niall again.

CHAPTER FIFTEEN

A continual burst of speed soon put them past Forlaith forest, the subtle pull of magic and nature enticing Neri to wander inside the trees. She knew to ignore it, to focus her mind elsewhere. As if she'd summoned it, a strong hit of *liliam* wafted around her so sharply she missed a breath. Wherever he was, Niall was thinking about her.

They only stopped as the next day waxed and waned to rest the horses, and by time they were close to Jakiris according to Livia, Neri was irritable with nerves and ready to riot.

"Oh, look!"

Mik's quiet awe brought her attention back to the group and she smiled as he pointed to a small pool of water nearby. Moments later, a bird with brilliant blue plumage shot out from beneath the water's surface.

"That's amazing!" he marvelled. "How do they breathe underwater? I've never seen one of those before."

Neri shrugged. She had put it down to the wonders of Kirelonian nature, but there was so much of it she didn't know, so much she wanted to explore.

"Our land has many wonders," Livia said. "We saw the dragons recently. Neri freed them, but they're every bit as fearsome as the legends suggest. Do you not have watellow birds where you're from?"

"Is that what those are? Fascinating. We don't have those, or dragons, but we do have araciduls." Mik cast a conspiratorial glance at Finn. "They're large eight-legged creatures the size of big dogs. Some are rumoured to have at least a thousand eyes."

Livia shuddered violently and made Neri jump, which set the horses off snorting and stamping.

"Mik's only teasing." Finn winked at them. "Araciduls are quite friendly and they love to shake hands. They consider it really rude if you don't."

Neri couldn't tell how much of that was true, but she hadn't seen or heard of an aracidul before. It might be fanciful nonsense to pass the time, but none of it was getting them home any faster.

Assuming I'm even welcome anymore now that he's back in Jakiris. The Jakida might insist I leave, and since when is he cosy enough to have counsels with her?

"I bet you're keen to get home," Livia prompted.

Neri hesitated. She was, more than anything, but Niall was somewhere in Jakiris and she would have to face him, to fight it out.

"I'll be interested to see what's waiting for us," she muttered.

"You'll be surprised. There were quite a lot of fighters massing outside the walls when we left."

Neri frowned. "How many?"

She had no doubt that Ciena would be happy to find fighters, but she'd assumed convincing them would be another matter entirely.

"All I'll say is you'll be surprised," Livia repeated. "Rumour has it even shades are showing up. Ready to find out?"

She pointed at the gap in the trees in front of them and Neri's heart lifted. Niall or no Niall, she was finally home.

Fiora picked up on her excitement and her hooves

danced toward the edge of the hill that led down to the stretch of grassland and the settlement.

Neri let her reach the top of the hill then reined her in with a soft gasp. Viljo and Livia's riverbed, carved into the earth during the last battle, was full of water and forming a small lake that several tents were camped by.

So many tents.

"Come on, let's go!"

Livia urged her horse down the hill and Neri let Fiora charge into a snorting canter to follow. The wind whistled against her and she laughed as they pulled up on the fringes of the camp, several startled faces pointed in their direction.

"Look, your welcoming committee is here." Livia pointed.

Neri eyed Ciena stalking toward her and grinned as the woman drew level with them.

"This is unbelievable," Neri insisted by way of greeting. "You managed all this?"

Ciena grinned. "Not me."

She turned to nod her head at the nearby cluster of tents, and Neri followed the line to an achingly familiar man stood in deep conversation with the Jakida and the captain of the Jakirian guard. Niall lifted a hand to sweep a handful of chestnut hair back from his face and Neri's heart squished with wanting.

"He did this? How?"

"Called in some favours, racked up some future debts." Ciena shrugged. "Came raging into Jakiris a while back looking for you, so I told him what you asked me. He decided to get you your horde as an apology instead of raging across the land to fight you instead."

Neri had no words. Any moment now Niall would turn

in their direction and she would need to speak to him.

What do I even say? I left again. Even though his attitude contributed to it, I'm a grown woman. I can't blame him entirely.

"Go easy on him," Ciena added. "He's not slept much since, and the Jakida has threatened to sedate him twice."

Neri let the sight of Jakiris ahead make her decision for her. She would be mature and greet him and the others, then let the excuse of the long journey drive her inside. If he followed, they could talk. If he didn't...

Niall's head lifted in one swift movement and he twisted to face them. Neri slid down from Fiora's back as he turned her way, and his gaze burned across the short distance between them. She kept one hand welded to the reins as she walked forward. His expression was clamped down tight, any emotions hidden.

She slowed when they were almost in reaching distance at the sight of his shadow flicking irritably over his skin.

Fiora snorted and tried to reverse with her eyes rolling wide as Niall stopped in front of them.

Then he sank to his knees.

"There's absolutely nothing I can say to make what I did any better," he announced.

Neri mouthed over countless words before settling on an indefinable squeak as his arms wrapped around her waist. He pressed his forehead against her and she looked around to see several folk laughing. She settled a hand against the side of his face but he refused to lift his head when she pushed.

"We both regret things," she said. "It's been a tough journey, and I don't know what-"

"I let the *mekhan* into my head. He twisted my worries into realities and I couldn't avoid them. Next thing I knew,

I was waking up hidden away with Cori. She got me, Finn and Mik out of Apeklonia and I came straight here."

She didn't need to ask who he was cursing about. Viljo's change in demeanour and Amis being present for it was all she needed to see.

"Ciena said this mass of folk is your doing," she said instead.

He nodded against her middle.

"I called in a few trades, mostly based on lineage which the Jakida wasn't happy about, but I think she's too worried about losing you to say no to me."

Neri snorted. "I doubt that. What do we owe, and to who?"

That was enough to make him lift his head, his dark eyes swimming with hope as he gazed up at her.

"There's still a 'we'?"

"Well, you are on your knees begging." She bit back a smile.

He stood and wrapped her properly in his arms, her chin fitted on the dip of his collar bone where it belonged. She nestled her face into his neck and breathed in deep, not even caring that he smelled way better than she probably did. She'd left the dress behind in Carahdyl but the slippers needed cleaning. Or burning, she wasn't fussy.

"You can have me on my knees begging anytime," he murmured. "I would have come to fetch you myself the moment we heard you were at Mary's, but I figured you would appreciate the fighting numbers more. Oh for the love of-"

"Let her breathe Niall, *ej-va*!"

Livia's amused voice was enough to make Neri lift her head off his shoulder as his arms tightened around her.

"No, go away," he grumbled.

"She looks like the bottom end of a dung-pit and probably needs to eat. I dragged her right out of Carahdyl in the dead of night like you insisted."

"Thanks." Neri pulled a face. "I do need to eat though."

She smiled as Livia hugged her, dung-pit stink and all, as well as Niall who stubbornly refused to let go.

"What state are we in?" she asked.

Niall waved a hand at the massing forces camped outside the settlement walls as the Jakida strode toward them.

"We've enough," he said.

The Jakida frowned. "We don't know that. We still need to discuss this before we drag anyone halfway across the land. Your brother-"

"-is beyond reach," Niall snapped back. "If you don't believe me, believe Livia. If you don't believe her, believe Neri. The man who was 'advising' the old lord has wormed his way into Viljo's head with some kind of mind-control gift, and they both need stopping."

Livia huffed loudly enough to gain everyone's attention.

"Enough. Neri and I need to eat, or bathe at the very least. I've got dirt in places that I never even knew existed."

"Bleurgh." Niall wrinkled his nose.

"My point exactly," she continued. "There's time enough to rest and convene before deciding anything, and I'm sure Neri had stuff to add."

When the Jakida didn't reply, Livia remounted her horse and Neri did the same. Niall walked alongside as they passed the camps of the gathered fighters toward the settlement with one hand resting on her thigh, as though he didn't trust her not to vanish again.

I'll let Livia go her own way, Neri decided. *Then it's straight to the cottage to sleep.* She glanced at Niall. *Mostly.*

CHAPTER SIXTEEN

Niall smiled to see a spark light in Neri's eyes the moment they reached the settlement gateway. He noticed the low bow the guard afforded them, and realised it was aimed at her, not him.

Neri halted her horse and swung down to the ground.

"Hi Silu, it's been a while. How's your boy doing?"

The man swept his hat off of his head and held it in both hands clasped in front of him.

"He's doing well, Lady, thank you. Not really a boy any more but he always will be to me. My girl's had a daughter of her own too."

Neri smiled and gave him a nod, but her horse grew restless after their rapid pace and she smoothed her hand across its neck.

"Business is still good?" she asked.

The man grinned at her, his reverence somewhat forgotten as he relaxed in her presence.

"It's as good as can be expected. I have a hue of red wood I've been working on that will dance with your flames. If you're staying a while, come and see me."

Neri nodded again and moved to pass through the gate. She caught Niall's gaze and flushed, her eyes darting down to her toes as she rode the horse up the main path toward the palace.

Niall had no idea she'd commanded that much respect in the short time she'd been in Jakiris. He'd been so caught up trying to win her over during their last stay in Jakiris together, that he'd not noticed anything else.

He saw her humility at having been noticed as well. He wondered if she remembered that the reason for their recent separation, the stupid fight about his inheriting the village. It sent a rumble of love through him and he decided to increase his attempts to regain her trust by whatever means necessary.

No doubt the others would understand him using a few devious methods. They would spend the evening at the palace and talk late into the night planning. Perhaps they would even throw her a mini-homecoming. If he could get Neri to relax enough, she would open up to him and talk fully.

Looking up the path toward the palace, Niall smiled. Walking down toward them, a broad smile on her otherwise ethereal face, Zel had her arms spread wide. On anyone else it might have been an invitation for a hug, but on Zel Niall knew it meant she saw their return as a victory. Neri didn't appear to gather the same conclusion.

Niall chuckled as Neri, overwhelmed by being in the place she loved most, dropped her reins and cannoned up toward Zel, almost knocking her over.

To Niall's surprise Zel tolerated the contact for a moment before patting Neri on the shoulder and moving her back to arm's length.

"I'm so glad to see you two side by side that I'm letting my guard down," Zel teased.

Neri glanced at Niall, merriment and embarrassment mingling in her eyes. Knowing to take advantage of any opportunity, Niall curved his arm around Neri's shoulders and pulled her close to his side. The enticing flush graced her cheeks and Niall grinned down at her.

"She can't get away from me that easily."

Not wanting to push his luck, he knew he had to let her go. Just for a moment though, before his arm slipped away and broke the contact, he thought Neri pressed herself just a little closer to him. Emboldened by this, he relaxed and they turned to wait for the rest of their party.

Zel issued greetings to them all. Niall caught sight of the Jakida handing her reins to a servant and sweeping straight into the palace.

They fell into step with Zel until a few steps more and Neri whirled off again. Niall recognised the next turning ahead of them to the left, his grin widening as he rolled his eyes at the others.

"She's worse than Emelyn in this place."

Everyone laughed, even Emelyn who protested without much vigour. They suggested he find Neri and meet them in the main hall when they were ready.

The suggestive nudge of Ciena's shoulder against his, more of an incitement to violence from anyone else, cheered Niall's spirits further and he turned down the lane after Neri.

The little stone and wooden cottages hadn't changed but Niall only had eyes for the one at the end. The stone walled front garden grew wilder than before, Livia's attentions in their absence not extending to manual labour.

Niall came to a halt behind Neri, the subtle scent of lavender and springtime flowers catching in his nose. He tried to read her emotions without seeing her face. Neri turned to look at him with a dazed smile and pushed open the wooden gate.

Niall's feet sank into the springy earth of the path, following her toward the front door. He wanted her to fully immerse herself in the happiness of being home.

On stepping inside, Neri stood in the middle of the room next to the round wooden table. Spinning on the balls of her feet in a slow, awestruck rotation, Niall wondered whether he'd be able to tear her away. After several timeless moments, she faced him. The last vestiges of worry and pain drained from her eyes. Her shoulders fell and her head tipped back, the sound of her relieved sigh transmitting to Niall and relaxing him too.

"We should go to the main hall." He interrupted her with much reluctance. "I expect Livia will want to throw some kind of homecoming party. But you can do whatever you like."

Neri would be incapable of unhappiness for a while, but he let her make the choices and the moves, watching and anticipating as she took his hand in her own. He stared at their fingers interlaced together and then looked up at her.

"We still have things to sort out." She couldn't meet his gaze. "I mean, now isn't the right time but- We need speak to everyone and sort out what's going on first."

She loosened her grip on his fingers, anxiety clear on her furrowed brow as she stumbled over the words.

Wishing he could fold her in his arms like old times and tease her, he tightened his grip before her hand could slide away from his.

"We're okay," he promised. "Let's go and see the others, then you need to sleep and eat properly. There's a lot to discuss, and I have some idea what you want the fighters for, but we're okay."

She relaxed at that, but he kept hold of her hand and led the way out of the cottage again. Her smiling face settled the restlessness inside him as they turned back onto the main path and started up toward the palace steps.

"Did you get out okay?" she asked quietly. "We don't

have to talk about why and what, I don't really want to, not yet, but are you okay?"

He nodded. "I'm fine. There's a detour Zel made us take on the way back I want to share with you but that can wait."

"There's a few things waiting we need to discuss first I suppose."

With her not fighting the hold he maintained on her fingers, he decided he could risk baiting her just a little more.

"I agree we have to sort out what's going on first, but can I suggest what happens after?"

He kept his voice low, intimate and secret. A delicious blush fired across her face, and moments later her hand tingled with exhilarating warmth against his. She didn't respond but he caught the slight flicker of a smile on her face so he settled his wickedness for a while.

He knew then, given her reaction, she would need time. He would take a walk through the village and get to know the guards. With enough friendliness and incentive, he could ask them to keep an eye out for a few nights, just in case Neri did find a reason to flee the village. Then he would offer to take his room in the palace, the one that had once been her room. She could let him know when she was ready to invite him back in.

Neri led the way to the main hall, constantly pausing to spin round and look at everything. Various maids curtseyed to them as they passed and Neri issued many joyous greetings whether they recognised her or not.

Niall forced himself to let her go once they reached the main hall. Neri headed straight toward Zel, who smiled and held her hands out in front of her.

"I hoped you'd find your way back home sooner rather than later," Zel said. "We have much to talk about, and I understand you have lots to do."

Zel's suggestive wording, always succinct and ever-knowing, widened Neri's eyes.

"Ciena seems like a very determined woman," Zel added with a conspiratorial smile. "She and Niall have a league of westlanders under the banner, and they will be ready to follow you when the time comes."

Neri squeaked. "They won't be following me."

"Well who else are they going to follow?" Niall grinned, unable to help it. "You called them here after all."

"No I didn't!"

She looked so horrified he started laughing, elated when she lashed out a hand to thump against his shoulder.

A howling noise made them both jump as Livia came crashing through the door, evidently pleased to be home with no sense of regality left in her.

"We will have a celebration!" Livia grinned round at all of them.

"Have you spoken to the Jakida?" Zel asked, amused.

Livia shrugged her delicate shoulders and rolled her eyes. She had changed from travelling clothes into one of her floating dresses more befitting a lady, but she was also pink-cheeked which suggested she'd taken more time to swing by the kitchens and into Orin's stash of wine.

"I'm sure she will not object," Livia retorted. "The townsfolk need uplifting after the rumours of dark times that runners and East folk are bringing us. We will celebrate Neri returning!"

Niall watched Neri, noting the slight narrowing of her eyes and the subtle quirk of her knowing smile.

"Organised a feast, did you?" Neri asked innocently. "Spent some time in the kitchens?"

Livia rolled her eyes. "So what if I did? The town square

can be cleared after the market. It's almost nightfall now. The locals seem very keen. Several are eager to hear of the plans to come and tomorrow we shall open the training rings in the valley."

Niall guessed Neri would want to rest, but she smiled along with the others. He watched her take responsibility for Emelyn, who seemed bewildered at all the commotion. Even Finn and Mik had gathered around her. Niall edged closer, wishing he could send them all away and have her to himself.

He turned just in time to see a maid come hurrying in. She bobbed a frantic bow to the group and then her eyes settled on Neri.

"The Jakida says you are to go and meet with her in the library, Lady."

The maid bobbed again and scurried off. Neri raised her eyebrows and rolled her shoulders. Niall heard the clicking and wondered how long it would be before he could ease the sore muscles for her like he used to.

It surprised him to hear the maids calling her Lady. Only noble blood had that title, like Livia. Had he been raised in Jakiris he would have been called Lord. The title sounded like the borderlands now to him, and the memory of darkness swelled at the thought of his brother.

Neri turned to him with a sheepish quirk on her lips, and he realised she was wordlessly asking him to go with her. Pleased, he moved to her side and took her hand. The touch seemed to warm her from the inside and her skin tingled against his own.

As they left the hall, Zel followed them. She walked a few paces behind but her presence was there all the same, so Niall held in all the things he wanted to say. He'd have time to tell Neri about the shadow-folk, and the frustrating conversations he'd had with the Jakida since about needing to fight back the dangers massing across the forest.

He opened the door to the library and let the others pass through before him but clung onto Neri's hand as he shut it behind them again. The Jakida stood at one of the openings to the valley, and she too had changed into more regal attire since leaving the plains outside the settlement. Her hair had been set, no doubt by a maid, and these familiarities seemed to give her strength.

"I will not see my lands descend once more into darkness." Her voice rang out clear and firm. "The high advisor has coerced himself into Viljo's beliefs and there will soon come a time where the east is not enough. I will not have folk of the westlands subjected to their ideals."

Niall wondered if perhaps the Jakida's reason for summoning Neri was the insight that he would naturally follow. He couldn't help a tiny dig, however petty, in the silence that followed.

"Perhaps your faith in your family has been misplaced."

Neri clenched his hand warningly, her shock spiking as a wave of heat. He ignored it and focused instead on the subtle ripple of anger that narrowed the Jakida's eyes. He would never see her as his *ama*, and no doubt she didn't want to claim him as her son. But he was her flesh and blood, and they would have to make the best of it.

"The most important thing to do is find ways to bring them down, all of them if necessary." Niall stood strong and took comfort from Neri beside him. "Then we will reassemble the fighters and march on."

Expecting resistance, Niall looked on as the Jakida turned to face the valley once more.

"You think it's easy to take folk into a war. You assume we'd gain a victory without even knowing the land or the folk you'll be fighting. It's easy to draw folk to a cause when they've known safety and a few battles won, but it's much harder to take them out of their homes and force them to fight in the enemy's territory."

Niall opened his mouth to retort, but Neri beat him to it.

"You assume we haven't considered all of this," she said softly. "I've seen what the Governance have done. Niall might have lived a few winterspans there too, but I've been there all my life. They killed my maman- sorry, I mean *ama*, and my gramma. They killed Hamlin, my friend. They kidnapped Emelyn, and tried to recruit me."

The Jakida's shoulders were tense, but she didn't argue as Neri stormed on.

"I remember the east being beautiful. We had herbs and plants and animals I've not seen here. It was green in summer with golden and purple fields, and the bell-flowers used to dance in the snow in winter. They tore it to the ground and I will tear them to the ground, with or without you and your fighters."

Niall slid an arm around her waist and squeezed tight.

"We will tear them to the ground," he murmured.

The Jakida said nothing for a long moment, although Zel gave them both a fond smile in the silence.

"I will think on it," was all the Jakida said.

Niall took that as a dismissal and tugged Neri out of the room. A few paces down the corridor, Neri stopped.

"I hate speaking to folk like that." She sighed. "I have no right to be telling anyone what to do, but someone has to do it. Does she even have any friends to lean on? I have Livia and you and Emelyn. Who does she have?"

Niall frowned, already feeling guilty for his cheap shot.

"I won't bite any more I promise."

"We should apologise." She hesitated with a reluctant

look on her face. "If we start discord between us we've got no hope of standing together against the enemy. That was the whole problem in the first place."

Niall's chest squeezed as he took her hands and forced her to look up at him.

"You're right, I'll go back and apologise for us." He paused as he raised her brow at him doubtfully. "I'll be diplomatic about it, I promise. Anyone would think you're trying to reform me."

Neri laughed at that. He hated how tired and weary she looked, but at least she seemed happier. There would be time for her to sleep and for them to talk. In time, there would be space for them to be together properly.

He refrained from kissing her, wondering if it would be too much too soon. She smiled at him, and that was enough as he watched her walk away down the hall until she was out of sight. He slouched back toward the library and the door he'd left ajar, stopping as voices floated out through the gap.

"-still have a part to play in this. They are your children, whether you acknowledge it or not."

Niall held back from entering the room at the sound of Zel's voice within.

"I acknowledge it." The Jakida actually sounded disheartened. "But you see how the servants and the maids are with her. Orin is more likely to take orders from Neri or Livia than she is from me. In time, and that time will come soon, I won't be needed at all. Niall and Neri will rule Jakiris together. Livia will likely take over the east if all Neri hopes for happens. I have tried to shield them all and I have nearly ruined them all."

Niall frowned. He hadn't thought of the Jakida as a person with feelings, not for a long time. She was the entity that had given him away as a baby because of what he was. Even after Zel told him she'd taken him to the tracks in the forest in the hope the shadow-folk might help him, he'd not spared a sympathetic thought for her.

For the first time he began to wonder.

"Niall would have experienced so much derision," the Jakida continued. "The first-born Jakid a shade."

"One of the shadow-folk. There was no guarantee he would have become a shade," Zel said.

"Even so, I couldn't take the risk with my claim on the west being in doubt. Then the second son, I drove so much duty into him, fearful of losing another child. Now he is ruling the borderlands with darkness so easily in his mind. Livia never listens to me."

Niall didn't stay to hear any more. Guilt settled in his gut and he walked away just in time for Livia to flap up to him and grab his arm.

"I can't find Neri anywhere."

Niall's guilt guttered into panic. He threw Livia's hands off of his arm and looked up and down the hall. Catching sight of his face, Livia's hands flew to her wine-flushed face in alarm.

"No sorry! I didn't mean she's gone!" She gasped and grabbed his arm again. "She said about visiting some old friends before the party. I checked the cottage and asked about, but I can't think who her friends are."

Niall tried to breathe and get his heart beating less wildly, even as he sought his mind for all the ways she might have escaped from the settlement. She wouldn't have had time to build another portal.

He tried to think of anyone she might have mentioned being friends with but drew a blank. He'd never even asked her anything about her time there without him, and they'd spent the rest of it arguing and making up again.

Livia looked over his shoulder and her body sagged. She breathed a huff of relief and Niall whirled round to find Neri behind him.

She approached them both, a large dark blue circle of fruit in her hand that he recognised as *calideh* and a smile on her face. Niall frantically tried to reign in his shadow. He didn't want her to think he'd doubted her again.

She didn't seem to notice and held out half of the fruit for him. He took it, noticing a smear of the fruit's juice in the corner of her mouth. He lifted his thumb to rub it off and she blushed.

"Very touching," Livia grumbled. "You two need to change and come down to the square. Don't be too long!"

Niall took Neri's hand in his own and tried to smile, but her expression was distant even though she made an instant effort to shake the thoughts away.

"She no doubt has a dress she wants me to wear." She pulled a face.

Niall nodded. "I've been using your room here at the palace. I didn't feel I had the right to stay in your cottage."

At least she rolled her eyes at that. Still, he would keep the palace room until she felt ready to invite him into her own home.

Neri led the way through the palace to her room and, true enough, Livia had left a deep green Jakirian dress out on the bed for her. The covers were rucked up from his last sleep there, but Neri didn't seem to notice as she rolled her shoulders and sighed happily.

Livia had even thought to lay out a pair of Jakirian trousers in smoky grey for him and a shirt. It would be rude not to wear them, especially as they matched the dress, but Neri picked up the dress and hesitated.

She wants me to leave. His heart sank. *It shouldn't matter. I can't expect it to be like it has been before, not now,*

He sought for something suitably irritating to say, anything to get her to snap at him and play like they used to, but he couldn't dredge up a single taunt.

Without a word, he picked up the clothes laid out for him and left the room.

CHAPTER SEVENTEEN

Neri stood in silence, staring at the bedroom door long after Niall had closed it behind him. She couldn't tell what he was thinking, not even a little. He seemed happy to hold her hand and to be around her, but all his teasing ways were gone. She had hoped he'd make it easier on her, baiting and taunting her so they could be like their old selves once more. But he didn't.

Knowing Livia would come and find her if she didn't appear soon, Neri took the time to sink into the bathing pool in the middle of the room. Despite the heated water being pumped through pipes, Neri allowed her gift to heat the water a little more to her liking.

Once she had washed and combed the tangles and knots out of her hair, she got out and set about drying it.

The dress fitted, as she had expected it would. She hoped that Niall at least still thought she was beautiful. She had no idea what he thought these days.

She took a deep breath and got used to walking around without her boots on. Niall wouldn't be coming to escort her; she couldn't wait around hoping for that. Instead she opened her door and squeaked out loud.

Niall stood leaning against the wall. This time, Neri took notice of the dark grey trousers and shirt he wore. The shirt, open at the neck, displayed the wax charm she'd made him a long time ago.

His eyes were shadowed as he stared back at her, but

whether in longing or due to some other thought she couldn't tell.

He held his hand out without a word and Neri took it, repaying the favour of silence. Together they walked through the corridors and onto the palace steps.

Neri grinned to see Emelyn in a similar dress, no doubt a gift from Livia. Emelyn's dress was dusky pink and suited her blonde curls so well. Neri took a furtive glance at Mik when nobody was looking. It made her smile and she forgot the awkwardness, nudging Niall in the ribs and nodding her head. Mik stood staring at Emelyn, not noticing a word that Finn was saying to him.

They walked as a big group down the main track, past lanes and houses, folk waving and popping out to see them go past. It appeared everyone would be coming to the celebration, but some folk were readier than others.

Neri took great delight in saying hello to anyone she recognised. They turned into the square and she had to stop. Niall stopped beside her, his silence indicating he understood.

The last time she had seen the square she had abandoned Niall, or attempted to, shortly after.

Her desire to open a portal save her friends, a task she had succeeded in, had started here. Almost as though she was officially ending her quest, Neri looked around at the folk gathered and breathed a deep lungful of home.

She left Niall's side, determined to go across to everyone she knew. Silu bowed his head to her, his lady and family all doing the same. Neri grimaced, not used to folk she knew being so formal.

"I wanted to thank you, Lady." Silu's wife seemed almost shy around her. "The centrepiece you made, it has pride of place on our table."

Embarrassed but pleased with the praise, Neri turned the tables on Silu and complimented his woodwork. Then she pretended to chastise him for not completing her bookcase yet.

"I have that red wood. I will make your bookcase from that," Silu promised.

Neri moved on, smiling and sitting occasionally to chat to folk. She had already visited the kitchens and found nobody she knew there. Now she spied Orin chivvying her workforce by the mouth-wateringly tempting buffet.

Neri waited until Orin was finished shouting and had turned around to see her. Orin had no sense of propriety and clapped Neri on the shoulder. They talked and Neri asked after the young girl who had been orphaned in the kitchens the last time she'd been home.

"We can't get her to stop talking. I remember that's your doing." Orin threw her hands up in anguish. "She's clever too."

Neri grinned, remembering the dirty young woman who hadn't spoken a word after being found in the kitchens.

After speaking to Orin, Neri moved on again until she found most of her friends clustered together around one of the long tables.

"Amis has darkfire at his will now." Zel held the group's attention. "I don't think the dragons will be the way to defeat him."

Zel's eyes flickered with something Neri couldn't interpret, a darkness that shouldn't have been there. Zel leaned forward a little more and Neri settled into a vacant bit of bench to listen. She jumped as Niall's hand thudded on the back of the bench behind her, millimetres from touching her shoulder.

"Darkfire is not to be messed with." Zel continued.

"There are ways to curb its effects on folk and methods of dousing it, but to destroy a person who walks amidst its grip is unheard of. If a solution is to be found then caution is needed. The east is more powerful now, more than we thought."

Neri resisted the urge to groan and slump over the table like a petulant child. She recognised the signs of tiredness as her gift grumbled inside her, and Zel's affectionate smile of knowing pity didn't help. Niall's sudden inability to annoy her with contact irritated her even more.

She stood up, which brought the others to their feet as well. She made excuses of tiredness with as many smiles as she could manage and slipped away from the table. She hoped Niall would follow her but didn't look back until she reached the relative quiet of the lane. Torches lit her path and a few revellers moved about nearby, but she and Niall stood mostly alone.

"Are you going to be using your cottage now?" he asked.

Neri nodded. She wanted him to ask to come with her, but he remained silent.

"I'll use the room in the palace then."

Desolation curled inside her chest, but if that was what he wanted, she would honour it.

"Fine."

She continued to the turning for her lane, knowing that as she walked down toward her cottage, he wouldn't be following her.

Perhaps he's waiting for things to calm down before we talk properly. There are still so many things unsaid, like me leaving without him.

After letting herself in, Neri used the grumbling remnants of her *ai-tan* to light a few candles on her window ledge. She stared around and found a weary smile.

Home at last.

So what if Niall had developed as much inner fire as a wet sponge. He might shake it off. If not, she would just have to scream at him until he either snapped or told her what was going on.

Neri took off her dress and found a warm bed-robe hanging nearby, then she clambered up the wooden ladder to the little indoor balcony that served as her bedroom. Without a single thought for anything else, she collapsed on the bed and fell asleep. Dreams taunted and teased her in equal measure, but she woke the next morning feeling rested and ready.

Livia had mentioned training rings and she wanted a chance to practice fighting. She had her bow and quiver, but after not using them for so long her sight was bound to be off. She would need practice with blades as well. Neri washed in the wooden pail, and idly wondered who had thought to fill it with water for her recently. Then she dressed in her finest Kirelonian trousers in russet colours and a matching waistcoat and shirt.

Outside she half expected to find signs of Niall lurking, but she only saw a neighbour who bowed and waved in greeting. With her blade at her hip and her bow and quiver in hand, Neri strode toward main lane leading up to the palace.

It was still early and in the absence of anyone she recognised, she went inside and found a maid.

"Can you show me to Livia's room please?" she asked.

The maid grinned. "Lady did not get into bed early miss. She might be still sleeping."

Neri shrugged and waited. The maid continued to smile, no doubt knowing what late nights did to young women, or at least having a fair idea. When Neri didn't back away, the maid shrugged and led the way through the halls to a door at the end of one of the upper-floor halls. With a quick word of thanks, Neri threw open the door.

Livia didn't even wake as the door thudded against the wall, so Neri went right up to the bed and shook her. Livia grumbled and clutched her blankets tighter but Neri leaned close to her ear.

"It's fighting practice today. I'm using flaming arrows."

To give Livia her due, it only took her a few moments to struggle out of her bed. Neri left her behind with the various groans about late nights and lethal berry wines. She knew the way to her room in the palace, which she still thought of as hers despite Niall using it, but she refrained from going there to wake him up.

Instead she met Livia in the main hall a while later, reminiscing over many breakfasts there previously. Livia ate little but Neri managed to put away a vast amount of fruit and soft Jakirian honey-bread.

She'd just cleared her second plate when Niall came in, but although he sat beside her and smiled, it wasn't one of his seductive, teasing ones.

Fondness. It's like he's only fond of me now.

Grateful for a distraction, Neri smiled in delight at Orin entering the room. Next to her she had a young girl who smiled brightly the moment their eyes met.

"Neri you remember Star. She still has the fruit you carved for her, although it's gone a bit mouldy now."

Neri grinned as the girl ran forward to give her a hug. Overwhelmed by the enthusiastic greeting, Neri tried to choke back the bizarre urge to cry.

"I'm glad you're home. Orin says you might teach me lessons if I don't talk too much. I'm always told I talk too much. Orin threatened to cut my tongue out."

Neri gasped in mock horror and Orin rolled her eyes.

"Enough of your words, girl, and clear the plates."

Neri wanted to tell Star to stay and talk a while, but she knew that Star worked for Orin. She wouldn't interfere in that situation, not when Orin made the food and had more blades than Ciena probably did. She said thank you when Star took her plate and returned the happy smile.

"Right, we train!" Livia stood up.

Neri got up too, eager to begin, and gave Niall a hopeful look as she passed him.

"Have fun, but not too much," he said.

Ignoring the sinking feeling in her chest, Neri focused her attentions on training as Livia dragged her outside. Nobody had arrived to train in the rings set around the valley yet, so Livia commandeered one nearest the wall as Emelyn approached.

"I never learned to fight," she said, hope swimming in her eyes.

Neri smiled. "Livia taught me."

"I learnt in hidden corners." Livia shrugged. "It's fine for women to fight but *Ama* didn't want me to. I taught myself. My brother did too, the one that isn't Niall. Neri learnt remarkably quickly."

Neri grinned. "I'm probably beyond rusty. I doubt I'd even be able to parry your worst shot."

Livia swung her blade to challenge but Neri twisted hers until she could hold it out hilt first to Emelyn.

"You might want to train Em first. Here, take mine."

Emelyn took the blade with wide eyes as Neri grabbed her bow and an arrow instead.

She set her focus on a target nearby with the sound of clumsy blade-play echoing merrily in the background. Her first few arrows almost missed completely, but then she remembered how to feel the bow, to absorb its weight and balance as a part of her.

"Not bad." Ciena's voice caught her attention. "But you need better practice with a blade."

Neri lowered her bow and faced Ciena with a grin. She stood a short distance from Livia with Finn at her side. While Finn had a huge hunk of bread in hand and showed no signs of exerting himself, Ciena was dressed for battle with two long-blades in hand.

"She's fine with a blade," Livia said, a tad haughtily.

Ciena wrinkled her nose.

"Could be better," then, as an afterthought, "Lady."

Livia scowled. "I trained her myself, I'll have you know."

"It shows."

Neri couldn't remember ever seeing Livia speechless. She swiped up the blade Ciena tossed at her feet before Livia could find a suitable comeback and took her stance. Even as she fought, parried and narrowly avoided each swing of Ciena's blade, her mind journeyed back to their first sparring. She couldn't look up to see if Niall was lingering, but this time she really hoped he was.

"Be aware of your feet, not just your arms," Ciena insisted as she lowered her blade. "Finn, you want in?"

Finn grinned. "No, I don't need any practice waving bits of blade-metal about. That's your arena."

"You're rusty," Ciena retorted.

"I can see an opponent's move before they make it. I'm fine. Go terrorise someone else and leave me be."

Neri wiped a hand over her sweating brow and dropped the blade again in favour of her bow. She took an arrow dipped in wine and passed her hand over the head, flame flaring. Aware of the others watching, she took aim. Livia laughed as Neri's arrow hit the target and the fire remained, so Neri focused on using it to trace letters, charring the wood underneath.

"It's still amazing," Emelyn said in awe.

Neri pulled her gift back and collapsed to sit on the grass for a rest with Livia flopped beside her.

"Will Niall practice?" Livia asked. "I have to admit my brother is a gifted fighter when he tries, but I've not seen much of him. Weird, considering you're here."

Guessing her friend's intention to bring the conversation round to her real aim, Neri rolled her eyes.

"Smooth. I'm sure he won't disappoint you when the time comes. Shame I can't say the same."

The words came out harsher than she expected. Neri caught Livia's dismayed expression and sighed.

"I'm being mean."

She leaned over her crossed legs with her forearms on her knees and let out a frustrated sigh. She shut her eyes and focused on the clean, sweet air and the warmth on her skin instead.

"I'm not used to him being so passive," she admitted. "We made our peace and now we're home together, but he doesn't want to be himself with me anymore. It's like he feels guilty because he's fond of me, but he doesn't, *want* me anymore."

Livia cleared her throat, but Neri ignored it.

"I keep expecting him to rage or taunt or toy with me but he just doesn't, and I hate it."

Neri flinched as a slap stung her bare arm. She lifted her head to scowl in Livia's direction, but Livia was looking up toward the large window behind them.

Realisation thudded in and Neri groaned.

"He heard me, didn't he?"

She didn't have to look at Livia to know the answer. She looked anyway. Livia nodded. Neri groaned again.

"Well that's just great," she grumbled.

Getting to her feet to go and find him, she gave Livia a weary grimace.

"If you want to practice, ask Ciena. She won't hold back."

Livia pulled a face. "I doubt she'd see me as worth training with. She's made that abundantly clear."

Neri smiled at the thought, but before she could utter any reassurance the scent of cake-spice swirled around her and firm fingers grabbed her wrist.

Niall's shadow was a cloak across his skin, and his eyes whirled dark with intent. She opened her mouth to apologise, or to argue, she wasn't even sure, but Niall walked away still holding her wrist. It took only a moment of struggling for her to realise she could follow or he'd be dragging her on her knees behind him.

Oops. She choked down the urge to grin.

He hauled her away from the training ring and down the main track, ignoring folk nodding to them as he stormed past.

"That was rude," she grumbled, fully aware she was only making it worse. "I was in the middle of a conversation."

She tried twice to free her wrist but he just squeezed tighter as he turned down the lane toward her cottage. Her *ai-tan* tingled but she couldn't bring herself to fight him off, too intrigued by this sudden reappearance of the Niall she knew. He marched right up her garden path and then turned to face her. He jerked his head toward her door, angry but apparently not enough to invade her home without her consent.

Realising her own anger was still buried deep beneath the layers of shallow relief, Neri glared her own anger back at him. She pushed open her door, walked in and turned with her hands on her hips, just in time to see it slam shut behind them.

His hands landed on her hips, his fingertips digging into her skin as his mouth landed on hers. He kissed her deeply, his fingertips gripping less when she didn't try to push him away. When she conceded, moving her hands from his upper arms to around his neck, he broke away, kissing her cheeks, her forehead, her chin, any part of her he could reach.

"Thought you'd lost interest," she muttered.

Niall growled and bit the side of her jaw gently.

"Then your head is full of sand."

Neri dug her nails into the base of his neck, hard enough to extract a yelp.

"Don't blame this on me!" she yelled. "You push me away, you want me back, you don't want me but hate the idea of anyone else having me."

"That's because *my* head is full of sand." He chuckled, the sound full of dark promise. "I will always want you. I tried to die for you before, and I'd do it again. I wasn't sure if you'd forgive me this time, that's all. Thought I'd try taking it slow, give you time."

He brought both hands to her cheeks and stared down at her, his dark eyes whirling.

"I didn't want to rush you and chase you away again."

He held her close as she sighed, the last dregs of worry finally ebbing away.

"You're hopeless." She couldn't stop the smile breaking free.

He nodded. "Hopelessly yours. Do you forgive me?"

"Is it the last time?"

"I'll vow it, if I have to."

She frowned. "No, no vows. I don't want you tied to me unless it's by your choice alone. You're always free to leave, it just kills me when you do."

"Then I won't." He claimed her mouth in another frantic kiss. "I promise, no more doubt. My brother could walk out of here naked with his fancy tiara hanging off his bits, and I'd still trust you loved me."

Neri choked over a startled laugh, but he didn't give her any time to recover as he snared her in another dizzying kiss, his hands roaming over her clothes.

"These come off," he demanded.

Neri nodded. "Yours too."

She clung to him even as the flurry of clothing scattered across the floor, soaking in the sensual slide of his bare skin against her own.

He followed her up the ladder to the sleeping level, lips kissing any part of her he could reach, until he lost restraint and wrapped his arms around her waist to haul her onto the bedding.

"In some parts of the land, folk mark each other," he murmured. "Some kind of permanent salve on the skin." He kissed over her knee, heading up her thigh. "I'd put my name here."

She laughed, breathless and giddy as she reached down for him. So much time had passed since the first time she'd been intimate with him, so much time spent *not* being intimate.

She intended to have so much time going forward.

"Where would my name go?" she asked.

He grabbed her hand, trailing her fingers over his chest

to his heart.

"Here." He grinned and moved her hand to his ribs. "Here." And lower. "Definitely here."

She let her fingers slide over him, revelling in his sharp breathing as his mouth found hers and his fingers went exploring.

Time, she chanted in her head, his touches maddening after so long apart. *We have time.*

She shattered easily in moments when he touched her, and then he moved his fingers slowly up her stomach, watching their path even as his chest heaved with the exertion of holding back.

Using her legs to guide him, Neri took control, wanting him as close as he could get.

"I could die happy like this," she whispered, her lips gliding over his ear enough to make him groan.

"No, no dying." His pace increased, his body curling possessively over her. "You're mine and I won't let you go, not to death or anyone else who tries to take you."

Neri gasped as her mind fragmented into delicious shards, his guttural moans telling her he was almost right behind her.

"Let them try," she whispered. "I'm more yours than my own."

He broke so utterly that she couldn't stop laughter spilling out, even as he recovered by raining uncoordinated kisses over her face. Content to lie beneath him, she wrapped her arms around him and held on tight. He rolled to hold her back and nestled her head against his shoulder.

She listened to the faint sounds of life going on outside, as though a war wasn't waiting for them. Natural irritability begged at her to get up, to be doing things, to carve or go outside, but Niall seemed content to simply lie holding her, and for him she would make all the time in the land and then some.

"Are you wanting to unite someday?" he asked, with the tone of someone asking for the last piece of bread.

"Excuse me?"

Niall's laughter filled the entire cottage. She wondered if he was making fun of her but found that, as long as he was teasing her, she didn't mind too much.

"In most eyes we already are, but it's like saying officially to everyone across the land that I'm yours and you're mine."

Neri settled against him. "For what it's worth, I don't care about having land or any of that. Jakiris is my home, and you're mine too, with or without titles."

"I know. The problem has always been me. While I'm at it, I didn't get a chance to apologise the other day, to the Jakida I mean. I overheard her and Zel talking. It's the first time I've thought of her as a person with feelings. She thinks you've pretty much taken over Jakiris as it is, and Livia will go to govern the borderlands, or maybe even the east when the battle is won."

Neri tried to back up, but Niall growled and held her still as he continued speaking.

"I'm not sure about me but I think she's right. The folk here love you and they respect you. You're the one leading the fight to protect their livelihood and their home. Jakiris might as well be yours."

Neri's gift bubbled awake, the trilling in her mind taking on a jubilant note of lively, leaping birdsong. She did think of Jakiris as hers, but not in the sense of governing it. Niall would do fine if he chose to take the role. If not, Livia would do just as well in a different way.

She smiled as he lifted his head and dropped a ragged

line of gentle kisses over her shoulder.

"Are we done with fighting each other?" he asked.

She nodded. "I hate us fighting all the time. When I left Apeklonia, I'd waited up all night but you didn't come back. I didn't have any option to stay longer, and I didn't know when you'd be coming back. I went to Mary's for information, but deep down I think I was scared of finding out you'd given up on us."

He sighed, the warmth gusting across her neck.

"I'm sorry I doubted you." His tone almost broke her heart. "The empath got into my head, I told you that. I'm convinced I'm not good enough for you and he knew it. He went on and on about Viljo having the true kingdom, about you wanting the best for the future and those that will come along in time. He said you loved Viljo once, when I went away, and you never really stopped. The darkness crept in and I let it."

He loosened his hold on her slightly but she didn't dare say a word.

"You just can't understand how destroying it is for me," he muttered. "Every time you have to 'save' someone or even the entire land, you just dance off into danger. It kills me to think you might get hurt or I might never see you laughing or smiling again."

She tried to lift her fingers to her eyes without him noticing and wiped away the subtle burn in her eyes.

"I can't change who I am," she said. "I will include you though, and fight with you about it. No more leaving. All it seems to do is make us fight and the big ones, they hurt too much. I never stop loving you and I don't care about anyone else, but you keep doubting me. I don't know if my feelings are enough for you and I don't know how else to show you."

Niall reached around her and she closed her eyes as he moved her legs over his lap and folded her body tight against his chest.

"You're mind-addled." He chuckled. "I'm so clearly besotted with you, but the fault is mostly mine. I'm sick of talking about it, of staring at you and wishing I can just hold you, so that's what I'm going to do until you stop me."

"We face what comes together, okay?" she murmured.

He nodded. "Hand in hand, like we promised."

Neri lifted her head and smiled at him in answer. His eyes were dopey and brown, his shadow no longer visible as he smiled back at her and dropped his lips to hers.

One or two feverish kisses later, she pulled back and looked up at him.

"Out of curiosity," She pinched him somewhere suggestive for effect. "Has Mik actually told Em how he feels?"

CHAPTER EIGHTEEN

"Stop grinning at everyone!"

Niall grinned wider as Neri hissed loudly at him.

It was a very good morning. The suns were shining, he was home and Neri walked beside him as they made their way up to the palace. He'd refused to let Neri leave her cottage the day before, or the evening before, but now after an extremely satisfying morning, he grudgingly got dressed and let her haul him outside.

"I can't be happy?" he asked, clutching her tighter against his side.

She swatted his arm, failing to hide her amusement.

"That's not happy, that's beyond smugness."

"I can't be smug? Not even a little bit?"

He waved at two women walking down the other way, both of them staring for a moment before nodding and carrying on their way with hushed laughter echoing behind them.

"Everyone's going to know we, you know." Her cheeks flushed as she gave him a meaningful look.

"Had sex?" He offered happily. "Several times? Admittedly, my sister is going to be unbearable when she realises, but there's no hiding it."

Neri groaned as they reached the palace steps and he settled his wickedness.

"We could go back," he suggested.

She shook her head. "No we can't, not yet. There's still

the rest of the land to think about. We might be safe but so many aren't."

He decided to ignore that, the thought of her dancing into danger yet again something he wasn't going to sully his good mood with. He steered her toward the main hall instead, guessing most would either be breakfasting or convening to talk before joining the morning training. Neri was the love of his life, but she wasn't the greatest at keeping her kitchen stocked, so at least they could eat in the main hall.

It wouldn't hurt to let Finn see us either.

He knew deep down that Finn had no designs on Neri beyond using her to rattle him for fun, but his pride needed that win all the same.

"There was something I didn't get a chance to tell you," he announced.

Neri frowned as he halted their pace outside the dining hall and took both her hands in his.

"When we were on our way back from the borderlands, Zel came to meet us. She took us into a forest, and I remembered it, even though I've never been, not that I remember."

"You remember a forest you've never been to?" she asked doubtfully.

"No- well, yes, I have." He sighed. "The Jakida took me there when I was a baby. Zel said that there used to be shadow-folk, half-shade but with emotions like me."

"So, you're not a shade, you're part of these shadow-folk? Can we go and meet them?"

He smiled at her instant enthusiasm. "Not exactly. They weren't treated very well and disappeared, whether into the mountains or beyond them, who knows? There were tracks though from older times. It means that there's a whole part of my history and my gift I never even knew existed, and I don't want to hide anything from you."

"I appreciate that." Her smile dimmed. "Actually, about that."

She took a breath, but Livia rushed out of the hall and pounced on them before she could say anything.

"There you are! I wanted to come and fetch you, but figured it best to let you work things through your systems."

She cackled loudly and Niall grinned to see Neri's cheeks go even deeper pink. He followed them into the hall and they sat with Emelyn. He glanced around at those gathered, aware of Mik studiously grinning at a book and Ciena leering at him.

Having friends around him and Neri sitting so close she was practically on his lap gave him a sense of calm and strength he'd so rarely experienced. Even the Jakida sweeping in with Zel behind her couldn't dim his mood.

"We've had reports that there are small patches of the cursed forest that are now non-existent," the Jakida announced, taking her seat at the head of the table. "They're further south but we can't delay much longer. The moment the east realises this, they'll be pushing through."

Neri sat straighter and Niall took the opportunity to shunt her sideways so she was sitting on his thighs. He rested his chin on her shoulder, reassured when she settled back against his chest.

"Do we have enough to force them back if they try?" she asked.

The Jakida frowned. "Initially, we might. But we still don't know what their full strength is, and Viljo's missives are becoming increasingly hostile and insistent."

"His latest demands that we join him before the beginning of the cold season to discuss a peace between the two sides," Zel said. "It also included a list of suggestions about what we can offer to gain their favour."

The Jakida scoffed, her shoulders rigid.

"We will not be making any offers to gain their favour, be assured of that. Our ways of living and theirs will never coincide, if what you've told us is true."

Niall nodded. "The east will have total dominion under one banner led by a group of power-hungry fanatics that don't care who they kill to achieve it."

"So what's the plan?" Neri asked. "We can't exactly march through the borderlands, not without taking it by force. That's more lives than we want to ruin. Maybe we can increase defence along the borders of the forest in time?"

She's planning to stay. Niall's heart sang at the thought. *She's aiming for defence, not attack.*

He dropped his hand to rest on her thigh, letting his fingers roam over the soft fabric of her trousers. She shifted at the contact and he watched as her cheeks flushed.

"Focus on the meeting, not me," he teased quietly.

He flinched a moment later when she squirmed against him, her body glowing warm.

Ciena cleared her throat to draw the room's attention to her next.

"It might be worth considering attack," she announced. "Not just because I want to fight, and trust me I do, but our folk in the east are marching on Apeklonia. They could do with a hand."

The Jakida's lips thinned. "That may be, but they aren't my folk to mind. If the passage through the borderlands were even safe to take, what's to say I would have anyone coming back to defend when they come for us?"

Niall sighed. She would never see further than the edges of her own land. Even in his youth, abandoned by her because of what his shadow represented, he recognised that she would defend not just the lives of her folk but also their freedoms. She simply didn't see any further than that duty. Much like she'd disowned him as a son, she disowned any folk that weren't westlanders.

"They're still folk," he said. "They deserve every bit the same as we do. West, east, the divide is part of what keeps the problem alive. We're not talking about protecting the west, or saving the east. We're talking about decimating the decay spreading through those that rule as our enemy."

Neri's hand slid over his, her fingers weaving and squeezing tight.

"We can't lock our land up as a pretty little box while the rest of it gets ravaged. Keep them out for this generation, what's to stop them killing our children, or their children down the line? We can't wait this out. We can't hide from it."

"Neither should we," Livia agreed. "Harelda will let us through if we ask her. She wants the safety of her folk as much as we do ours. If Viljo is the problem, we bring him home. If his advisors try to stop us, we remove them."

Ciena grinned as she stood and braced her hands on the table.

"If it helps, a friend of mine has managed to get a message all the way across the forest."

Niall frowned. "How?"

"By bird. Even if folk are still failing to find a way through, the creatures are finding it easy now. Apparently your new lord of the borderlands has been invited to Apeklonia as an honoured guest. He'll sit and play pretty with the Governance council, be their puppet, all that, but it does mean-"

"The borderlands will be free of them." Neri sat up and Niall groaned at her sudden excitement.

Ciena nodded. "They will all be in Apeklonia for the great event."

"Is that *the* great event?" he asked.

He had no doubt Lavian had planned something fiendish to take down the Governance, or the heads of it at least, but if he could take even half of the west's fighters through to aid them, it could turn the tide of the entire war between both sides.

An idea Neri had first. Maybe I won't mention that unless she does though.

"Yep." Ciena sank into her seat with a cat-like grin. "So if the west did intend to send anyone through to fight and unite the land, now would be the time."

The Jakida looked to Zel, who nodded. When she stood, bringing everyone else out of their seats, Niall remained seated.

"I will consider this," she announced. "It is still dangerous to send any fighters into an unknown land."

Niall tensed as Neri cleared her throat.

"I have to ask," she began. "On my ride to Carahdyl, I came across a mine near the cursed forest, Acerinth I think it was called?"

Niall frowned. It wasn't a place he was familiar with, which worried him. The Jakida's shoulders stiffened slightly, but she nodded for Neri to continue.

"There were shades mining there, running back and forth. Several looked... in need of a rest."

Niall tensed, even with the knowing hand she settled on his arm.

"We have shades working in Acerinth, yes," the Jakida admitted. "They're mining for *freirer* ice, among other things."

Mining, like the mine they were left slaughtered at.

He took a step forward, his face twisted in instant fury as shadow flicked over his skin.

"Why send me to that death-ground out west if you had shades further east?" he demanded.

The Jakida eyed him for several moments and he fought the urge to let his shadow flare fully. He'd seen the subtle twist of distaste on her face when he wielded it in front of her, and he needed her to admit what he now knew.

The Jakida sighed. "We had report a while back that many of the shades in the east mine were showing signs of dissent. It was almost entirely depleted, so we removed the loyal ones west."

"And slaughtered the rest?" Neri couldn't keep the horror from her voice.

"We couldn't risk them falling out of line with the borderlands at stake. Shades don't feel emotion or pain, but they can become... intransigent."

With that one word, Niall saw the true map of his past laid out across the room. After what Zel had told him about the shadow-folk, he'd slowly started considering the possibility that the Jakida was a young woman, newly titled and afraid. But no, she'd seen her firstborn was a part shade, a person who might be able to disobey her without regret, and the rest was irrelevant.

She abandoned me without even waiting to see for sure.

"I'm not surprised," he sneered. "For someone who despises shades, you definitely seem to behave like one."

The taunt found its mark, but the Jakida's expression didn't falter once despite the subtle flushing on her face.

"We need the spice the shades mine to be able to continue trading in the south. Without that, we don't have enough blade-metal to fill the armoury or-"

"Enough." The bite in his tone silenced her. "Dissent is the sign of a conscious mind, even if there are no obvious feelings you recognise. You throw around decisions and toy with lives you know nothing about. Even knowing you sickens me."

He ignored the awkward glances flying around the room and faced her down. The only thing keeping him anchored in place was the steady warmth of Neri's hand on his arm.

"That is a private matter," the Jakida said. "The taking of westlanders through the borderlands to the east is not. It's still an unknown land where we will be at a disadvantage."

He shook his head. "It's not unknown to some of us. I know the east well enough, as do Ciena and Neri, and our other friends."

Neri didn't know the east as well as the rest of them, but he guessed throwing her name in might appease the Jakida somewhat. Something about Neri seemed to give her confidence.

"I will think on it."

She turned away and Niall forced himself to bank his fury. He'd never expected her to like him, or even feel anything other than repulsion. It changed nothing. They would likely be marching with or without her blessing, but it would be in Neri's best interest and therefore his to play nice if they could. After that, they could focus on liberating the shades in the mine. Until then, he didn't want to waste time when he could be back in bed.

As he steered Neri away from the table, Livia dodged

in front of him.

"Don't you dare. She's training with me today."

He pulled a face. "Who says?"

Neri folded her arms across her chest, flicking an amused look between them.

"Don't I get a say in this?"

"No."

"No."

She shrugged. "Fair enough. Fight it out between you and let me know. I'm starving."

She moved toward the tray of fruits, Niall following with one hand locked around hers. Livia stomped after them as the hall cleared, leaving Emelyn staring at them wide-eyed, while Mik tried not to laugh and Ciena and Finn didn't bother to hide theirs.

"I've had hardly any time with her," Niall grumbled.

Livia scoffed. "And I have? When we go east, there'll be even less time."

"As if the Jakida will let you go."

"She can't stop me. Besides, if she did, all the more reason Neri spends time with me now."

Neri turned and shoved a thick wedge of fruit between Niall's lips before he could find a suitable retort.

"I'm going to take the morning to rest," she announced. "Then I'll join everyone in the fighting rings for the afternoon. Then you two aren't fighting over me like some toy, okay?"

Niall grinned. "I win."

Livia scowled. "Fine, but I get the evening too!"

Niall watched her storm away in a flurry of angry skirts, doing his best not to look too smug. Neri only rolled her eyes at him and continued eating. Mik and Emelyn left the room together, Finn and Ciena following shortly after, so

Niall took Neri's hand and brought it to her lips.

She laughed as he licked the fruit juice from her fingers, her expression shadowing when he finished.

"Are you going to get all sulky about me going to fight?" she asked.

Niall hesitated. It did sound like something he would do.

"I won't, as long as you promise the only fighting you'll be doing is with me," he tried. When she didn't reply, he sighed. "I won't stop you fighting, but I'll be fighting beside you. On that I'm not budging. Give me that at least."

Her brow lifted, surprise holding her silent for a long moment, so long he started assessing what he'd said.

"You're not going to make this difficult?"

He shook his head. "No point, it only makes things worse between us, and I don't want that. But I will keep you safe or die trying."

A devastatingly beautiful smile broke over her face, and he pushed aside the tremor of panic at the thought of what might be to come. Today was his morning, his and hers. He wasn't going to waste it worrying.

"You promised me the morning," he reminded her.

"Actually, I promised myself the morning. But you can have it if you want."

He wrapped an arm around her waist and towed her toward the doors as fast as they could walk, delighting in her laughter as they hurried through the halls.

"I do want, more than you can possibly imagine. I want- oh, look."

He stopped, halting her alongside him at the front entrance to the palace. Further down on the steps, Emelyn sat with Mik.

"We shouldn't eavesdrop," Neri whispered, her eyes

wide.

"Go past them then."

"Shhh." She pressed a finger to her lips as Mik's voice floated up to them.

"I know you want to hang out with Neri, but she and Niall have been apart for a while."

Emelyn's frustrated huff echoed halfway down the lane.

"I do know that, I'm not stupid. It's not like I don't understand what folk do when they love each other. They're lucky they've got each other to enjoy."

When Mik tried to hug her she pushed him off, hard enough for him to stagger backwards.

"Don't keep trying to placate me! I'm not a child, I don't need pandering to. I get that you're just my friend, so you don't need to always be patronising me!"

Niall tightened his arm around Neri's waist as she started forward.

"Let them work it out," he murmured.

"Stop being such a brat."

The cold anger in Mik's voice brought Emelyn to a standstill, and even Niall balked to hear it.

"I've been quietly in the background of your story for years," Mik continued. "You fell for Finn and I stepped back, even moved to my own home so I wouldn't have to see it. You wanted my friendship and I gave it to you without caveats. Now you're yelling at me for giving you what you wanted?"

He seemed to have gained several inches in height, the anger making him draw himself up tall. Niall let go of Neri's waist reluctantly, half-inclined to step in himself.

Mik turned and started up the steps, Emelyn almost stumbling in her rush to follow him.

Before Niall could guide Neri out of sight behind a

nearby pillar, Emelyn grabbed Mik's sleeve.

He shook her fingers off but she tried again until he turned to look at her.

"I don't think I knew what I wanted," Emelyn babbled. "I think I do now. You, you never said. You never told me. I didn't know then and when I did know it was too confusing, because it was different."

She stumbled over the words, unable to see any sign of thawing in his expression or his body language.

"I don't want to be just your friend anymore."

Mik didn't move, didn't change. He stood as an almost haughty statue in the middle of the corridor. Even Neri had both hands over her mouth, waiting. Niall had some vague idea he should try and lead her away, but Emelyn was sensitive in a crying kind of way and would need her friend if everything fell apart.

And I'll be the one who has to stop Mik fleeing from his problems into the wilderness.

Mik and Emelyn stared at each other, lost in their own existence. Then Emelyn lurched forward and brushed her lips across Mik's.

"*Finally,*" Neri whispered.

Niall grimaced. "They're not doing anything."

"Shh!"

Even as Emelyn stepped back, Mik's arms came around her waist and she squeaked loudly. He ignored that and pulled her close, enough for Niall to know he wouldn't need to be chasing any friends across the village any time soon.

"Let them be now," he murmured in Neri's ear, rewarded when she shivered. "We have a room here that will do for us."

Neri grinned, still slightly misty-eyed.

"Will do for what exactly?"

Niall bent low and anchored one arm around her legs, ignoring her less than dignified squeal as he hauled her over his shoulder and set off back through the halls.

It was most definitely a very good morning.

CHAPTER NINETEEN

Neri sat in bed, Niall asleep beside her. Tingling with trepidation about what might happen in the coming days, she managed to slip out of bed without waking him.

She rummaged through the things she'd unpacked into her chest at the end of her bed. Today they would leave Jakiris and begin the march back to the borderlands. She kept thinking about the future one step at a time. The thought of heading into battle once more scared her.

Neri made it down the wooden ladder and across the floor to her little kitchen by the time someone knocked quietly on the door.

She opened the door and slipped out to meet Livia.

"Folk are massing now." Livia tried to smile, fear of the future in her eyes too. "I thought you two would like to be at the front, part of the pep talk."

Neri nodded and promised they'd be on their way. She watched Livia go back down the lane and took a moment to soak in the sight of her front garden and her lane. She didn't know when she might see it again. *If* she might see it again.

The moment she entered the cottage again she saw Niall leaning against the ladder. Darkness swirled around his eyes as he saw her. The smirk that curled over his mouth sent excitement bubbling but Neri saw the wistful resignation in his dark eyes.

"Is it time?" he asked.

Neri held out her arms until he embraced her tightly.

"I won't ask you not to fight, I know you too well," Niall murmured onto the top of her head. "But please let me protect you. Don't fight or argue if I get in your way."

Neri nodded. She had a fair idea of what the battle would bring, but she agreed with him to keep him happy. Niall pulled back and looked deep into her eyes.

"When we get home, *when* not if, we'll figure out what we want to do about this place, about Jakiris. Let's just get there first."

His serious expression made her smile. She would protect him just as much as he protected her.

She waited for him to get dressed and made sure she had everything in her pack, then they stood together looking at the cottage. Neri didn't know if she would see it again, but Niall gave her time until she tugged on his hand and they left it behind.

Neri refused to turn and look back right until they reached the end of the lane. She turned and Niall threaded his arms through hers from behind, letting her stare.

At the end of the main track, just outside the village gates, Livia stood with the reins of a brown mare in one hand, which Neri had seen Niall ride many times before. In the other she held Fiora's reins.

On hearing the noise beyond the gates, noticing it only now, Neri took Fiora's reins and stared ahead.

The plains she knew like her own garden, her own home, had morphed from rolling green beds of grass churned up by the occasional stampede of travellers' horses. A wave of purple, a guttering, dancing vision like the flag of the West spread across their land. It seemed to billow, the movements created by thousands of westlanders preparing to fight.

Neri saw Ciena standing in front of them and now she understood Ciena's jubilation.

"More have been arriving while you've been cavorting," Ciena announced with a grin. "I've been making friends among them."

Turning her awestruck face to Niall she noticed he looked less impressed, his eyes fixed only on her.

As they walked the horses forward, Neri leaned her head close to Niall, near enough to impart secrets and set his pulse racing as her arm brushed against his.

"If we win the war, we'll see how long you can handle me for and keep me entertained when there aren't any wars to fight and I go crazy with nothing to do all day."

Veering away from his side to let the message sink in, she hoped the tease would kindle some kind of fire in him to get them both through.

Neri mounted Fiora and took her place riding with Ciena on her left and Niall coming to hem her in from the other side.

The hordes of warriors, villagers, carpenters and stable boys that had signed up to fight for the home and the land they loved waved to them as they passed. Ciena rambled at length, discussing potential strategies, but Neri's mind dwelt on the moments before battle commenced.

The Jakida rode at the head of the groups with Livia at her side. Neri urged Fiora forward. She saw Emelyn riding Zel with Mik on horseback right beside her. Finn rode nearby and Ciena made a beeline for him.

Their progress began to move, a curving snake of purple winding across the plains and around the settlements.

"We stop to rest at nightfall." The Jakida addressed their group alone. "The final night we will move through and rest before dawn. Then we make our stand."

Neri nodded along with the others, taking this as an order. Frowning against the glare of the suns, she noticed their gradual descent by how much more she could open her eyes. The glare dissipated and Neri looked at Niall once more. Cloaked in shadow as he sank deeper into his thought, she reached her hand out on instinct.

"Stop here, pass it back!"

Ciena's yell made Neri wince, causing Fiora to whinny and dance about beneath her. She struggled to gain control and laughed at her hopeless attempts. She only managed a squeal when an arm came around her hips and hauled her clean off the horse's back.

Clinging to Niall with her hands clamped to his shoulders, Neri blushed as he loosened his hold. She slithered down to the ground, landing on her feet with her palms pressed against his ribs.

Niall looked at her for a moment, checking that she stood firm, and then kissed her hard. Neri swayed on her feet, gasping for breath as he moved away again. It appeared her previous taunt as they left might have worked.

Folk were moving around to set up camp. Fires were built and stakes were hammered into the ground to tie horses to.

Neri eyed the Jakida in low conversation with Livia, and her mind travelled south to a supposedly deserted mine. She hadn't found time to ask about the shades she'd seen, but as Livia stomped off muttering under her breath, Neri saw her chance.

Niall appeared at her side without a word as she approached the Jakida, but she didn't divert.

Perhaps he of all folk should be hearing this.

"We will make good progress," the Jakida said by way

of greeting.

Unable to think of a suitable beginning, Neri nodded and launched in.

"I wanted to ask your opinion. Just before we left the borderlands, Amis was talking to someone about having Viljo under his control. I'm wondering who he could have been talking to. Is there another faction maybe that we need to consider?"

The Jakida sighed, loudly and without restraint. In that moment, illuminated by the flicker of the fire, she looked weary and aged.

"There are so many more ancient forces that ebb and sway across the land. There are tales of Kiren in the mountains that are entirely lawless, barbaric. Then word has it the south is ungoverned and awash with chaotic land-magic. We cannot fight all those forces. We can barely find enough folk to fight this one. If he was speaking with someone else that we need to worry about, then we need to wait for that to be revealed.

"Focus on the manageable ones then," Neri said.

"One enemy at a time."

So now is not the time to have the shade mine debate again then.

She eyed the short stretch of grass to the next fire, where Niall was thankfully sitting next to Ciena and Emelyn.

"I don't expect him to forgive me," the Jakida added softly. "I made a grave error and have lived with it every day since."

"You should tell him that. Him being shadow-folk doesn't make him a bad person, and there's no guarantee shades are either."

"He wouldn't understand."

"No, but I'm beginning to worry that you don't either."

Neri hesitated when that sharp gaze swung her way. "Shades are living beings, emotion or not. They aren't like rocks or hammers or things you can use and discard. When was the last time you actually spent time with one, or even knew one?"

"Niall isn't entirely shade, and he never has been. You can't use him as a shining example of humanity."

Neri held in the flare of *ai-tan* with great effort as it reared up, white-hot and raging.

"Maybe not, but at least he wouldn't slaughter beings for the sake of coin and glory without even taking time to make sure who and what they are first."

She walked away with the fraught silence echoing loudly behind her. Only when she could be sure of making it to the fire with the others in quick enough time did she look back.

"This will be on your conscience for a long time," she tried to say it softly, sadly, so it didn't sound like the threat it was. "I don't want any strain, especially not for Niall, but if we have to fight you on it, we will."

She hurried across to join the others and sat right next to Niall. He'd shifted his anger quickly enough around the others, but he sat in silence with his hands on the grass behind him, his eyes turned to the last light of the day on the horizon.

As Ciena passed around a small bag full of food, Neri pulled out a blanket and settled it next to Niall. She sorted their food in a small wooden bowl, splitting the bread into two halves and spreading the rest of the greenery and the berries.

"Food."

She held the bowl out to him. When he didn't take it, she gave him a look and ate her half with one hand while holding the bowl out with the other.

"It's not poisoned."

His smile, small but still a relief after his sombre mood, gave her the incentive to scoot a little closer as Emelyn shuffled up next to them.

"Let you go for a moment, has he?" Neri nodded in Mik's direction.

Emelyn blushed and stuck her tongue out. She seemed to be fidgeting due to some internal turmoil. Neri didn't press her, waiting for it to splurge out.

"I'm worried about coming across Amis." Emelyn pulled a face despite her distress. "I told you he can get into your head and folk say he now has full empathy skills."

Neri had hoped Emelyn wouldn't find out. She had a plan forming her mind that might involve Emelyn at some point, but hopefully she wouldn't ever have to bring it to light.

Sighing, she took Emelyn's hands.

"If he does, and he gets in your head, you'll be safer than most. You can take that and twist it. I know you're afraid to use your gift but on him, whatever happens, you can use it to turn his mind against him."

Neri felt Niall stiffening beside her but she ignored him.

"I'm not saying you'll ever have to face him. Steer clear, fight if you have to, but you don't have to come in with us. Mik will keep you safe."

A look of scorn passed over Emelyn's face despite Neri's comforting words.

"I go where you all go." Emelyn's voice grew stronger. "We fight this evil together. Jakiris is your home but I hope one day it'll be mine too. One day our children will play together in the streets. They'll laugh and pretend to fight in the wars as though they're just legend. That will be because we fought for them, for what they might one day become."

Neri knew Emelyn's gift worked, perhaps without her even realising it. She squeezed Emelyn's fingers in her own and nodded.

"We have things to protect now." Neri whispered.

Emelyn nodded and clambered to her feet. Neri sighed and flinched in surprise when Niall took her hand. Smiling apologetically at him, she stared at his eyes gazing into her own.

Memories of their first ever kiss echoed, of trekking through the onslaught of an eastern summer. Back then Neri had no clue if Niall could even be trusted, despite being already half in love with him anyway. Unable to stop the naughty grin at the thought of all that had followed since then, Neri pulled Niall by his hand so that his head bent lower.

The moment her lips passed over his, one soft brush of skin on skin, the overwhelming hit of spice and man whirled through her senses. She clutched at his arms, drowning in the consuming urge to get closer.

Niall's shock at her brazen contact, stilling him for several moments, broke as his hands gripped her thighs. He pulled her legs over his own so that she sat nestled against him. Groaning when Niall pulled away, Neri bit her lip and glared at him.

The drain of darkness from his face, the dopey brown of his relaxed eyes showing nothing but happiness, calmed her. When his arms clenched tight around her as though she might disappear, it made her breathless with wishful thinking. There would be nowhere along the journey for them to be alone.

Niall flopped sideways and his arms dragged her to lie against him. Curling her body into his, she hummed out a satisfied breath and let the world slip away.

When Niall moved in slumber, pulling her even closer to him, Neri didn't wake. When one horse kicked out at another and a hoof fight broke out that six burly men had to subdue, she slept on. Only when Niall's grip lessened did Neri shake off the sleep-dust and open her eyes.

The suns were about to rise, dull hints of light on a bruised horizon. Neri's gaze strayed to Niall. He held her close to him with anchored arms, his closed eyes still angled down toward her.

Yearning to be at a place where she could pretend to pull away and wake him up in a mood, Neri sat up and shook his shoulder. Bleary eyes became wide and bright, as though he'd forgotten the previous days and couldn't believe she sat so close.

"I still wake up thinking you're going to be gone." Niall grumbled.

His sleep-dredged candour sounded accusing but Neri let it go. She smiled down as he tried to give himself a mental shake, honing in on their memories as her most powerful tool.

"I know you don't like to wake and find me not there, or I would have been up and about by now. But I think everyone is ready to go."

Niall's pale cheeks tinged with colour, bashfulness coming out above any other emotion. He took hold of her fingers with his left hand, playing with them, in no rush to get going. Neri looked over to Ciena, issuing directives. She grinned at Niall and stood, holding out her hands to help haul him to his feet.

"Come on sleeping beauty. Ciena will have your head

if we don't get going."

Neri mounted, already aching from the constant riding. She tried to bear her pains with no complaints. She chose instead to start a lively debate with Ciena on the merits of different types of weaponry.

"I don't think you're being rational!" Neri couldn't stop herself smiling. "The bow has saved folk's lives before *and* from a distance, whereas a sword is more for defence."

She laughed and knew her words were causing the frustration in Ciena's eyes. They stopped arguing when Neri noticed Niall getting off his horse. She pushed Fiora round and trotted back along the line to him. He stood next to his horse, looking at its hooves.

"She's cast a shoe and hurt her leg." He looked dismayed. "I'll have to walk her in hand."

Neri swung down, holding the end of Fiora's reins. She looked at a swelling on his horse's leg and sighed.

"She won't be able to walk on that." Neri looked around in despair. "We'll have to find the nearest settlement and drop her off. I can walk with her if you like."

Niall grumbled something to someone behind her. She didn't even have a chance to walk. A man stepped in front of her, dressed in uniform and vaguely familiar. He took Niall's reins and led the horse away.

Neri frowned, wondering how Niall would continue the journey. He clasped her round the waist and threw her up into Fiora's saddle.

About to grumble and argue her disagreement by dismounting again on the other side, she caught the sight of Niall's expression and her resolve failed. His eyes whirled with darkness and his mouth pressed with unhappiness almost unveiled. He'd been attached to the horse, so Neri didn't argue.

Fiora snorted and tried to bolt when Niall swung onto her back behind Neri. Not in the mood for games, Niall took her reins and pulled. Fiora's head shot up and Neri elbowed him back.

"Don't manhandle her." She warned him.

She stroked her hand down Fiora's neck and whispered soothing words. Heeding her warning, Niall took a looser rein with one hand and his other hand gripped Neri's hip, pulling her further back against him.

"I won't my darling, because she's your horse. However, when we get there I've half a mind to get off and send her clattering back to Jakiris with you on board."

She guessed that Niall hoped to wind her up to get her fired up for fighting. Gritting her teeth, she allowed herself to relax back against him.

"You're a shining example to us all I'm sure. I know you're trying to wind me up. Just remember, you've known what I'm like all along. I'm not going to sit at home and weave when I should be standing up and fighting."

Neri held her breath, wondering whether her taunt would enrage Niall or pacify him. He sighed and his shoulders sagged weighty against hers.

"I wouldn't expect you to sit home and weave." Now he sounded almost amused. "I can't imagine you'd have the patience for needlework."

His arm edged around her waist as they rode, just a little more each time until he had her anchored against him. With the hazy heat of the two suns glaring down upon them, the horses laboured to walk on. Neri marvelled at how the grass and the foliage they passed remained deep, nourished green.

Her eyes closed and her head lagged back onto Niall's shoulder before she realised how tired she felt. Only when

Niall chuckled and kissed her cheek, thinking her asleep, did she open her eyes. She smiled and stretched her arms over her head.

"When we get back home, after this is all over, I'm going to take a holiday." She wanted to tease him. "I'm going to sleep for a month and not open the door to anyone."

Niall's arm tightened a fraction and Neri grinned into the heat.

"You'd better behave yourself and let me fight for you then." Niall was back to goading her. "I haven't taken you to the lake lands yet. They're beautiful, tiny islands floating in endless clear water. The suns shine and the skies dance at night, reflected in the lake. If we get a chance to unite properly, we could call it our union-fayre. We have those in Jakiris where the united pair go off and spend some time alone before returning to the less enjoyable whims of life."

Flushing and unable to hide a grin at the banter, glad Niall couldn't see her face, Neri forced her lips to pout. She decided to pass the time by playing with him a little. Turning around so she could see him, Neri bit her lip.

"You're assuming that you're the better fighter out of the two of us."

Niall's arm tightened again, a warning squeeze. Neri yelped as his teeth grazed her earlobe and his voice rolled gravel against her ears.

"If someone comes near you then I'm the best damn fighter anyone's ever seen."

Neri grinned at his sudden display of dominance. Niall's hand rubbed her hip and his nose nudged the spot he'd bitten to soothe any hurt.

Before she could find some way to toy with him further,

because the boredom was making them both irritable, a round of shouting echoed further back.

A shadow passed over them and Neri lifted her head with her heart plummeting.

"DRAGON!"

Similar shouts echoed through the air but Neri urged Fiora faster so that they could get to the Jakida and Livia further ahead. As they broke the front line of the procession, Neri hauled Fiora to a stamping halt.

The rhythmic thudding shook the land beneath them as the dragon landed to block their way. Shining earthy green scales covered its entire body, from snout right down to the lethal grey claws gouging into the earth. Neri glanced over her shoulder but there was nowhere to hide, not even a wide enough swathe of forest nearby to take cover in if the dragon decided to start picking them off.

Ciena's horse and Finn's halted next to them, with Mik and Emelyn on the other side.

"That's... a dragon," Mik announced, his eyes wide with awe.

Neri nodded. "Yep. Definitely a dragon."

"Is this your doing, Em?" Finn asked.

"No and will everyone please stop assuming that!"

"We need to move slowly," Niall said. "Get everyone moving backwards and see if we can't draw it along until we reach the last crop of rock. It might not be able to get to us in there."

Neri didn't even flinch as he grabbed the reins from her hands and hauled Fiora into a snorting reverse as Finn held up a steady hand.

"Wait. It's not going to hurt us, not for the moment."

"Oh, suddenly communing with animals, are you?" Niall snapped. "No, we back away slowly and hope we don't have to fight."

Neri bit her lip as the dragon flicked its enormous tail and took out three shrubs and a young tree with one swipe.

"I know truth, and I hear it too," Finn replied calmly. "I can hear emotions like voices, whispering and screaming. The dragon doesn't want to harm us, but it will if provoked."

"Then what does it want?" Livia asked.

Sunslight glinted off the scales as the dragon lowered its long, ridged snout and huffed the tiniest flicker of smoke. The birdsong in Neri's mind fluttered awake and trilled an insistent note.

"We've no way of knowing," Niall insisted.

Finn gave him an irritated look. "Dragons are balance. They wouldn't approach an entire horde on horses unless there was a reason."

Mik nodded. "He's right. Several fables talk of life's unicorns and deaths dragons meeting at the end and beginning of all things, but they all say that they're creatures of balance. Maybe it owes a debt?"

"Does anyone recognise this one?" Finn asked.

Neri flinched as the birdsong trilled again and the dragon angled its head in her direction.

As if it can hear it.

She thought of Sav and the way he'd tilted his head when he spoke to the bird and whatever unnatural affinity she carried in her mind answered.

Niall's hand went to his blade as the dragon snorted again, but she dropped her fingers over his. A hint of silver glimmered on the left side of the dragon's head, nothing more than a remnant, but she understood then.

"It's one of the ones we freed, look."

She lifted a hand to point and waited a second for Niall's

attention to waver. He made to grab her as she swung her leg over Fiora's neck but he missed, and she took a couple of hesitant steps forward with the enormous dark eyes boring into her.

"We can't be sure that it won't eat us and the horses, debt or no debt," the Jakida hissed.

Neri ignored her and glanced at Zel instead, who nodded with a soft smile.

"Touch him. He won't hurt you if you're respectful."

Neri stopped just out of reaching distance and lifted a hand. The dragon lowered his enormous snout, the broad length of his nostrils larger than Fiora was long.

She could see Niall mirrored in the dragon's eye, but he stood a respectful enough distance with one hand on his blade.

The dragon edged the tiniest tip of his jaw to her hand and she inched across the remaining gap to make contact. The trilling in her head became a caw and she flinched back at the unyielding aura of icy fire that leapt up to meet her fingertips.

Sav had told her dragons would know about darkfire, but she could sense it thrumming through the dragon like sensing someone else's *ai-tan* through their skin.

What? She demanded as the cawing in her head grew more insistent. *What is this telling me?*

Zel had told her to touch the dragon, who stayed within reaching distance, as if he wanted her to understand. Neri let a kernel of her fire warm her hand and reached out again.

"I'm not going to hurt you," she murmured.

She winced as her heat met the chill of the dragon's darkfire, but the trilling in her mind calmed as the essence of her *ai-tan* met the core of the dragons.

It doesn't hurt. She frowned. *It's not bad, just different. My fire and darkfire, like water and wine.*

She lowered her hand and took a step back. The dragon turned his head to a bare patch of grass nearby and snorted out a steaming plume of burning smoke. A strange mix of thick black liquid with a pearlescent sheen hit the ground with a hiss, bubbles leaping to the surface as it charred the grass and continued to burn.

Neri lifted her hand on instinct and her fire flared, the flash of it covering the short distance to land on the puddle of darkfire still sizzling. She could feel that unyielding chill biting into her heat, but also cooling. Calming. She recalled her *ai-tan* and watched with her heart sinking as the darkfire dissipated along with her flames, until there was nothing but a patch of burnt earth.

"I get it," she mumbled. "Thank you."

She focused the warmth in her hand and reached above her head. Unable to reach the side of the dragon's head beneath his ear where the remnant of *freirer* ice glinted, she let her fire flare in an arc.

The dragon huffed as the last of the *freirer* ice attached to his scales grew hot and dribbled free. The moment it splatted on the ground, he wheeled around. Several shouts of alarm went up and Neri ducked an outstretched wing even though it passed far too high over her head to do much more than gust a breeze through her hair.

The dragon arced overhead and in moments he was a mere dot against the bright sky on his way toward the tips of the Kahlen mountains.

She watched him go, unflinching as solid hands landed on her hips.

"That was dangerous," Niall said, his tone full of unspent bite. "Do not do that again."

She ignored that as Zel caught her eye, a grave knowing hidden behind her smile.

I know what I have to do then.

She didn't say a word as Niall guided her back to Fiora and helped her up, and she didn't say a word when he took control of the reins.

Let him think it's the shock of seeing a dragon.

Nobody said a word as the procession moved on, and soon enough it was time to stop and make camp for the evening.

"You're not going to tell me off?" she asked as Niall sat by their fire and pulled her onto his lap.

"No point. It's a strange thing, but I'm learning to trust your judgement."

"*Ej-va,*" she muttered.

He laughed. "Exactly."

She let that calm her thundering mind and curled in his arms to listen as Ciena challenged the Jakida's plan for attack. When Niall leaned forward, his shade-self throwing shadow out to loom over the fire, Neri squeaked and thudded onto the ground.

"We move tomorrow." He took command like it was the most natural thing in the land. "We'll make it to the outskirts of the Apeklonian walls and those nominated will go through the tunnel. Those of us known to them will need to be seen leading the front of the charge but then we'll slip away, through the tunnel and try to arrive unseen. I can believe his *lordship* will be in the fray, but I doubt the Governance members or his adviser will be."

When Niall settled back down he instantly claimed Neri once more, his hands on her hips guiding her to him. Anchored to him, Neri turned her attention on her companions.

Emelyn's wide green eyes sparkled as she looked at Mik, who sat with one arm slung over her shoulders. He smiled at her with such uncomplicated devotion that Neri couldn't help but smile as well. Niall smirked up at her, mocking her sentimentality, but in such good company she couldn't be grumpy with him.

Sticking her tongue out in childish retaliation instead, Neri's *ai-tan* bubbled when Niall's eyes clouded with suggestion. He leaned close, snapping his teeth in mimicry of biting.

Neri yawned and raised her arms above her head, fidgeting a little on Niall's legs just to tease him. She bid everyone goodnight, standing and tilting sideways, her little finger snagging around Niall's. The smallest little tug of intention and Niall stood to follow.

She curled up on her blanket, happy when he curled his body around hers and covered them both with his own blanket.

"I might well make you behave yourself." Neri teased him.

"Don't worry, I know we can't have any intimacy. It's enough that I have you near me."

Niall kissed the top of her head and she got trapped in the scent of him, her eyes closing with sheer relief and contentment. Niall's arm curved over her stomach and she rolled into her side. Her cheek fitted into the special space on his shoulder where she could sleep in comfort as his embrace secured her.

As Neri rested she listened for the change in Niall's breathing. The sudden slow deepness indicated his slumber. Smirking against the cloth of his t-shirt, Neri closed her eyes. When then suns streamed upon them she opened them again to find emotive brown orbs floating in shadow above her. Blinking away the dregs of sleep, Neri recognised Niall and smiled to see him balanced up on one elbow.

"Did you sleep? You look tired."

Niall grinned, the upward curve of his mouth teasing her. His eyes glinted against the early rays of the suns and made her realise she might not have many more opportunities. Before she could raise herself up and antagonise his sensibilities, his fingers landed on her collarbone, a light touch but firm enough to keep her in place.

"You looked so peaceful asleep I reckoned I could keep you out of mischief as long as possible to save my nerves. But unfortunately, the troops will be up any moment now."

The crooning roll of Niall's low tone tickled at Neri's humour and she smiled up at him, feigning innocence. He rolled his eyes and lowered his head. Thinking he would kiss her, Neri closed her eyes. Moments later she opened them to find him nose to nose with her, the same playful smirk on his lips.

"Anyone would think you wanted me to seduce you. You've got that devilish smile again and I'm two shreds away from losing my restraint."

Giggling, unable to take his urgent desires seriously and knowing she wouldn't care if he did lose them, Neri held her palms up to the sky and smiled. When Niall's lips descended, they glanced off of her cheek and slid down to the sensitive skin on her neck, his attentions wiping the giggles away.

Someone cleared their throat above and Neri blinked up to see Livia laughing down at them.

"Not that I blame you, but everyone's watching."

CHAPTER TWENTY

The line of the borderlands approached quicker than Niall expected. He had Neri in front of him, her soft weight calming against his chest, but the closer they got to the border, the closer she was to danger. He could make out a long line of guards at the gates as well, a far cry from the reception they received on the east side.

Almost as if we're the enemy, not the east.

After the random dragon visit, which thankfully Neri hadn't taken as some kind of omen that she needed to follow it, or try to convince it to come with them, he wouldn't be assuming anything.

He pushed the thought aside as Emelyn rode up beside them on a horse as flighty-footed as she was.

"What if it's a trap?" she asked. "What if your brother is still there, and has archers waiting?"

Neri shrugged. "Then we fight. Standard formation, healers at the back, spare reserve of horses if all goes wrong."

Emelyn pulled a face but didn't reply.

They rode up front behind the Jakida, Zel in her horse form for the span of the day, and if Niall squinted, he could see the gates opening.

"Someone's approaching," the Jakida called back.

Neri nudged her horse's sides to take them forward.

"They won't take a horde of fighters on their doorstep lightly," she said. "Let me go ahead and talk to them."

"Let us go ahead and talk to them," Niall grumbled.

The Jakida and Neri both ignored him, a look passing between them.

"Fine. Speak for us, but no agreements are to be made."

Neri nodded and Niall anchored his arms tighter around her waist as she urged the horse into a trot.

"That's Harelda, isn't it?" she asked.

Niall squinted. "Yeah, looks like, with less guards than she should have beside her."

"Viljo's probably taken them all with him," she muttered.

Niall reigned in the flare of delight to hear her talk so dismissively of his brother, letting it settle his nerves as they stopped a respectful distance away from their own group to wait for Harelda to join them.

"What brings you and a whole horde to our gates?" Harelda called out.

Neri raised a hand and swung her leg over the horse's neck. Niall lunged to catch her but her weight dropped downward before he could, and she walked forward alone.

He grimaced, riding right behind her until the horse was all but trampling on her heels. With one hand on the reins, he kept the other on the hilt of his blade ready.

She will be the absolute end of my sanity.

"We need to pass through, all of us," Neri announced. "Without trouble ideally."

Harelda's brow lifted, a hint of amusement flitting across her face.

"What for?"

Neri shrugged. "What else would a group like this be for? Am I right in thinking you don't actually agree with how Viljo or his new friends treat your folk, or anyone else's for that matter?"

236

Harelda sat silent for a long moment, before dismounting her horse and handing her reins to a guard.

"You are, but there's little I can do when anyone who speaks up is cast out."

Niall frowned. "Cast out?"

Even as Harelda turned her gaze to him, he understood.

"Anyone who speaks up, fights, or even thinks of dissent is cast out through the east gate, left with nothing. I hear most are picked up by grey-cloak patrols and taken nobody knows where. Families are frightened, and we can only release so many through to the west without suspicion."

Niall's mind flickered back to the tunnel, and to Cori insisting he needed to stay behind. He'd mentioned too that Amis could control minds, read thoughts much like Finn could. If he had mastery of darkfire too, they were truly facing a dangerous enemy.

"It is clear that this cannot be allowed to go on any longer." The Jakida's voice rang out clear behind them. "We should look at fortifying our control here while we can."

Niall heard Neri's tiny groan as Harelda's posture stiffened. She took a step back, using a guard's foot to remount her horse, an instinctive defence move.

Neri grimaced an apology in Harelda's direction, before turning to face the Jakida with a level of calm Niall couldn't fathom.

"We don't own control of the borderlands," she said. "We're asking for passage through, not invading."

The Jakida's eyes flared with fury but Niall lowered his hand and forced Neri to remount in front of him in an undignified scrambling of limbs that spooked her horse.

Better undignified than ready to be trampled.

"It would be best if Niall stays behind and takes control of the borderlands. Anyone who wishes to pass through can do so, but we still don't know the state of the east or if this is even a prudent plan."

Neri's body burned hot but she held her fire in check. Niall had no such calm and let his shadow flick over his skin.

"No. I won't be taking control of anything, not today," he announced. "If anyone should lead the borderlands, Harelda should."

Neri's hand squeezed over his as she settled back against him, a reward only he understood. She charged into these situations, but she was yielding to him instead of acting alone, honouring his control alongside hers.

Harelda chuckled. "I admit that surprises me. Not many noble families would pass up a chance to rule."

"We're not normal," Neri announced cheerfully.

"No, you don't seem to be. I would be honoured to lead my folk like my kin once did."

"We would follow you," one guard announced, his tone ringing with clarity.

He pressed a fist to his shoulder, arm across his chest, a movement the remaining guards followed without hesitation.

Harelda smiled. "Whatever my faults, there are those that will always be loyal to fairness, and to my family's legacy. Amis and Viljo and their kind would pale in comparison to how much I love my folk."

Neri nodded. "It's settled then. No more talk of taking control, not here at least. Can we count on you to let us through?"

"I can't offer you shelter, but I can open the gates and demand that nobody stops or harms you."

"That's more than enough," Niall agreed. "We've got a long way to go yet, and we have some serious dangers to face. Do you know anything about darkfire by chance?"

Harelda grimaced. "That I tell you for nothing. Amis has always been part of the borderlands, even since I was a child. He served the old lord even after the old lord took the title from my older brother. Rumour has it there's some dark sorcery at work though, as it wasn't a gift from the land, not one he always had."

Neri leaned forward. "Do you know how he came by it then?"

"No, but he used to be visited often by a wandering man, always hooded and cloaked. When that man started coming, Amis started wielding darkfire."

Neri tensed. "Amis maybe."

"I can't be sure. I've tried to study it, to find ways of dousing it when he uses it on my folk for fun, but it's near indestructible. The only thing I've ever seen calm it is actual fire, and that could have merely been him panicking about being burned by it."

Niall squelched a groan in his throat as Neri's hand warmed over his.

"This is all information we should be taking away to assess," the Jakida insisted, her tone sharp.

Niall wheeled the horse around to face her, Neri huffing as the horse snorted in alarm.

"You wanted to make me the next ruler of this place, right?" he demanded.

The Jakida's nostrils flared, guarded hope lighting in her eyes.

"I believe you at least would hold a firmer line to keep our boundaries safe, yes."

It was as close to a compliment as he would get from

her, a concession that he might succeed where her favourite child had failed.

"Fine, you've bestowed the charge on me, I'm lord of the borderlands, yay me."

Neri laughed as he wheeled the horse around again.

"I'm officially abdicating my lordship to you," he told Harelda. "Enjoy."

He waited for something, some shouting, a threat, anything. But for once it appeared the Jakida was rendered speechless.

"I don't think Niall would want to live here anyway," Livia piped up from behind them. "No offense."

Harelda shrugged. "None taken, Lady. We don't want to risk delaying your journey, so follow me and I will lead you through the borderlands."

She turned her company around and set off back toward the open gateway, and Niall urged Neri on after her. Livia's voice echoed back through their group, passing the message on to each section to follow on, but Niall focused on Neri as she turned her head to grin up at him.

"That was smooth," she teased.

He grinned. "No sense being showy about it. Harelda seems fair enough to not be an immediate to us. Once we start through the east though, we'll be in danger."

"We'll be fine as long as we stick together," she insisted.

He kissed her cheek as they passed through the gateway and into a sea of astonished faces watching them pass.

Harelda reined back enough to ride alongside them.

"We won't announce our agreement now," she said. "There's been enough change already. But if you do end up slaying the enemy, let me know. I quite fancy myself a titling ceremony."

Neri grinned. "I couldn't imagine anything worse, but if we're invited, I promise to wear a suitable dress this time."

"Wear whatever you like, I don't care. Once you pass through the east gates, I'll be closing them permanently. Unless you return victorious, or folk need sanctuary, they won't be opening again."

Neri laughed as the east gate came into sight, but Niall's gut was furling into knots at the sight of it. He shook away the more sombre thoughts, forcing himself to focus on the others.

"I'll hold you to your promise, Neri," Harelda insisted. "When the war is over, I will visit you in Jakiris."

Niall smiled. "Trust me, after this you are welcome anytime."

CHAPTER TWENTY ONE

The skyline of Apeklonia drew ever closer and the mood of the group soured. Niall stuck to Neri wherever she went, to the point she had to insist he leave her alone for a few moments to do her personal business, but he demanded to stand guard instead.

They made a grudging truce of a short distance, but the squabbling kept them busy. A few grey-cloaks chanced attacks on the fringes of their group, but they were sent fleeing by sheer numbers. News would reach Apeklonia fast enough that they were approaching, but Ciena received increasing birds with short missives scribed on scraps of paper to say that the performers were in place in the citadel, ready to attack.

Neri eyed the long trail of fighters tailing behind them, framed against the late morning horizon, then the enormous settlement ahead. Set against the towering Kahlen mountains, the winding streets were tiny lines weaving from a dark stone palace set against the rockface to a vast expanse of the great water beyond. High walls surrounded the settlement, and she guessed there would be guards everywhere ready to defend it.

"It looks impenetrable," she muttered.

Niall sighed. "It's supposed to be, but if anyone can get a fighting force through, the Jakida will manage it."

It almost sounded like grudging praise, but Neri didn't call him on it.

"Not our problem," Ciena grumbled. "The route you've planned for us is much less exciting."

"Tell me the plan again," Emelyn begged her.

"I have told you the plan again. And again. And again. Fine." She relented easily. "We have half our group marching on the gates, while a smaller group of us will be meeting Lavian to take tunnels through the mountains."

"And we're definitely sure the messages you've had are legitimate?" Niall asked.

Ciena nodded. "Definitely his hand."

"Unless he's been captured and forced to lure us into a trap," Finn suggested.

"Not helping."

They rode on in silence, but no matter how thorough their planning, Neri doubted they'd get everyone out alive.

Ciena halted her horse beneath the ragged line of the cliffs and Neri reined Fiora alongside her. She wished Emelyn hadn't insisted on coming, or that Mik hadn't encouraged it. Emelyn didn't know how to fight and yet she insisted on riding up front with the rest of them.

Warmth crept around Neri's fingers and she looked down at Niall's hand, following the tanned line of his arm until she turned and looked up into his face. Hints of shadow swirled around his shoulders and his frown owed more to the situation than to the waning daylight.

Livia and the Jakida trotted past them and Niall's grip tightened. He pulled on her hand until she had to pay attention to him. Fiora had quickly become used to carrying both of them but Neri's neck ached from constantly turning around.

"The empath will try and get in all our heads," Niall whispered. "I love you more than living, but if he tries to tell you otherwise you can't believe him."

Neri stared into his dark eyes for a moment before the smile crept over her lips. Despite all the recent upheaval and their reunion, her cheeks flushed pink.

"I know that. I think the warning goes both ways."

Niall's mouth twisted in annoyance and he dropped her hand. Neri sighed and made no attempt to recapture it.

"I don't want to argue," he growled. "If I had my way you'd be back in Jakiris, but I've given up holding you back."

His shadowed expression looked decidedly sulky. Neri reached back on instinct and her hand landed on his arm. She twisted and moved her fingers to the small lump beneath the fabric covering his chest.

"Everything I've said before is still true. It's not about holding me back. I'm just not going to stay behind while everyone else is defending their homes, the folk they love."

Neri forced Niall to look at her by grabbing his upper arm and digging her nails in. She knew inciting him to anger would enable him to fight harder when the inevitable battle found them, but the thought of him fighting at all zapped the energy out of her.

As the lines halted behind them, Neri urged Fiora to join the Jakida and Livia.

"You're sure about this?" the Jakida asked.

Neri nodded. "I trust those I'm listening to. We take the tunnels and draw Amis and Viljo out. You keep their forces busy at the gates. We can't risk fighting them as one force, and we don't want to risk Amis retreating either if he thinks he can avoid capture."

The Jakida eyed the towering walls of stone ahead with a grimace.

"It's a tall ask to put before a ragged line of fighters weary from travelling," she muttered.

Livia rolled her eyes. "Inspiring. Perhaps let me make the speech this time if you're going to be so gloomy."

Neri snorted over a bubble of laughter and tried to choke it back down. There would be no rousing speech for her. She glanced at Mik and Emelyn who shared the space on Zel's back nearby. Beneath a brittle smile, Emelyn's fear radiated but Neri had to trust Mik would keep her safe.

"What's the signal then?" the Jakida asked.

Ciena pointed skyward. "The moment we make our move inside, you'll see blue birds flying and a flash of spark stones over the walls. That's your sign to attack."

The Jakida glanced at Neri, and she had to nod. She trusted Ciena, but she had to hope that those Ciena was putting faith in could also be trusted.

When Niall took her hand again, she interlaced her fingers with his and held on tight as a faint cheer echoed across the otherwise calm air.

"That's our cue," Ciena announced. "The tunnel Lavian told me about is just up ahead so let's get this done. Wishing you all good fight and fortune."

She didn't bother waiting for anyone and set her horse at a smart trot away along the edge of the cliff. Neri dropped Niall's hand and grasped her reins to keep Fiora steady as she broke into a canter with Finn, Mik and Emelyn following close behind. Echoes of cheering sounded behind them, growing fainter with each pace as they set a fast pace.

Ciena pulled to a halt a short while later and swung down from her horse's back.

"Found it."

Reluctant to leave Fiora in a position where she might wander off, Neri dismounted and kept hold of the reins as they approached a large cut in the cliff. A convenient boulder hid it from view and Neri let the reins drop. Fiora nudged her shoulder and dropped her head to graze on bits of shrub growing between the rocks.

Ciena had already disappeared into the hole with Mik and Emelyn following, and Zel gave Neri a soft smile.

"I will mind the horses. The battleground is no longer my arena."

Neri nodded and stepped forward to follow, but Niall held her back. The shine in his eyes displaced her thoughts for a moment until she realised how close he stood, his hands possessive on her hips. A kiss dropped onto her upturned lips and she inched her feet to get closer as her hands skimmed over his shoulders. With no time left to them, the brief kiss was all they could have.

Niall held her close after, her cheek against his shoulder and his chin resting in her hair. Neri half wished a shimmer would throw them into a completely different realm entirely, until Niall pulled back and smiled down at her.

"We'll have time for that," he teased. "But not if you go around doe-eyed when you're meant to be saving us all."

His sudden playfulness sent a rush of heat through Neri's skin and the familiar prickle of fire started to grow. It was a promise and layer of protection, something to keep them both strong when the fight began.

Refraining from leaping on him and sending them both flying out into the wilderness to hide, Neri took his hand and faced the mountain.

"Come on, come on," Ciena muttered. "There's plenty of time for that once the fight is done."

Finn sighed in mock despair, but he held up a small lantern and Neri clicked her fingers to summon flame to light it.

"Useful when you want to be, sweet thing," he said,

grinning at Niall's instant glower.

Neri ignored him and faced the tunnel ahead, the firelight flickering off the bare rock.

"Is it far?" she asked.

Ciena shook her head. "Shouldn't be. No talking and keep your steps light."

She took the lead and they fell into a single file trail behind. Neri stubbed the occasional stone or embedded jut of rock and the noise bounced with a dull echo ahead, but soon the sound of each step was drowned out by the ominous rumble from above.

She didn't want to think of what might be causing it, because Lavian's group were meant to be performing and the Jakida was waiting for the signal to attack, but time had them prisoner and she could think of nothing else.

Ciena stopped and they all followed her gaze as she looked up. Finn held the lantern higher to illuminate a small wooden hatch, and Niall cupped his hands to give Ciena a boost toward it.

Ciena grunted, then a stream of murky light framed her body as the hatch lifted. She scrambled around out of sight, then her face loomed back through the gap as she held her hands out.

The echo of noise reached them as Neri pressed her hand on Niall's shoulder and he pushed her up to Ciena's waiting hands. She gritted her teeth as Ciena hauled her up, moving aside with her hand on her blade to wait for the others. Once Niall stood beside her, the others peering around at a storeroom full of sacks, Ciena crept toward the door.

"We turn right, then left, and we should be at the square," she whispered. "It sounds like Lavian has made his move already, so we can only hope the westlanders are ready at the gates."

Neri clung to Niall's hand as they followed Ciena outside. Emelyn and Mik were staying behind to help folk escape the citadel through the tunnel, anyone sent to them through Lavian's forces already fighting.

Neri took a deep breath and stepped into the lane, aware of Finn drawing alongside her as Ciena stormed ahead.

Doors were hanging off hinges, and signs of debris littered the ground. The fight had spilled through the citadel and left chaos behind, but no doubt Amis, and even Viljo, would be holding court in the square.

"The fight will come fast once we're in it," Finn said. "Let Ciena do what she does best. We'll clear a path, but you both need to get as close to the real enemy as you can. Distract them, play to their vanity. When the time comes, take them down."

Neri nodded. That was their role in the wider plan, to attack the real evil while the Jakida distracted their defences into battle from outside.

Even as Finn's words died away, a surge of fighters in deep red uniforms charged at them. Niall's hand slipped from Neri's hold and she raised her blade, dodging one assailant and parrying a blow from a second.

The man grinned at her as she ducked his outstretched hand, but the blade he swung toward her in retaliation had all of her attention.

"The Governance want you alive," he called out.

Neri grimaced and met his strike with a clang.

"I have no intention of disappointing them."

Her next attack scraped his shoulder and his amusement turned to venom.

"They say he wants to carve you up and see what makes you burn," he snarled.

Neri shrugged and danced out of the way of his blade, her *ai-tan* bubbling through her limbs.

"He can try."

Arms wrapped around her neck and her waist before she could twist them around again, tightening enough to strangle. The man's lip curled with glee as he lowered his blade.

Neri kindled her heat and let it spike over her skin, but her assailant clung on even as they seethed through their teeth at the pain.

She dropped her weight downward, tilting their centre of balance forward. Thanking all things she could think of that Ciena had insisted on making her wear a wrist-wrap, she palmed the thin blade from underneath it and angled it.

The scream barely registered as the arms disappeared from around her. She twisted before either of them could react, the woman behind her clutching at the puncture wound in her thigh, and the man staring in horror.

He never sensed the shadows massing behind him, or saw the billowing hand that grabbed him by the neck and slammed him into a nearby stone wall.

"You okay?" Niall asked.

Neri nodded. "Nothing I can't handle."

He grinned as a small group of men dashed toward them.

"That's my girl."

Before she could do more than raise her blade to defend, he knocked two men unconscious and sent a third running back toward the square.

Neri eyed Finn fighting three at once, his blade weaving even faster than Ciena's. She stared in horror as he narrowly missed a savage slice to his chest. She lifted her head, Niall and Ciena holding back a wider group together, forging a clear path back toward the square.

With a grunt, Neri shunted her shoulder into one of Finn's enemy, sending her flying and blocking a return below.

"You won't win," the woman spat. "Even while you tire yourself out, he's waiting for you. He'll always be waiting for you."

Neri let her fire flare out from her palm, forcing the woman back even as she had her blade ready to chop any reaching hands away.

"I'll be finishing him too, don't worry," she hissed. "All of them. You still have a chance to run."

A pained curse echoed behind her. The woman grinned, stepping back.

"I might, but he doesn't."

Neri twisted sideways, slamming her back against the nearest wall so she could turn while keeping the woman in sight.

Her skin chilled at the sight, one man dead and another trying to crawl with countless injuries.

And Finn, bleeding out on the stony ground.

Neri let her fire flare and the woman stumbled back, her laughter raging as she ran back toward the square. Niall and Ciena were out of sight but Neri dropped to her knees beside Finn.

"Don't fuss," he grunted breathlessly. "I knew it was coming. Better me than him."

Neri grimaced, fumbling for something to staunch the blood, even though she could see there was no coming back from such a gaping wound.

"Don't say that."

He rolled his eyes, a ragged gasp passing his lips.

"I do wish we were parting as friends. I never... didn't

mean you any harm."

Neri tore her cloak off and pressed it against the worst of his chest wounds, even though there were too many to across the rest of his body to cover.

"We are friends. I just thought you hated me for part of it."

He shook his head, the movement sluggish and uncoordinated.

"Stop flapping, there's no saving me."

"I have to try." She blinked away tears, furiously trying to spread her cloak wider than it could go. "We may not have always been friendly, but-"

"Never your enemy, Neri. Remember me for that." He inhaled a sharp breath. "You'll always be the prettiest girl who punched me in the face."

She snorted over a choked laugh, drowned in tears.

"Don't tell Ciena that."

He nodded, his face comforting with pain.

"Tell her... I died taking down six... fighters... something... glorious."

"I will, I promise. Finn?"

His head rolled and her heart twisted, the spark of life leaving his eyes as he fell still.

Emelyn would be distraught. Mik and Ciena too. Ma, Moonshine, all of them would suffer.

Neri lifted her head, searching for a quiet place. The clamour of fighting raged on ahead, but for the moment her lane was quiet. She heaved Finn's body against her own, scrabbling toward the nearest open door.

The small grain store was deserted, so she settled him behind some sacks and found a piece of cloth to shroud him with. Her cloak was ruined so she left him with it, then reached into his trouser pocket and pulled out two coins, closing his eyes with shaking fingers and settling the coins over his lids.

Her limbs ached and her insides felt raw, scraped clean of panic.

No more. Not today. No more death but theirs.

Unsheathing her blade, she focused on the rage simmering deep inside, uncaging the constant burn as she stalked out of the store and toward the chaos.

Someone came flying at her but she sent a flick of flame at them, lashing them back. No more death, not even theirs.

Only two more need die today.

She found Niall crouched at the edge of the square, the mouth of the lane giving him cover as Ciena whirled through the throng of fighters facing her, a grin of pure elation on her face.

"Finn?" Niall asked.

Neri stood beside him and shook her head. Niall's grimace said all it needed to. They weren't friends, but Finn would be remembered.

Niall stood and leaned his head close to hers.

"I'm going to go out on my own." He pressed his fingers to her lips as she opened them to protest. "Let me draw them out before you reveal yourself. I have some kind of sense that Viljo is standing on the steps with the empath and we'll need an element of surprise."

Neri glared at him, indignant without really knowing why. Then she nodded. Despite her adrenalin urging her to jump into the fray and send fire blasting all around the square, Niall's plan made the most sense. He was the best fighter to stand alongside Ciena until the rest of their forces turned up, although she could see Lavian fighting in a group on the far fringes of the square.

Niall drew a second blade. Before she could even grab

him and hold him close one last time, he cloaked himself in shadow and stepped into the square.

"Back again so soon. How have you managed to hide from me in my own city?"

Viljo's voice filled the square and Niall's shoulders rose ever so slightly as he turned in the direction of the palace. Neri clenched her hands into fists, one gripping the handle of her blade, and waited for a chance.

"I have my ways. I'm surprised you're not leading your army. You may be drowning in dull sensibility, but I never took you for a coward."

Neri hissed through her teeth at Niall's taunt and glanced around to check nobody had crept up on her. The lane behind and the square ahead were both far too deserted and the idea of a trap trickled into her mind. Amis would be aware of her *ai-tan,* and that it could be the only weapon they'd have against his darkfire.

Niall shook his head and glared up at whoever stood assembled on the steps.

"Don't try getting in my head either old man. We might not have exactly your numbers outside the gates, but they'll be here before you can spit."

The sound of someone spitting out of sight almost made Neri laugh out loud. She would give Niall a few more moments of his charade and then she would burn the city and its leaders to the ground.

"We have other ways of controlling errant rebelliousness. Do you know what it feels like to burn black inside I wonder?"

The oozing slickness of his tone brought the final remnants of her fire to the forefront. With a growl, she dodged out from behind the building and set a flame on the regal fabric hangings adorned with the Apeklonian crest above the steps.

Despite the blood thundering through her veins, Neri saw no sign of trepidation on the faces of those assembled. Three guards in Apeklonian battle dress stood behind Amis and Viljo, who looked down upon her despite the fire burning above their heads. Viljo showed no sign of emotion and Amis looked amused.

"It's lovely to see you again my dear." Amis' voice curdled the very blood in her veins. "We've been having some talks about your particular skills, and it appears you've been holding out on me."

Neri blinked, the sense of being watched trickling into her head. The unwelcome sensation crept like fingers across her skull. She clenched her fists harder to push out the threat.

"I'm sure you have. I'm surprised you're not holding court here already, but then again manipulating folk as puppets is more your style."

Viljo laughed but a bite of discontent echoed beneath the bravado even as Amis smiled on. Neri glanced at Niall standing beside her and took strength from his presence.

"I'll take that as a yes," she continued. "It's interesting how snakes like you always give folk the ideas that further your own ends, but enough is enough."

Neri glared at both of them and wished she'd refrained from the theatrical fire throwing. Now she didn't feel able to call it back to her. She focused on being vigilant whilst keeping the fire from dropping onto the enemy's heads as Viljo stepped forward.

"You know so little of this world and yet you say you're fighting to save it. Do you know anything of running lands and tending to folk?"

Neri caught sight of a small measure of concern in his

eyes as he stepped into the harsh glare of the suns. Memories of the last war echoed through her head, of the old lord whose head he'd sliced off on the battlefield. That lord had worn a crown made of *freirer* ice, the same substance used to subdue dragons, and the one Viljo was wearing looked much the same.

"No, I don't, but more importantly, do you? Have you ridden the lands? Have you seen how sick and poor the folk are?"

A crash reverberated across the city. The ground quaked in the wake of a victory, whether theirs or the enemy's she couldn't tell, but she force all thought of friends from her mind.

"It sounds as though we've broken your gates already."

The lie came easily to her and she began to pace, keeping Niall behind her and those atop the steps clear in her line of sight as she called her fire to her.

'I see you're not swayed enough to believe your lover unfaithful, but what about your friends. I'm sure they have seen others die at your hands and how long before they're next?'

Amis sent his voice into her mind and she gritted her teeth. He might be able to worm in and speak to her but she wouldn't give him the satisfaction of making any impression. But using it for hitting back at him, she could do that.

With a wicked smile from the not-so-slumbering darkness she kept bedded down deep, she started to pace.

"I wonder how much trouble you get into with that little trick." She lifted her voice for all to hear. "Who knows what you whisper into the ears of others? If you're encouraging me in my power, what does that mean for those who stand beside you against me?"

Viljo's eyes narrowed. If he had ever had feelings for her, then now would be the time to call on them, but Amis strode forward and blocked the fragile gaze between them.

"I know you're only trying to do what you think is right, but you don't understand our vision."

Neri sucked air through her teeth, the memory of Emelyn's terror fresh in her mind. She wondered if somewhere, deep down, Amis' true power was casting fear into hearts and minds, like the icy prickle needling inside her own head.

"I believe you're misguided," he continued. "There might be hope for you yet. You have great power and it could be used to change our land for the better. Why wouldn't you want to align yourself with that?"

Neri rolled her eyes. She couldn't understand why he assumed such vapid trickery would sway her, but she saw Viljo's stiff shoulders hunch more.

'He hasn't targeted me yet, but Niall was so easily taken in by it all.'

She growled as the prickle intensified and her *ai-tan* flared. The words in her head weren't her own, and Amis frowned when she glowered back at him and refused to relent. Then his gaze flickered sideways, and it took a moment to realise he wasn't targeting her.

Niall stared at her with his lips twitching over unspoken thoughts. He blinked several times and clenched his fists tight, trying to hold off the torrents of a mental storm.

Neri gathered her gift and sent a warning boomerang of fire shooting toward Amis. He scrambled out of the way and his hold on Niall fractured.

"I'm not doubting you," Niall muttered, even as he wiped a hand over his face.

Neri recalled the fire to her, fuelled by the sudden flash

of anger on Amis's face as he lifted both hands.

Niall roared beside her as she lifted hers in answer, a circle of golden fire burning a path around them.

Black flames licked through the air toward them, but her own gift leapt to meet it.

She grimaced against the elements, the square swept clean of anything for the fire to grab hold of.

"Need straw, parchment, fabric, anything," she hissed.

Niall shouted the demand back rather than leave her as she shuddered at the biting attack of the darkfire raging against her. Even as she surrounded the darkness in a circle of light, it stayed inside the boundary like a splinter deep in skin, but through the haze she could see Amis, his shoulders tense and his face crunched with effort.

When he called the darkfire back, he staggered to stay on his feet. Neri sucked in a breath of air as a feral gust of wind swept straw toward them, all the sweeter because she saw Livia wielding it from behind a pillar. It fed the fire and gave her a moment to rest, but she had to force Amis to attack again.

She paced a small semi-circle to keep them all in sight, taking strength from the subtle squeeze Niall gave her hand as she passed him.

If I keep Amis attacking me, he can't take Niall.

Viljo looked nervous now, the innate facade of emotionless responsibility shattered as the clamour of crowds grew louder nearby.

"It seems I'm more used to my *ai-tan* than you are to yours," she taunted.

It landed exactly as she'd hoped as Amis forced himself upright again and lifted his hands, but Viljo stepped forward before he could attack. His eyes darted from Neri to Niall, and Amis lowered his arms again.

"We can fight with gifts if you want, brother," Viljo called out.

Neri eyed the fringes of the square as fighting spilled into it, but several folk were choosing to climb atop stalls or posts above the battle to watch what was going on instead.

"I've always preferred a straight fight." Niall swung his blade through the air with a wicked grin. "Remember who you are, because if he's controlling your mind to make you fight me, he won't be controlling mine."

Neri's chest constricted but she couldn't humble Niall by keeping him back from the battle he had to fight. One brother would come out a leader and one would lose. If they were lucky, both would get to keep their lives.

If I keep Amis busy, they might both survive this.

She sent a warning shot of fire and seethed through her teeth as he tried to dodge it. She whipped another higher to burn the hangings above him, and let the flames pin him to the stone wall.

He attacked in kind and she grimaced against the onslaught. Even the feel of the darkfire trickled damp and cold against the mental tendrils of her *ai-tan*, but the clashing of metal, fast and lethal beside her, kept her mind sharp. If Niall got hurt then she wouldn't be able to keep Amis from him.

With her concentration centred on the flames and the sound of Niall's battle beside her, she didn't notice the first rumble. The second came louder, and she almost sagged to her knees with relief as the darkfire receded.

Amis threw his hands out before she could recover, and sent the darkness flying toward her. She screamed as it passed her and twisted to see Livia right behind her, wide-eyed as Neri deflected the stream of darkfire toward the edge of the tower. The black flames leeched into the stone, spreading like oil before the stones cracked and flew out toward the square. Neri stumbled back to Livia and shoved her behind the nearest hitching-post.

The sound of rubble settling on cobbles rumbled on and Neri peered out with Livia's arm still gripped between her fingers. Niall and Viljo had missed the onslaught, their blades swinging and clashing almost too fast to be seen.

"This is madness," Livia shouted. "You need to end him. End him and Viljo can take the punishment."

A rush of wind blew Neri's hair forward and the sudden sensation of being lighter lifted her shoulders. She lifted a hand over her shoulder to find her bow and quiver missing as a shining white horse with no bridle or saddle clattered in front of them with the Jakida steady on her back.

The Jakida held Neri's bow and one arrow, the tip pointed at Viljo's heart. Livia's arm quaked between Neri's fingers. Neri's gasp went unheard above the clamour of fighting that had spilled into the square.

Even as Neri fought to go forward and fight before the Jakida changed her mind and aimed for Niall, or Amis got into her head next, Livia clung on to hold her back.

Niall pushed his sword against Viljo's and sent him staggering. He landed on his knees and froze as he stared straight at the Jakida. The arrow whished through the air and left no room for error. Viljo's right shoulder jerked back as the arrow caught it, the tumble of his body to the cobbles just another soft thud in the melee of battle.

Neri risked a spike of heat to her arm and Livia let go with a soft yelp. It was enough and she promised herself she would apologise later as she dashed into the square to join them.

"Get him up, quickly," the Jakida hissed.

Niall shoved an unceremonious piece of cloth against the edge of Viljo's wound to staunch the blood, then hauled him to his feet and threw him up onto Zel's back.

The Jakida dropped the bow and sent Zel clattering back out of the square, sending folk fleeing at the risk of getting trampled.

Amis had one hand on the stone pillar beside him but his eyes hardened around the overwhelming tremor of fear in the air. Neri's glanced around, assessing their chances. Amis didn't have his puppet, but his fire could still harm so many, as could whatever mind-control gift he seemed to have. Her gaze flickered to the lane opposite, where Emelyn stood hidden behind the corner of a dwelling. Neri scanned the square again, wondering how to get to her. She sent her fire to the hangings above Amis again to distract him, then weaved through the crowds as quick as she could move. Emelyn's wide green eyes blinked at her as she darted into the lane.

"How are you holding up?" Neri asked.

She saw Niall making it to the spot she'd just vacated, his head leaning low to Livia's ear. His shadow would be able to blind their enemy to things that moved perhaps, but he couldn't send it from him as she could do with her fire or Livia could do with the wind.

Emelyn's hands shook as Neri held them, but she nodded and stammered that she hadn't had to fight yet.

"I'm going to have to do something rash," Neri whispered. "While all eyes are on me, move fast and get to Niall. He and Livia will keep you safe."

She couldn't bring herself to ask where Mik was, or why he and Ciena weren't at Emelyn's side. She sighed instead and clutched Emelyn's hands tighter.

"You'll need to be brave, but it has to be you to do this,"

she insisted. "If my sacrifice doesn't work, you need to turn the tide. I know you're afraid of what you can do, what you might be capable of, but you are good right down to the bone. Amis holds his power through fear but you can turn that story against him. I know you can do it."

Emelyn shook her head with tears springing to her eyes, but Neri had no time left. Soon the crowds would soon become unmanageable and control would pivot to whoever they sided with. She hugged Emelyn close and kissed the top of her golden hair. Then she let her go and stepped away.

"The moment I'm done, get to Niall," she murmured. "If you can't find Ciena then let Livia defend you, but above all keep Niall from doing anything dim. He'll need all of you."

"But who's going to stop you from doing something dim?"

Neri ignored that and forced her feet to take each purposeful step across the square. Her skin prickled with promise as she called the firebird to her. The burn inside her limbs grew to an almost excruciating hum as she walked across the silent square and up each stone step toward the man she hated so much.

She had to trust Emelyn knew what to do, and that Emelyn could turn Amis' power on him as easily as he'd tortured her with her.

As Amis caught his gaze, she let every essence of fury flare in her gaze. His expression was unreadable, but she could see the flicker of her flames reflected in his narrow eyes. Her stomach throbbed, the skin on her chest boiling and bubbling with burning. The echo of birdsong and the incessant chirping she'd been hearing on and off since leaving Jakiris through the shimmer grew louder.

She almost faltered, almost, as the sensation of control slipped and slithered away from her, but she thought of Niall.

I wonder if Livia and Emelyn will be able to restrain him alone.

She lifted her voice and a whisper of wind caught it, carrying it far louder than she could have managed on her own.

Livia was with her. She at least understood.

"You abuse the gifts given to you by the land." She let all her effort and strength pour into her voice as she faced Amis down. "You use everyone, the dragons, the folk, but you don't give anything back."

Amis laughed, but it was a strained sound and he hadn't moved to summon the darkfire back yet.

"What is taken must be repaid is the oldest balance there is," she shouted. "You're going to learn that today."

CHAPTER TWENTY TWO

"Oh my dear." Amis smiled. "Such passion, yet you've barely had your *ai-tan* for a winterspan, if that. What can you possibly know about any of it?"

He lifted his own voice, less powerful than hers with help from friends, but still able to carry across the square.

"Friends, we can build a land where the worthy are praised. There is so much to learn, so much freedom to be had yet."

Neri held her fire in check but the prickle in her mind kept her determination on simmer as the firebird cawed in anger.

'I am glad my dear that you were able to come this far.' Amis spoke into her mind. *'Perhaps in time you will come around to my way of thinking. Think of your friends, their safety is in your hands.'*

The tone that invaded her head sent a flash of memories screaming through. Emelyn's frightened face when she was rescued from the stronghold, untold horrors in her eyes. She refused to succumb to a wave of revulsion, lifting her head higher.

"You think you've won, but winterspans from now this tale will be told." She flicked a glance sideways. "Viljo's name may be mentioned as someone the folk overcame. The Governance will be a cautionary tale to tell the children around campfires. But you won't be remembered. You stand there, ready to bend the folk to your will, but you overestimate your power."

A cocky smirk spread over his face, his eyes dancing.

'Do you think you can harm me? You failed before, too sweet for your own good. Did thoughts of me haunt you when you thought I died at your hand?'

More taunts to play with her, to waste time. She smiled, her *ai-tan* rippling through her, the chirping in her mind getting louder and more insistent.

"You're in a land far more powerful than you," she countered. "You desecrate your gifts instead of earning them."

Emelyn had taught her one thing. Stories had to have a suitable ending. The worthy earned their freedom, and the wicked always learned their lesson.

"I may borrow power, but I have learned far more about this last and its histories than you will ever know," he countered. "I have walked with ancients and I alone am strong enough to wield their power."

Neri snorted. "You really believe that? Total dominion over folk, and you think you're the wise one? The good one? You're the enemy that gets slain, not the hero."

'But what are good and evil really?'

She glared at him as the crawling sensation of doubt tugged at her mind, wrapping around her head as a disconcerting pressure.

And so the battle began.

"Don't talk into my mind with your twisted words," she snapped. "Honour the folk by talking in front of them. What do you have to hide?"

He shrugged. "This assumption of yours that everything should be good and fair is naïve. No land is without its troubles."

"So the alternative is pain? Anyone can gain power

through threats and suffering. Some can even use it, but in the end your ambition will destroy you."

Aware he was still reaching around in her mind, she let the last thought sing into his.

'Unless I destroy you first.'

He chuckled. "So noble of you, one so young, so inexperienced, to talk of ambition. How can you be one to judge what counts as governance and what strays into abuse? Examples always need to be made to keep the peace."

"And what would you know about peace? What would you know of love and trust, or friendship and loyalty? How many folk must have betrayed you to cause such a bitter, twisted mind?"

The words flitted through her head, but unlike the bitterness of his gift, the words were soft and gentle. Neri risked a look behind her and found Emelyn in the centre of the square, looking tiny all alone. Emelyn nodded, her face set in determination.

Emelyn wasn't going to support her if she failed. She was going to support her to succeed.

Where Amis was a small, sharp pebble against her mind, Emelyn's gift flowed through her like sunlight after too much rain. All she had to do was trust that feeling, let Emelyn weave the words through her mouth.

Before Amis could take a turn, she forged on.

"You were probably the kind of child who pulled legs off insects and made the other children cry. You wanted to be liked, but there was something that made them wary of you. Then when you grew, you delighted in hurting others and that made others avoid you, right?"

He frowned, the tiniest chink of discomfort hidden beneath a mask confusion.

"I don't think cheap taunts are going to do you any good here," he snapped.

"Cheap taunts? When you've razed half of the east into ruin? Are you so bereft of love that you find so much pleasure in hurting others? Are you so broken that control is the only thing that works for you?"

"Stop this. I will not enter into these childish games with you. There is a cell with your name on deep in the Apeklonian keep, and I have my own plans for you."

"Plans for me?" She raised her hand, letting her flames play across her fingers. "Who are you to decide? Even now, after all this time you're just a wounded child lashing out. Pathetic. You've grown into a hate-filled, fearful man who has no real control of his borrowed power. Why aren't you controlling my mind right now like you've done to others? Why am I not cowering at your feet, begging for mercy?"

Neri hesitated as a powerful wave of heat rolled inside her chest, but Emelyn's gift continued talking through her.

"Is the magic of the land too strong for you to handle sometimes?" she demanded. "Have you defiled it so badly with your depravity that it turned to chaos?"

Amis lashed out a hand but the darkfire sputtered at his fingertips as she danced back, letting her fire flare enough to burn his hand.

"What if I turn your power on you, hmm?" she taunted. "How would you like it? See exactly what you've done to so many others?"

Neri's insides chilled even as her fire burned hot across her skin, a shard of Emelyn's pain somehow raging inside her. She had no control now, no ability to stop talking as the memory that wasn't her own flared into her mind.

A flash of a boy in a dank stable with a leaking roof.

266

Pipe burns and lashings with a belt, cruel jokes and humiliation.

A brother dead, cause unknown.

Children cowering to whisper as he walked past.

Her stomach bubbled with revulsion as she saw the extent of his pain and what had driven him.

Amis thudded to his knees with both hands clutching his head as Emelyn wove the truth even faster.

Fear feeding him as he killed his first.

Pleasure at having others die without even getting his hands dirty.

A woman lying dead beside a batch of herbs. Neri whimpered. *An older woman lying face down in a nearby stream, the sight of it satisfying him beyond all measure.*

The delicious sound of screams and torment from the cells his nightly music of choice.

The sensation of the pebble pressing against her mind crumbled. The visions faded and Amis fell to the floor. Nausea crawled up Neri's throat as he whimpered random exclamations that made no sense.

She gasped as he lurched up onto his knees and grabbed at one of the guards nearby. The woman drew back in horror, but Amis pulled himself to his feet by her clothing. Neri sent a lash of fire out as he grabbed the woman's throat and squeezed for some maniacal attempt at control.

"Your strength is failing," Neri announced, her voice strong even though she felt like breaking.

At the mere suggestion of it, Amis fumbled. The guard shoved him off and dashed away.

"Now." Emelyn's voice floated over on Livia's air. "If you have to do it, do it now."

"*DO WHAT?!*"

Neri winced at Niall's exclamation as the rest of their

words whirled away again. They probably didn't know exactly what 'it' would cost her, but she summoned the firebird again with all her might, calling to the soft tune trilling inside her mind.

It's time. I'm ready.

She wasn't, and tears burned down her cheeks as her skin heated until she was gasping at the pain of it.

Amis lifted his hand and his face contorted in horror as a piercing whistle of birdsong wrenched from her lips. She pushed herself forward as the pain threatened to scorch her, even as the haze of hurt brought a swoop of blissful numbness with it.

His darkfire leaked out to meet her, and through the battle of heat and darkness she could sense him trying in vain to pull it back. It answered too readily, choosing to feed on weakness over fighting strength, and rebounded.

Dark flames curled around his eyes and out of his nose, covering his mouth and ears. Little wisps of smoke curled up from his skin and he gurgled as flickers of it burst from his lips.

As light met dark, the two of them crashed together and Neri closed her eyes, listening to the bittersweet melody her bird was singing for her, a lamentation of her own.

Another song, older and darker and bittersweet in its own melody, answered hers. She sensed the darkfire exactly as it was, power so solid and biting it felt like plunging a hand into an icy bucket.

Ai-tan is nothing more than energy, no good or bad, righteous or wicked. It simply is.

Someone might one day come to harness darkfire, to wield it without malice, unlike Amis who used it to fuel his hatred. It seemed a wretched revelation to have at the end of her days, but in the last dregs of life as she tumbled down the stone steps, she focused on Niall.

One last time, she promised herself. *One last thought.*

His smile. That would be the one she took into the permanent darkness with her. Her life in exchange for everything his could now be.

CHAPTER TWENTY THREE

Niall fought even as his body betrayed him. Grief and panic fuelled every single punch and stab he aimed, but Ciena had him held down tight, Mik too. He barely noticed Emelyn standing in the centre of the square, so mired in desperation to get to Neri as her body shone as bright as the suns in the sky.

He struggled as her words rang out, and as she fought the enemy. He roared and kicked and bit and struggled as a golden head of flame reared above Neri's body, the effigy of feathers spreading out from her arms and leaving the human limbs behind.

She lunged toward Amis even as darkfire escaped his body, the *ai-tan* desperate to find freedom and join with the light.

Niall roared again as the two of them tumbled down the stone steps, each rotation a blow to every essence of who he was. They landed, Amis shrivelled to a soulless husk like the cursed forest decaying nearby.

Niall almost didn't register Ciena letting him go, or her low cursing that filled the pin-drop silence. Only when Emelyn moved forward did he stumble to his feet and dash past her. He dropped to his knees beside Neri and folded over her with his arms cradling his head. She lay without a mark on her, but her flames were extinguished and her skin covered with the pale mark of death.

"We still coin him," Emelyn murmured.

Ciena's disgusted grunt echoed, but she nudged a toe through the remnants and shrugged.

"Death coins don't burn," she said. "So arrogant, he didn't even think dying was an option. Definitely dead though. We need to be gaining control and fast. Niall?"

He shook his head, lashing out a hand at whoever appeared with coins for Neri's eyes. He wouldn't let them send her off. Until the land came for her body, she wasn't dead. When it did come, he'd be going with her.

He ignored Emelyn as she settled beside him and stroked a hand over Neri's forehead, her tears dripping onto her fingers.

"I can't write her alive again," she whispered, her voice breaking. "Please don't ask me."

He hadn't considered that, but he wouldn't ask. He could ask no more of Emelyn or his friends. If Neri didn't somehow return to him, if she didn't fight death like the natural chaos she was, he would follow her into it.

Emelyn stroked Neri's cheek and her hand flinched as feet appeared beside them.

Niall snarled in warning.

"Don't growl at me," Cori said, her tone gentle. "Let me look."

She ran a hand over Neri's forehead, then held one of her hands.

"I don't... it doesn't..." She frowned. "We need to get her inside. If there's to be rites for her, we want her out of the sunlight."

Niall nodded. It was the right thing to do. He lifted her in his arms, barely able to keep his chest from bursting as she lolled against him. He took a couple of steps forward until a shadow fell over her face.

The Jakida had dumped Viljo somewhere and stood in

front of him with her hand up, palm forward as though she had any control over him. He let his shadow drift forward to cloak his arms and wraith around Neri like a shroud.

"Niall, I know you're grieving but you need to think about the wider issue here. You could take control of the east, lead from here. We could unite the entire land under one banner, one…"

The Jakida couldn't bring herself to say family, even then. He didn't much care, but he noted the strain of momentary sadness, or perhaps regret, passing over her face as she glanced down at Neri.

None of that shifted the yawning nothingness growing inside him.

"Don't ask me to rule without her. Don't risk it," he warned. "I will become worse than any of them without her. Give Livia the chance she's more than earned."

His legs started moving, following Cori into halls he had no idea of. He might get lost if he tried to get back out, but either he and Neri would be navigating them together, or he wouldn't be leaving.

As they walked up the steps, he almost broke at the sight of the charring on the stone, but the Jakida's voice echoed behind him, the ruler taking every advantage of a new conquest.

"You may not know much of us, but in the west that we govern, there is freedom. We have abundance, and we would help you renew your lands to match."

A querulous muttering started up as Niall walked through the doorway.

"We don't want to take over," Livia announced, her tone soft. "We've had enough of that. Let us- let me help you rebuild. I'll take the responsibility for renewing this land until you agree a suitable replacement. We don't want power or control, or at least I definitely don't. Too much hard work."

Niall heard the awkward strain of laughter then sound was lost to him as Cori took them deeper into the oppressive darkness of the Apeklonian palace.

Cori accosted a nervous-looking young woman who led them toward a bedroom they could use, a large one with a balcony overlooking the water. Niall set Neri down on the bed and smoothed her hair away from her face as Cori felt her cheeks. She stood staring at Neri with a frown, until Niall glowered at her.

"What? What is it?"

Cori shook her head.

"Nothing. I-" She inhaled sharply, a purposeful grimace covering his face. "I'm simply wondering why the others burned but she didn't. Perhaps the last of her *ai-tan* preserved her. I take it you'll want to stay?"

Niall nodded and lowered himself to sit on the bed beside her.

"I'll have them send in food for you," Cori offered. "But they won't disturb you otherwise."

"Don't bother."

Niall stared at Neri as Cori left the room. With her eyes closed, she could be sleeping, but no matter how long he watched for, her chest didn't rise or fall once. He grabbed a pillow and curled around it, determined to watch over her. The land would claim her soon enough, it had its ways of dealing with bodies that not many folk understood, but until then he would fight to keep her.

When the ferryman came for her, he would be ready to bargain.

Blinking against grief-fuelled weariness, he thought back over every memory, from the very beginning.

So much time we could have had. He blinked harder, his eyes closing for longer each time. *So much time I wasted.*

"Niall!"

He jerked upright, the strange room around him baffling until his memories filtered back in. He stared wildly at Ciena in the doorway, then at the empty bed.

"*WHO TOOK HER?*" he yelled.

He swung to his feet, looking for a blade he'd long since abandoned as his knees caught in the ruck of the covers.

"Niall-"

"I swear I will end whoever took her, who was it?" He charged toward her and grabbed her shoulders. "Was it you?"

She fought his hold on her, but he refused to let go until she relented.

"A boat's been spotted," she snapped. "Apparently, Neri is in it!"

CHAPTER TWENTY FOUR

A gentle shaking started. Awareness began to blossom. The idea of pain remained a memory, but comfort echoed all around.

A trilling note called to Neri from somewhere far away. She realised the shaking was still going on. She could hear voices around her and tried to tune in, but they slipped and slithered away before she could make them out.

Neri opened her eyes and noticed an awful lot of wood. Wooden beams on the ceiling, wooden logs making up the walls, wooden furniture around her. She lay on her back and the only thing in her line of vision other than wood was the person shaking her.

A slim man, familiar without Neri knowing why, smiled down at her.

"You don't belong here my girl. Need to get you back quick."

He moved away from her and something about his voice filled her with calm.

He sounds like Mary somehow.

She struggled to sit up. The room around her was looked odd but she couldn't work out the reason. There was something about the kettle carved out of wood that didn't seem right. Even the wooden oven had a wooden door. Now that she stared around, it looked like a wooden carving of the kitchen back at the sanctuary.

The only things in little room not made of wood were a

heavy grey cloak, a wide-brimmed grey hat, and a lantern on the table that had a strange, murky blue flame.

Neri pushed herself to her feet and stared at the man. He looked deceptively ageless, no skin wrinkles and a bulky physique, but there was something about the eyes that screamed ancient. They changed colour and she couldn't look at them for longer than a moment or two. The skin of his hands were gnarled, but the joints were deft and the fingers moved too quickly for her to see as he pawed something from the table.

"Outside you go. I see reflections of all that those come to me have done and there will be no games this time."

The man threw on the coat, pulled on the hat and grabbed the lantern. As he opened the door to sunslight and the waft of salty air, Neri recognised him. The thought of dying brought all the memories back. Amis, the darkfire, her firebird rising from her from where it had nestled since leaving the east, and Emelyn finally taking control of her power.

She had no idea why the ferryman was being nice to her, but he was smiling and she knew she wouldn't be going anywhere without his help. She looked back over her shoulder and her mouth dropped open. The door to the wooden room she'd just left through was now the mouth of a large cave.

"No boat this time? No cards?" she asked.

He grinned. "No cards, no coins, but the boat is unavoidable where you have to go. I never seen someone die quite so much as you. Usually it's just the once, but your part of the land is whole now, and the peace means I have less tortured souls sent my way. Not nice to see. Perhaps next time you stay a while, play some cards. The seas have a way of finding me."

Neri nodded, wordlessly confirming a promise that one day, hopefully in the far distant future, she would greet him one last time as a friend.

The boat was moored to the grey jetty on the grey, airless beach. Neri got into the boat and sat down as he cast off and sat to face her.

"What does it feel like to die?" he asked.

Neri shrugged. "The pain is endless but also fleeting. They say the shock makes you numb so I suppose it depends on your mind and how you die."

The ferryman laughed, his bark deep like a dog's. Neri thought of Dog, of Ma and Moonshine. She hoped they were safe. She wished with all her heart that Emelyn would accept that she wasn't bad for using her gift to help turn the tide of the war, and that Ciena had fun fighting while she got the chance.

"Did Finn come this way?" she asked.

He tilted his head. "Many come this way."

"That's not an answer."

"It is, and it isn't. I've been busy today thanks to you folk fighting, but the dead are all accounted for, save one."

"Amis?" She had to ask.

"Darkfire is never gifted. The powers of creatures beyond mere folk are not ours to meddle with, and he delved too deeply into ancient power for me to find him at the end."

It didn't comfort her like she'd expected it to. She remembered the memories Emelyn had pulled from his mind, and of her friends, she had to admit that Emelyn's *ai-tan* was perhaps second in power only to Livia's control of the weather.

"I only ventured east once." The ferryman's quiet voice made her jump. "I made a deal with a man who made candles."

Neri frowned. "Hamlin?"

"He believed and so I came. His was the first sacrifice for you, and that one didn't sit well with me. But this time there is no sacrifice, no debt to be paid. I make that choice. For good or ill, the bird chose you and life cannot be whole without death."

Neri wiped a hand over her face. Whether the whole thing was happening as a lingering flicker of her dying mind or there was actually a ferryman of the dead talking to her, she had to make sure she understood.

"Hamlin died so that I could live, and then the firebird chose me, so you have to do the same?"

He shook his head, the grin never fading.

"Life and death always have choice. You could say that is our own little game she has me dancing through."

The beginning and ends of all lands dwelled in his eyes, the minutiae and vastness curling into one tangled mess of infinity. She shook her head and dragged her gaze away from his face, knowing no good would come from losing herself in the thought of it.

Vague memories of Mik and his fables about unicorns and dragons flickered in her mind.

"Did you send the dragon?" she asked. "The one that came to show me the darkfire could be calmed by mine?"

He laughed. "I don't deal in the ebb and sway of debts. That's firmly in the domain of life. I only deal in the finality of the beyond."

It wasn't much of an answer, but then it could be seen as a personal question.

"This may not feel pleasant," he added.

"You're going to throw me overboard again aren't you?"

He chuckled and stood up to point behind her. When she glanced over her shoulder, she saw a short expanse of red sand formed a small beach amid cliffs.

As the boat glided toward life and the living, the ferryman laughed.

"What would be the sense in that? I won't offer you my hand, but if you want to get yourself into the water, the waves will do the rest."

Neri groaned as she leaned over the edge of the boat and stuck her fingers in the water.

"Cold," she muttered.

"Of course it's cold. Life often is, but also full of warmth. In you go now. There are still many souls I need to fetch."

Neri swung a leg over the edge of the boat and held her breath. The icy water swirled around her face, snapping at her skin as she kicked up through the surface. It didn't surprise her to find the boat and the ferryman nowhere to be seen when she blinked water from her stinging eyes, but she couldn't stop the bubble of laughter bursting out.

The waves seemed determined to sweep her toward the shore, so she lay on her back as best she could with aching limbs and focused on keeping her head above water.

Her mind was scattered and hazy, but in the sort of way where it would clear with enough rest. And probably a lot of screaming.

She sank inside her mind and the weary flicker of warmth answered her. The firebird hadn't taken its gift back when it was reborn, and she let that blessing carry her until the shore started to catch her back and rocks scraped her legs. She listened, but there wasn't any clear echo of a battle still raging. Then her head skimmed a soft patch of sand and the rest of her got stuck, the water and her sodden clothing lapping gently around her body.

I should probably try to get up. I'm going to catch cold. Niall is going to kill me.

A shadow fell over her, followed by the sight of a familiar face. Beneath the tumble of shining yellow hair, Livia looked terrified.

Neri smiled. "Hello."

"What are you- why are you- how-"

Livia burst into tears and stumbled as Emelyn appeared beside her.

"Get her up," Emelyn sobbed.

Neri wanted to help, but as they tried to lift her it was clear that she didn't have the strength for it. She shook violently and it took all of Livia and Emelyn's combined strength to get her up to drier sand. She lay basking in afternoon sunslight instead.

"If you two are here, is it over?" Neri asked.

The ferryman had told her Amis was gone, but there was still the folk and the land and titles to be squabbled over. Emelyn tried to smile but she was still crying too hard.

"It's done," Livia promised.

She put an arm around Emelyn's shaking shoulders, and that gave Neri enough shade against the sunslight to see them properly.

"Viljo is nursing his pride," Livia added. "*Ama* has insisted she will deal with him at home. We've sent Ciena to fetch Niall. Figured she might have some hope of holding him down if she couldn't get through to him. We should help you up to the palace now. Tower. Castle, whatever they call it. It's ghastly and I have to *live* here."

Neri lifted her head with a groan.

"If you really want to help me, you'll bring me a

waterproof box I can write on, two coins and a pack of *chekana* cards. I'm happy here for the moment."

Livia and Emelyn made motions to stand but Neri reached out a sluggish arm and grabbed Emelyn's wrist to hold her in place.

"I'm not glad of what I did." Emelyn choked out the words the moment Livia was gone. "My power got away from me a bit, but I wanted to give you every chance I could."

Neri squeezed her wrist gently before letting go, her arm falling onto her stomach.

"I knew you'd be able to, although I didn't expect you to use me as a puppet, that came as a bit of a surprise. I'm sorry I even had to ask you to. I'd love to say it's over now but no doubt the mending of the lands will be a struggle in itself."

Neri would tell of her ferryman story in good time. First, she wanted to thank him. Emelyn glanced over her shoulder as the suns started to go down over the water.

"I'll be back," she said.

Neri frowned, but then a subtle breeze brought the scent spice to her and she realised why. She wriggled until she could see behind her, in time to almost get a face full of sand as Niall skidded to a halt beside her.

"You're alive, are you okay?" He gasped the words out. "What happened? I was sure-"

"Will you unite with me?"

Her voice came out cracked and unsure, even though she had absolutely no doubt or reservation.

He stilled. "You're asking me?"

"Is that a no?"

He sank to his knees beside her, hands hovering halfway between holding her and respecting her space.

"Of course I will, to the end of our days and beyond."

His voice faded as he pulled her body against his, dropping kisses on any part he could touch. She sank against him, fighting the urge to cry.

"Can you tell me what happened?" he asked after a while.

"It's a long story," she mumbled. "I'm okay, or I will be. Emelyn said, or Livia said, one of them said that it's over?"

He nodded. "It's done. Livia will be taking over the east until they choose a suitable replacement, apparently. We will go back to Jakiris where I can keep you out of trouble."

She chuckled, nestling against him until she hit something hard and pointy. Frowning, she lifted a hand and tapped it.

"Happy to see me?" she asked.

He inched back just enough to reach between them.

"Oh, Livia threw some box at me and said you'd asked for it."

He unearthed a small box made of a strange sort of glistening blade-metal.

"*Freirer* ice, exceedingly rare. It'll keep whatever you need safe. What do you need it for?"

Neri shushed him and used his body to get herself into a sitting position. As she listened to her body without distraction, she could sense her *ai-tan* strong inside. Niall didn't interrupt as she used the tip of her fingernail and a flow of her gift to carve some words into the top of the box.

She took the coins, purely symbolic, and placed them inside. Then she held the pack of playing cards and pulled one out at random. She stared down at the 'blessing' card in her fingers, the image of pale skies and suns in the distance, stormier weather closer to the eye.

It would be a fitting choice.

She put the blessing card into the box and sealed it, re-reading just once the words she had carved on top.

'The beginning of a promise to a friend'.

The Ferryman had told her the seas had a way of finding him. She found it almost impossible to stand, her body still so weak. It took all her remaining strength to reach the edge of the water on her hands and knees and push the box into the water.

It floated on the waves and soon she lost sight of it. Her limbs shook and she used the last of her strength to push until she lay on her back once more.

"So, are we fighting each other?" she asked lazily. "I can't remember."

He pulled her against him again, his hands stroking over her aching limbs.

"Of course not. I still think you deserve the best and I still worry that isn't me. I can't give you riches and I doubt I'll be able to give you any lands if the Jakida has her way. She's not my biggest fan, especially after I keep rejecting her offers to take over places."

Neri smiled. "She offered you this place?"

"She did, and I refused. Said I'd be worse than everyone else without you."

"It's a good thing I don't want riches or land then. All I ever wanted was you."

She smiled to see the worry fading a little from his eyes, something that might never fully disappear. She raised a feeble arm and pushed her fingers against his chest, feeling for the wax tulip under his t-shirt.

"I almost don't believe that you're safe, that this is all over. We were so sure you were gone."

Niall's fingers found her cheek as he spoke, his touch moving over her hair and down to her arm. He clasped her hand in his and Neri shook her head lazily at him.

"Not dead, just visiting an old friend."

Niall frowned, his eyes darkening. Neri could barely see him now in the shadows that blocked the lights of the city, but he leaned closer and the signs of worry had lessened slightly.

"It seems as though the fight is done." Neri yawned loudly. "It's a relief as I could do with a rest now."

The sounds of revelry carried over to them on a sudden breeze and Neri suspected Livia wanted them to return. This reminded her that Niall had been in conversation with Jakida and Viljo for hours. It wasn't necessarily her place to know what had been said, but she felt like being nosy. When she asked, Niall smiled one of his seductive smirks that promised misdeeds.

"Don't feel too shocked, it wasn't a loving family reunion. She wanted Livia to take on the east with us staying on to advise. I think the idea was to save Viljo's pride by letting him 'help' her run Jakiris."

"What of the rest of the Governance? Amis mentioned a council."

Niall sighed. "They've been rounded up. The folk here are leaderless now and there are several noble families who need to be monitored. They'll likely try to get their own choices to power, but the Governance have been soundly renounced by all."

"That's something. So, Livia's going to be staying here?"

"So it seems."

She hesitated. "What about us? We can go home? Let this all pass?"

"That's up to you." He kissed her nose softly, then her mouth, as though he simply couldn't stop himself stealing a kiss. "The Jakida wants me to look at taking over Jakiris in time, although I think that's more her respect for you than it is favouritism toward me."

He stuck his tongue out and Neri laughed. The laughter made her chest hurt but the idea that she could laugh without having to be on guard all the time made her dizzy with happiness.

She held her arms out to Niall and he took hold of her, lifting an armful of sand as he brought her to sit up. Her body ached and her skin tingled with sensitivity, but she nestled against him and sighed the last of her worry away as he continued.

"I said I'd speak to you about it but that I had no plans and was making no promises. That was after someone came in to say you'd been found. I had no idea you'd even gone missing but Cori came in soon after to tell us you were awake."

Niall pulled Neri closer to him and kissed her hair. With his free arm he pulled her legs over his own and folded her to lie properly against him.

"I can't even remember most of what happened." His voice almost got lost in her hair. "I fought Viljo and then you were on fire. Then the fire disappeared and you were just lying there. I think I blanked out, I don't know what happened. But then Emelyn said she felt a pulse of sorts inside you and I had to hold out until it was certain."

Neri closed her eyes. No doubt Niall would cause an uproar if he had to carry her through the streets but the longer she sat there the more inclined she was to sleep there until she could stand unaided. Niall asked if she was chilly, but the shaking came from so much previous effort rather than cold.

"Zel came in at some point and kept saying that things don't happen when we want or expect them to, but when it's their time. I thought she was mad but then she said that sometimes on occasion we get granted a bit of luck. I don't know what happened to you, but I think it's more to do with luck."

Neri murmured a sleepy agreement. She could tell him about the Ferryman and her family, someday she would, but today she didn't want any long in-depth conversations. There would be time for that when she gained her strength back. Now she wanted luxury and frivolity and some time alone with him, preferably in a room where being horizontal was comfortable.

"More like luck and choice." Neri yawned again. "We should try to get up to the castle. There will be mass celebrations and I want to see everyone and hear their own stories. I might steer clear of Ciena until my stomach settles though."

"We'll steer clear of everyone, don't worry. I have plans for you that definitely don't involve others."

She chuckled. "I like the sound of that. You should make peace with your brother though."

"No." He shook his head, his voice stony in an instant. "I'll never be able or willing to accept him."

"Why not?"

"Some folk just don't get on and that's okay. Like you and Hareili."

She flailed against him, struggling to sit upright.

"She tried to steal you! Her whole existence is annoying."

"And Viljo didn't try to steal you? Several times? He'd do it again too if he thought he had a chance." Before she could argue, he pulled her tighter against him. "No, we're allowed to have our rivalries, as long as there's no fighting."

"What about fighting each other?"

"I'm the only one allowed to fight with you now." His kiss was a soft caress of lingering wine and promises. "Do you mean it, about uniting?"

"What do you think? You're mine as I'm yours. There'll be nobody else for me, not ever."

"Not ever," he echoed. "Nobody else would be able to handle you."

Neri grinned, letting the insult slide as he hauled her to her feet and supported her. With one foot in front of the other, they began the slow walk toward the city.

"I still can't believe you're safe. I'm almost still in shock. The bird came out of you and left you behind on fire."

Neri smiled and tried not to think about it. The firebird emerging was the only aspect she didn't understand. Perhaps it had become part of her when she last went through the portal, only to be born when she needed its power most. She had time to ponder that another day.

Her feet hit the solid ground of the lane and Niall slowed his pace. The party goers appeared to be in full swing, dancing in and out of each other's houses. Front doors were left wide open, folk mingled over garden walls and children ran madness and joy through the streets.

Folk gave Niall and Neri a wide berth, smiling and moving aside for them. Neri wondered if they knew how close they might have come to Niall becoming their lord, had the conversations with the Jakida gone another way.

"I didn't know when to rake things up." Niall clutched her tighter to him. "I'm sorry if I ever gave the impression I doubted you. I still don't feel I deserve you but at least now I can keep you safe."

Neri scoffed and almost stumbled when he halted and turned her to face him. Her body sagged with weariness but Niall's arms anchored her tight enough to keep her upright. She smiled at his serious expression.

"Despite you being a complete idiot, I still love you." Her voice cracked with tiredness. "I don't think you ever really doubted me; you always came back. As for keeping me safe, I might decide to go crazy with boredom and then you'll need saving."

Niall kissed her, his attentions capturing her breath and making her dizzy. She didn't much care about passing out as long as he kept hold of her.

They walked on slowly until the square came into view. Neri doubted she'd be able to look at it and not remember what happened, but Niall took charge and marched her up the steps.

He seemed to know where to go and Neri lagged along beside him, allowing him to support her weight and whisper sweet things in her ear.

When he pushed open the door to the bedroom they'd shared during their last visit, Neri frowned.

"I thought we were going to see everyone."

Niall rolled his eyes and continued to manhandle her into the room, her entire lack of strength laughable against him.

"We will tomorrow." He promised. "I want you to rest for a while more. Tomorrow you can do whatever you like, but tonight you're all mine."

Neri smiled, relieved. She waited until he'd folded back

the bedcovers with his arm still around her and then collapsed onto the sheets.

Her skin tingled against the cloth but she ignored it, weary and wanting to sleep. The sensation reminded her of the Mathoen blankets in Carahdyl and she made a mental note to visit Sav soon and buy some of her own.

Even before Niall could join her in bed, Neri's mind forced her into slumber. Dreams stayed away and she woke again as the suns rose, casting gentle rays through their window.

A few moments of calm silence lingered. Then the sensation of fingers moving idly through her hair told her Niall was already awake.

She shifted and rolled onto her stomach with one arm balanced on his chest. He smiled down at her, his eyes a dopey brown and still lidded with the after effects of deep sleep.

As she stared, Neri realised she'd never properly managed to take time and look at him fully. She knew him of course, knew his features, but now she examined him.

She asked if he could isolate his gift and bring shadow into one hand. He raised an eyebrow and shrugged.

"I don't think I've ever tried." He admitted, raising his hand.

Neri watched as his shadow began to form across his arm, curling down over his fingers. Even as he focused on it, the shadow began to creep into other parts of his body until he dropped his hand with a sigh.

"It doesn't look like it." He took her hand in his. "I won't ask you to do the same; I want to keep my eyebrows."

Neri giggled and continued to notice little things about him, revelling in the time she now had.

One ear was a little higher than the other, barely noticeable. His eyebrows were thick and his lashes fairly long. His knuckles and arms bore signs of old scarring and Neri continued exploring. He seemed happy to let her, remaining still and quiet as her fingers trailed here and there. When she finally looked up, he smiled at her.

"All done?" He pulled her a little closer. "I promised you that you could do whatever you wanted today."

Neri wanted to see everyone, to set a plan in motion and have everything sorted so that she could go home. Even though her skin still tingled with weariness and her mind seemed hazy with flu-like symptoms, she didn't want to spend the day in bed.

"We should get up and at least see folk for a bit. If Livia is determined to take Apeklonia on she will need help, at least initially, and I want to get home as soon as I can."

Niall sighed as she sat up. He didn't make any movement to claim her back or to get up himself. Sensing a sulk imminent, Neri turned back to him and took his hands.

"I never thought to ask you what you wanted." She tried a different tactic. "I don't care, I really don't, about whether Jakiris or Apeklonia are 'ours'. But what do you want? Do you want to run any of them?"

Niall rubbed his thumb over her knuckles, the sensation soothing her irritated skin.

"I honestly don't know. I feel as though I should ask you to decide, but I know it's my decision to make. Jakiris is our home, at least I think so. I don't want to rule the East, I know that much. But the West? Maybe, in time."

Pleased she had a proper answer from him, a meaningful one at last, Neri relented. She settled down with her body nestled against his and turned her face up to kiss him.

She smiled. "Then that's what we'll do."

"The Jakida suggested we take over now." He admitted it so casually.

Neri tried to sit up, but he held her firm against him. She struggled but he wouldn't relent.

"That's not what you want though." Neri said.

She had to settle, no match for his strength. Niall shrugged his shoulder beneath her head, still holding her tight.

"I've told you before, I want you. I want us to be together. If I need Jakiris for that, so be it. If I don't, then I'd prefer to wait. She can go whistle."

Neri gulped down the urge to giggle. Determined to tease him, she pretended to disapprove.

"She's still your family, you shouldn't be so rude." Neri tried to frown at him.

Niall scoffed and tugged on a strand of her hair, looking grumpy.

"I don't care. Everyone pretends it's a nice gesture, her handing me down a kingdom. It's like she's going out of her way to be generous, when really everyone knows that I'm the only choice left. It's either me or Viljo and look out he turned out."

Neri paused, staring at him. She caught the petulant tone and the whiny voice of Niall's inner child, but also, she thought he sounded ever so slightly sad too.

Relenting, wishing she hadn't pushed the subject, Neri ran her fingertips over his forehead and down to his cheek, forcing him to look at her.

"You're a good person though. You'll do right by the folk and everyone knows it. But you know you don't have to accept it."

Neri hoped he wasn't still stuck on the idea that she needed a kingdom, but he surprised her by smiling ruefully. His shadow had been creeping around him but now it receded again.

"I do though." His eyes began to sparkle playfully. "I wouldn't subject our folk to his tyranny. Also, I very much doubt you'd ever let me live it down if I walk away from them now."

Neri had to laugh. He teased her, but she didn't mind. Unwilling to spend any more time being serious, she went for the first ridiculous thought that came to mind.

"You could abdicate and ask Ciena to take over. She's the caring, sharing type."

Niall laughed and pulled her back down against him.

"She'd have them fighting to the death over the last piece of bread. No, I reckon Emelyn's a much better choice. She'll have everyone organising group dances and then start yelling that they're all making too much noise when she's trying to write."

Niall grinned up at her. Neri pretended to hit him, accidently landing her fist into his shoulder. He grunted, but the noise got drowned out by a loud hammering. Neri turned to look at the door and Niall groaned, his head thudding onto her shoulder in dismay.

"If we stay really quiet, they'll go away." Niall shouted out.

Neri doubted the exuberant knocker would be dissuaded by his loud hint. She began to giggle as the knocking got louder and more furious.

"I'll kill her hang on." He got up and off the bed.

Neri guessed it would be Emelyn. Niall pulled the door open a tiny crack and peered out. Moments later the door bounced into him. Emelyn steamed past.

Now that the doorway stood empty Neri could see Mik standing patiently in the hall.

"You can't monopolise her forever!" Emelyn grinned at Neri.

She then stood frowning at Niall with her hands on her hips.

Niall glared back. "Not even for a bloody morning it seems like."

His shadow started to swirl but his threatening growl didn't seem to hold any weight. Emelyn rolled her eyes at him, stamped her foot and then turned to Neri with a beaming smile.

"Are you well enough to get up? The others really want to see you. We're holding talks in the square for the townsfolk. Then there'll be a celebration there this evening too."

Neri floundered in the galloping stream of Emelyn's words. She could feign illness and return to the comfort of her bed. Niall would no doubt prefer that. But then, she did want to talk to everyone too.

Niall surprised her by reigning in his shadow.

"We have time." He took her hand and smiled. "I'll share you for now."

Grateful, Neri turned to Emelyn and promised she would bathe, change and meet them in the square. That was enough to send Emelyn spiralling out of the room, a hurried apology to Niall left floating in the air behind her. Mik thoughtfully decided to close their bedroom door behind her.

Later, as they walked together through the stone halls, Neri glanced around them.

"I can't imagine what it will be like for Livia to actually stay here." Neri held off a shudder. "It's so dark and oppressive. I worry it'll somehow dampen her spirit."

Niall moved his hold so that Neri nestled right underneath his arm. He stopped for a moment, kissed her on the nose and then continued on.

"I'm sure she will renovate accordingly. More windows, painted stone, that sort of thing. The folk here will be glad of the business. It will be interesting to see how she handles her first public appearance as their potential new Lady."

Neri appreciated his belief in Livia's strength, but still she breathed a sigh of relief once they reached the steps and descended into the fresh air.

Niall remained holding her tight as the crowd swarmed. Of those assembled in the square, Neri knew most if not all of them. The locals hadn't yet arrived, so Neri had to stand in the midst of a swarm of friends. She allowed herself to be hugged and congratulated and exclaimed over by everyone.

Ciena refrained from slapping her on the arm, although she almost attempted it until Niall glared at her. Emelyn bounced around, always with Mik guiding her patiently out folk's way. Ma and Moonshine were holding court near the food table with Dog at their feet, and Neri knew there would be time to honour Finn later.

Zel stood aside with the Jakida, separate from all the reunions and chatter. It appeared that any time to talk about the future of Jakiris would come at a later date as well. Neri didn't mind and smiled at them nonetheless. Cori and Ciena added their congratulations until finally Livia came forward and took Neri's hands in her own.

"I couldn't be happier to see you." Livia smiled.

Then she leaned close and pulled Neri forward to whisper.

"I'm petrified. What if they don't like me? Ciena's offered to stay and manage my guard, whoever that is. What if she tries to stab me in my sleep?"

Neri insisted on shaking off Niall's arm. Despite the uncomfortable skin and the unsteadiness, she tried to stand tall and be a good friend.

"They'll love you. Just make sure you get across that you don't want to boss them about, so much as govern. You're not here to take their livelihoods or their earnings, just to help everyone have a chance at a good life."

Neri stopped when she realised Livia was grinning.

"I think you'll make a good Jakida in time." Livia teased her.

Neri rolled her eyes and glanced back at Niall. He watched her but managed to keep his part in a conversation with Mik. When he winked at her, she marvelled that she still felt butterflies. Their time would come, time to be alone and make a life. Now it was Livia's time.

As the first few local folk trickled in, looking unsure now that the initial revelries had ceased, Livia drew herself up tall.

Decked in brilliant blue Jakirian robes, Livia looked every inch a ruler. Her blonde hair shone in the morning sunslight and her entire countenance radiated positivity.

"Thank you for taking the time to come." Livia approached the locals.

Neri marvelled at the instant reverence they seemed to show Livia, bobbing their heads in a bow to her. She conversed with them quietly for a few moments and then turned to welcome some other folk. Neri barely noticed Niall arriving back at her side to claim her once more.

"They like her already, look!" Neri whispered to him.

Niall chuckled and forced her to turn toward him, away

from the others.

"We should talk to the Jakida while the others are occupied." He didn't look too eager. "There might be things we can learn from talking to folk here as well for when we inevitably take over the West."

Neri raised an eyebrow, tempted to tease him. Instead, she nodded and let him guide her to the edge of the square.

The Jakida regarded them both for a long moment. Zel made excuses and then Neri wondered if perhaps folk were waiting for her to start the conversation. She couldn't think of a single thing to say.

"There will be time for discussions." The Jakida seemed the most awkward of the three of them. "Viljo has at least admitted his failings. He will return to Jakiris with me and I shall deal with him as I see fit. I doubt he will venture much into public life again. I have proposed to Niall that he look at ruling Jakiris when the appropriate time arrives. That is of course, up to you both."

Neri didn't want to have the serious discussion. She hadn't seen Viljo since the fighting and knew the Jakida would be harbouring some form of shame for a long time to come. But it should have been a happy time for them all.

"This is Livia's time." Neri had no idea if her words would help or make things worse. "I will do anything I can to help her but then I want to go back to Jakiris, back home. For now though, Jakiris can wait. I'm sure Livia will need your counsel in the coming days, although she seems to have grasped the basics already."

Neri glanced just once at Niall when she finished speaking. His eyes shone with nothing but adoration. She couldn't even be sure that he'd listened to her words. The Jakida's expression remained unreadable.

Thankfully, Neri was saved from any lingering

awkwardness. Niall nudged her and pointed toward the lane that led to the main gates. Neri had enough sense to excuse herself as she left Niall's side, but the sight before her eyes couldn't wait.

Emelyn walked toward her from the lane, holding Fiora by the bridle.

"They found her outside the gates." Emelyn handed Neri the reins.

A servant arrived, offering to take Fiora to the stable. Neri reserved a hug for her horse and then turned to find Niall. The excitement had all but exhausted her and she found the idea of leaning on him again quite appealing.

The day wore on with folk to talk to and stories to tell. Neri hedged around the idea of asking what had happened to Viljo, but Niall wouldn't leave her side and she didn't want him to assume she cared.

When she saw Zel standing slightly apart from the other groups, she used that as an excuse to leave Niall's side and approach her.

"Let you go for a moment, has he?" Zel asked.

Neri nodded. "For now. I'm still worried though. When we were in the borderlands, Amis was talking to someone but we have no idea who. It could be one of the nobles Livia will need to face, but what if there are wider enemies still roaming that we don't know about?"

Zel looked over the square and those assembled, her easy smile never once faltering even as her voice turned serious.

"There are often enemies within enemies," she said. "We have rumblings of ill-will creeping in all the time, just rumour but there's often a grain of truth in rumour. Palatril are massing in the south, and the Kiren in the Kahlen mountains are pushing their boundaries more and more as the winterspans go on."

"So, we're not out of the woods then."

Zel shook her head. "The cursed forest will crumble soon enough, but the mountains and the great water hold their own stories."

"No idea how we fight them back then?"

"Ready to fight again so soon? Poor Niall. No, we haven't managed to get much from Viljo, but he has let slip that Amis was often talking to someone hooked and cloaked when he thought he was alone. It could be anyone, but we will keep a careful eye as far as we can and meet the challenges as they present themselves."

"Great." Neri sighed.

"Until then, enjoy your peace. You've more than earned it."

Neri eyed Niall and his lips lifted as he caught her staring. She smiled.

"Good idea. Excuse me."

She dodged the groups of folk clustered around until she was at Niall's side. He lifted his arms and pulled her onto his lap before she could even make a move to sit next to him, so she snuggled closer.

Let the fight come another day. Hopefully a fair way in the future. For now, we're okay.

The suns began to fade and the palace torches and those in the square were lit. Only then did the subject of the future fully come up.

"So, Niall and Neri will eventually take over Jakiris and the Westlands?" Emelyn asked.

They all sat in a comfortable group on large cushions. Folk milled around and Neri enjoyed the sense of freedom that everyone finally seemed to feel. Even the Jakida had chosen to sit with them, although she perched on a high stool with the appropriate formality.

Neri glanced at Niall in the same moment that he turned to her. Niall took her hand and smiled.

"We will see," he said carefully. "For now, Apeklonia needs attention and the folk need freedom. We'll do whatever helps Livia provide that."

The conversation turned and Neri leaned close to him.

"Spoken like a true leader," she teased.

Niall pretended to glare at her, but if she hadn't of been looking up at him, she might have missed it. The dark sky with its bright multi-coloured dancing stars lit up in a stream of fire. She nudged him and pointed as several other folk did the same.

All conversation ceased as they watched the blazing streak of orange flame darting across the sky. A ball of fire swooped out of the natural arc, twirling up and down in a beautiful dance. Just like that, it disappeared as quickly as it had arrived.

Neri continued staring as conversations resumed around them. Folk would no doubt herald that into the legends to come as an omen of brighter days. For her, she could be content with knowing that her firebird existed somewhere, the entire realm its playground.

Niall squeezed her hand as she began to stand up. He held on tight to keep her sitting beside him and she had no strength to fight him. She glared at his amused grin and sparkling eyes, full of devotion as he looked at her.

"I just want a few more moments before you let the madness descend on you." Niall grinned. "You no doubt have folk to speak to, things to do and places to be. Fights to calm, because for some mind-addled reason, Ciena is angling to be the head of the Apeklonian guard."

Neri snorted loudly. "She and Livia can barely stand

each other. That I have to see."

"There will be time for all of it," he continued. "But I'll be trying to keep as much of your attention as I can, to keep you distracted from dragon hunting and war fighting."

He grinned and she had to laugh, but her limbs were aching and her mind felt hazy as Dog appeared. He seemed to sense her weakness and sat firmly on Niall's lap with his big dopey head resting against her knees. She copied him by settling her head onto Niall's shoulder and holding them both tight.

The sounds of lively normality started to hum around them, with clinking mugs and the sounds of raucous revelry. Neri looked up at Niall, a question smiling in her eyes.

"So, what are we going to find to fight about now?"

ACKNOWLEDGEMENTS

This book has been at least two decades in the rewriting, so thank you to everyone who encouraged me to keep writing, to my family and also my writing family as always, your support means everything to me – Anna Britton, Debbie Roxburgh, Samantha Williams, Sally Doherty, Marisa Noelle, Emma Finlayson-Palmer, Katina Wright, Alison Hunt, writing Twitter, everyone who joins #ukteenchat, the WriteMentor crew, libraries and shops who will take a chance on this series and give this indie author a chance to reach more readers, and to the readers who will find these books in the future.

THANK YOU!

ABOUT THE AUTHOR

While always convinced that there has to be something out there beyond the everyday, Emma focuses on weaving magic realms with words (the real world can wait a while). The idea of other worlds fascinates her and she's determined to find her own entrance to an alternate realm one day.

Raised in London, she now lives on the UK south coast with her husband and a very lazy black Labrador who occasionally condescends to take her out for a walk.

Aside from creative writing studies, an addiction to cake and spending far too much time procrastinating on social media, Emma is still waiting for the arrival of her unicorn. Or a tank, she's not fussy.

For the latest news and updates, check the website or come say hi on social media:

www.emmaebradley.com
@EmmaEBradley